The Artist Formerly Known as Adolf Hitler

The Artist Formerly Known as Adolf Hitler

A.M. Overett

The Artist Formerly Known as Adolf Hitler

"Thus I will harden Pharaoh's heart, and he will chase after them; and I will be honored through Pharaoh and all his army, and the Egyptians will know that I am the Lord."

Exodus 14:4

Table of Contents:

CHAPTER 1

A young man sits nervously in a waiting area at the Vienna Academy of Fine Arts. He thinks about getting up and walking around the room in an attempt to relieve the tension he is feeling. He finally summons up enough courage to walk over to a nearby window. He smiles at a receptionist who offers him a blank stare. At the window he looks out over the streets of Vienna. He loves the city and especially at this time of the year. It is early Fall and there is a cool haziness over the city. The year is 1910 and the country is at peace. After years of war with France in the previous century, the country, and specifically Vienna is flourishing. The city is again filled with poets, artists and musicians.

Adolf soon snaps out of his trance and begins to walk around the room looking at the various pieces of art hanging on the walls. Although he appreciates Impressionism, it is not his favorite art form. He has made a vast improvement lately in his work and he no longer avoids drawing and experimenting with the human form. Previously, he had been criticized by his art instructors for not including people in his street scenes or other paintings. Why was that? Did he hate people? While sometimes aloof and distant, deep down he loved people. It was more an issue that he just would become inward – sometimes self-absorbed, but mostly self-conscious, concerned about his appearance, how he looked, how he sounded. Looking inward was a way of protecting himself. The death of his mother, three years before, shook him deeply and the wounds never seemed to heal. His only solace was to throw himself into his work. And as a way to throw himself into his work even more, he heeded the comforting words of his teacher, Professor Franz Spielman. He began to study the human form; he began to look deeply into the faces of those around him. He started to enjoy drawing and painting people, especially their faces, especially their eyes. He was captivated by eyes – the so-called "windows to the soul".

While staring at Van Gogh's *Starry Night*, a door opens and a man pops his head out.

"Adolf, we're ready for you."

Adolf nods silently. He takes one more look at the image which he finds breath-taking. He wonders how Vincent did it. He is literally inches away from the painting. Looking at it that close, the painting looks like a mess, a fury of paint strokes produced after throwing several cans of paint at the canvas. And yet, as he slowly walks away, almost in a hypnotic trance, the true image reveals itself. It is exactly what he intended – a brilliant, galactic explosion of precision that is only evident to the true artist, the ones that can truly see.

Breaking from the pull of the painting, Adolf turns and walks toward the beckoning man. He tries to hold his breath, his heart pounding. He gives a nervous smile as he walks past the receptionist. He walks through the doorway…a doorway to another world, or just another doorway?

"Please have a seat Adolf." Professor Spielman offered with a smile.

Adolf quietly takes his seat. He carries a hat which he places neatly in his lap. He slowly looks up and sees the three men before him. There is his teacher Professor Franz Spielman, the director of the institute Professor Frederick

Rubenstein and Richard Leventhal, one of the board members and probably the most influential person on the panel.

"Well, Adolf, I've been talking to Professor Rubenstein and Herr Leventhal about the tremendous improvement you've made recently. I told them you have much potential."

Adolf smiled and nodded silently.

"Adolf, if admitted to our prestigious institute, what would you bring to our school? In other words, what makes you different from any other student?" Herr Leventhal asked with a stern look. Adolf, previously mute and stoic starts to squirm in his seat. He seems to look toward the floor. He quickly looks up and a light seems to fill his eyes.

"Well, gentlemen, I am not only a very good artist, but an excellent leader. The ideas I have will impress you. I not only want to be a leading artist in our great community but I want to help establish our institute as the leading institute for art throughout the world!"

"Interesting Adolf, but how would you plan to do that?" Queried an interested Professor Rubenstein.

Adolf paused for a moment. He looked at all three men. He felt like they were looking through him, looking at his soul, like they were judging him. He could sense that they were not impressed by him. He had heard rumors that at least one of the men found his work to be "uninspired". He could sense this was an important moment in his life. He could either shrink down into a self-absorbed and brooding intellectual who was angry at the world, or he could look these men in the eye and show them what he was truly made of.

"This institute means a lot to me. It means a lot to the community. With a little work we can make it the best art institute in the world. We can attract artists from all over the world. The first thing I would do is make sure that the admittance committee works with current artists here at the institute, that the artists would have a say in who is admitted to the school. They would work closely with the committee to ensure that artists of all genres are considered and that this would result in a school that celebrates diversity of artist, diversity of spirit."

Adolf was getting quite animated, to the point that he stood up and walked several paces from his chair. He turned and then continued…

"I would work with our advertising and publicity departments to ensure that we are sending out good communication, so that museums and other venues in Austria and around Europe know the quality of art we are producing. I will work tirelessly with the museums of Vienna and those throughout Europe to ensure that our artists have ample work on display, that there are multiple events that will promote our artists."

Adolf could feel he had the attention of the three men. He felt a surge of power, a surge of self-confidence that he had never felt before. He loved the feeling. He smiled for the first time in a long time. He met the three men's gaze and did not feel the least bit intimidated. This was surprising given ten minutes earlier he had felt like a frazzled lump of nerves.

Richard Leventhal leaned back in his chair as if surveying Adolf. Herr Leventhal felt that the institute was doing enough to filter out those who did not truly deserve to be there. He was not convinced that Adolf was right for their school, for their culture that they had worked so hard to create. Richard Leventhal, although not an artist, had been an art-collector for years. He was a banker by trade, having run several banks in Vienna and Salzburg. Like any banker he was an investor. He had invested in many works of art and his collection was considered to be one of the most valuable in the world. He had also been a major donor to the art institute and was held with deep respect within Vienna social circles.

Adolf looked at Herr Leventhal and began to think about what he had heard over the years about how Jews ran everything, especially the banks. He remembered how his father had cursed those "damn Jews", when he wasn't able to get a bank loan for a piece of property he wanted to buy. He also remembered his uncle also being anti-Semitic, when a local Jewish run law firm tried to collect on a loan he had been unable to repay. Adolf despised both his father and uncle and especially his father who physically abused both he and his mother. Adolf also remembered that he had several Jewish friends with whom he had always been impressed – their generosity and intellect were truly admirable. When Adolf had first arrived in Vienna, he had very little money and had stayed at a hostel. Two of his closest friends there were Jewish. They had helped Adolf secure work and even helped him to sell his watercolors to friends and family.

Adolf though was becoming somewhat torn. He had been reading various pamphlets as of late regarding how "Christian Austria" was becoming overrun by Eastern Jews. The mayor, Karl Lueger was anti-Semitic and was railing against all forms of immigration to Austria, not only against Jews. For Hitler, he did seem to notice that more and more of the population was Jewish, either by noticing the names he was doing business with or their appearance. Hitler fought hard to be neutral. Had he not learned in Catholic school that Christ was a Jew? How could the savior of the world be anything but good? But then he would hear the theological arguments that Jesus wasn't really a Jew, he was God who had chosen the Hebrew race to enter the world by. He could have chosen any race to do that.

"Herr Leventhal, you are a brilliant and creative man, I think you and I could work together." Leventhal's left eye-brow raised dramatically with a simultaneous crinkle of the lip.

"Imagine Herr Leventhal the world-renowned Vienna Academy of the Arts! If you and I can work together closely I am sure we will succeed! With my artistic background and your contacts and influence we can have our artists featured in the Louvre, in the Prado. Our artists will be well-known in Budapest, Rome, Moscow, and all over the world!" Leventhal liked that idea. He eyed Adolf up and down. Adolf was sporting a brown tweed jacket with matching pants. He wore a vest and a tie that showed he was aware of current Vienna fashion. Leventhal would not be embarrassed to have such a partner. Leventhal began to scribble some notes and looked toward Professor Rubenstein.

"Adolf, Professor Spielman has been impressed with your recent improvements with your artwork, he cites your improvement of the human form. I do see improvement but I still think your work with structure is your best attribute. Given that, wouldn't you feel like architecture would be better suited for you?"

"No Professor Rubenstein. I think what Professor Spielman has done for me is unleashed my true talents. I don't want to create soul-less buildings; I want to create images and paintings with soul, with spirit!"

Adolf took his seat and looked at the three men with pleading eyes. There had been a change in Adolf and Professor Spielman had seen it. There was true potential for Adolf, but there were only three spots left and two of them had been taken. For the final spot there were two other candidates and both of them were excellent artists. While Adolf may not have been on the same level as the other two, he did have the main quality they wanted to see from him – passion. What some great artists lacked in technical style they more than made up for with passion and ideas, Picasso comes to mind.

Adolf began to silently inspect each of the men. He looked at Professor Rubenstein. Professor Rubenstein as always was immaculately dressed. He had a bluish-gray tweed suit - a dark blue tie with alternating silver bands. He had a dark gray handkerchief extending from his top pocket. He also wore the most brilliant pair of black dress shoes that seemed to have been shined by the most elaborate of mechanisms that would have ever been created by human hand. The shine was so sheen. But what of Professor Rubenstein – what made him so that he would judge the likes of Adolf Hitler?

Frederick Rubenstein had been born in Minsk in 1853 and his family had immigrated to Austria after a terrible pogrom that had been administered by the local Russian authority. Rubenstein's family had run several kosher butcher shops and markets in the Jewish quarter of Vienna. Frederick, not forgetting his Russian roots had long studied the Eastern masters and was especially an authority on Ukrainian artists. He himself was an artist with more of a technical ability – also having become an architect. Rubenstein, unlike his colleague Leventhal, was always a "softy" when it came to the struggling artist. He sympathized with Adolf and wanted Adolf in the academy. If he failed as an artist he could always turn to architecture.

As for Professor Spielman, he also was fond of Adolf and after all, he had devoted many hours of tutoring him and saw great potential. His speech today had only solidified how he felt about the young man. He smiled at Adolf and nodded his head.

"Adolf, we have a couple of other interviews and then we should be able to make our decision. You will hear from us by the end of the week," Spielman offered.

Adolf was somewhat cool. He had hoped his ideas and enthusiasm would be enough to earn him a spot right then and there. He summoned the best smile he could create and then offered each man a handshake. He eyed Leventhal with his best stiff upper lip. He gave Rubenstein a warmer façade and for Spielman he gave a questioning look – *why couldn't you have done more?*

Adolf gathered all of his disappointment and hurt, turned toward the door and began a quick pace to escape before something unfortunate happened. As he quickly opened and closed the door behind him he spied the receptionist filing her nails.

"I sure hope that went well?" He asked, hoping for some sort of reply. The girl continued filing her nails, looking completely unsuited for a position in the highest art academy in the country. Adolf grinned slightly, turned and marched through the front door. He closed the door behind him and blew a deep breath.

"How did it go?" his friend Josef asked.

"Not sure, they looked a little crusty. I guess I will find out by the end of the week."

"By the way, Siegfried Mandle came by and bought your painting of Salzburg – 25 francs!"

"You're kidding, for that? That was not one of my best works. Oh well, at least we can get a pint of beer and a sandwich – let's go."

Adolf and Josef marched down the street like they were its lords. Everyone would bow to them, or so they believed. They were soon joined by their mutual friend Siegfried as they continued their assault on the streets of Vienna. Before they arrived at the local hofbrauhaus, a small bookstore caught Adolf's eye. He stopped and motioned for the two men to follow him. Adolf stopped by a small book rack near the front of the store and picked up a pamphlet.

"Ah, let's see what our dear Lueger has to say…" Both Josef and Siegfried leaned in, placing their hands on either shoulder of Adolf.

"Press: here, too, as always in the liberal press, abuses, invectives and the most insolent lies. After 15 years of fighting with the liberal press, I have developed a rather thick skin, thank goodness. Therefore I shall limit my comments and simply say that the liberal press, sometimes also classed Jewish liberal, or Jewish Press, is the most impudent press on the earth…In Vienna, only fools and those on the same moral level support it; all decent and intelligent people reject it with disdain…[Jewish press against clergy and religion, therefore], we believe: the Jews have no right to become judges, political officials and officers, and must be pushed back."

"Wow, clearly our dear friend had toned down his rhetoric," Adolf offered. Josef and Siegfried burst into laughter.

"Let's see what Herr Schönerer says," before Adolf could pick up another pamphlet, the two men pulled Adolf toward the door.

"C'mon, forget all that Adolf. You have a couple of steins of beer you owe us!"

"Alright boys, to the pub!!!"

Josef and Siegfried let out a cheer and then continued to pull Adolf toward the door. The three men made their way into the hofbrahaus and Adolf signaled to the barmaid for three beers. The men found a table by the window so they could observe Vienna street life. The barmaid, a healthy woman of Bavarian stock quickly brought three large steins of a local brew. Adolf flipped several francs on the able, giving the pretty young woman a wink and a smile. She returned his look, winking back.

"That my friends is good Austrian stock."

"Not good 'German' stock Adolf?"

Adolf smiled at Siegfried and the three men joined their steins together for a salute. Adolf felt like he was on top of the world. He had not been accepted into the art institute as of yet, but he felt that he was on the verge of success. Several of his paintings had sold and he knew that he had impressed the board at the art institute. Maybe not now, but soon he would be in a position to put his talents to good use.

"So Adolf, what do you really think of your friends Schönerer and Leuger? Do you subscribe to their ideas of Germanization?"

"Ah, they're all bluff and hot wind those two."

"Yes, but many of your fellow citizens share their beliefs."

"Gentlemen, I assure you that sentiment will soon blow over."

"So, how do you feel about us 'Jewden'"?

"I respect the Jewish people. They are intelligent, industrious, hard-working…"

"Wow Adolf, you sound like an honorary Hebrew!" The three men burst out laughing. Adolf though soon grew a serious expression.

"What are you thinking about Herr Hitler?" Josef asked, noting the somber expression on Adolf's face.

"Ah…I'm just thinking about my mother back in Linz. We had a Jewish doctor taking care of her when she got really sick. My father was no where to be found. The doctor did everything humanly possible to help her…I really miss her."

Adolf began to stare at the table, rubbing his finger around the top of the stein.

"To Fraulein Hitler!" Siegfried offered a toast. He looked at Adolf and could tell he was hurting - it was a significant loss for Adolf. Josef soon raised his stein as well. Adolf smiled and clinked his stein with his two friends.

After the men finished their drinks, they began their return to the hostel where Adolf was staying. In a park by the hostel, an orchestra was playing Mozart. The men increased their pace and began to check out the various female audience members.

"Pardon me Fraulein, but could we sit on your blanket?" an embolden Adolf asked.

"Sure", responded the blushing Austrian beauty.

For an hour or so, the four sat mesmerized by the beauty of the music. The park was situated in such a way where on one corner there was a completely unobstructed view of the Alps. A warm breeze was swirling through the park, given its occupants a pleasant sensation. Adolf didn't know if was the music, the company or the beer, but he was feeling enraptured. This was exactly why he was in Vienna. He loved the city. He never wanted to leave. This was his home and this is where he would make his mark on history, or so he hoped.

CHAPTER 2

The following Friday, Adolf was summoned to the art institute. This would be it. This would be the day that he found out if he would be accepted. He felt it was a good sign that he had been called to the institute, rather than receiving a rejection letter in the mail. As he arrived at the office lobby, he was greeted with the same receptionist having the same disregard for anyone who walked through the door.

"Adolf Hitler…to see Professor Spielman, Herr Leventhal and Professor Rubinstein," Adolf offered a polite smile. The receptionist, without acknowledging his presence, pressed a button on a nearby intercom.

"Yes?" barked Professor Rubinstein's voice.

"Ah, Adolf Hitler to see you, professor."

"Please send him in."

Adolf summoned all the courage he could. This was it. This would determine his career. He held tightly to the hat he had removed prior to speaking to the receptionist. A large lump grew in his throat. He smiled and realized that he had nothing to fear. If these men did not accept him, then he would find another school, or find another profession…maybe the military. He always wanted to learn to fly. He could join the Austrian Air Force. He shook those thoughts from his head, grabbed the brass knob to the door and pushed through.

"Ah, Adolf, please take a chair," a bright and happy looking Professor Spielman offered.

"Thank you, professor."

"Adolf, we have reviewed your application and have spent some time reviewing your work."

"Yes Professor Rubinstein," Adolf offered a humble acknowledgment.

"And while your work is a little rough around the edges, we feel you have potential."

Adolf shook his head and began to let out a small smile.

"Welcome aboard Adolf!" Professor Spielman offered his hand to shake as well as the two other men. Adolf had never recalled Professor Leventhal ever smiling. This was truly a remarkable occasion.

"Thank you, thank you gentlemen. You will not regret your decision."

"Yes Adolf we hope we do not. You need to apply yourself. This is a remarkable opportunity. You can develop your talents and become anything you want – a graphic artist, an architect, a painter…"

"Yes, but let's hope it's not a painter of buildings!" Professor Rubinstein let out a loud burst of laughter with Adolf and the two other professors soon joining in.

"Now Adolf, you will need to contact Fraulein Frankl, she will set up your schedule for the next term. You know how to contact her?"

Adolf nodded, but from that point on he could barely follow anything the three men said. He was in the heavens. His dreams and his prayers had been answered. He had struggled with believing in a deity, especially after seeing what his mother had gone through, but whether it was Jesus or Abraham, or Allah or Thor, he didn't care, he was truly grateful for the opportunity. The three men ushered him out of the office, Adolf still in a haze and speechless.

"Fraulein Gersin, please set up an appointment for Adolf here to meet with his course advisor. Again, congratulations Adolf!"

"Thank you sir, this is the greatest day of my life!" Adolf finally found the words and shook each man's hand as if he was experiencing and electric shock. All three men were amused, seeing the look on Adolf's face. The three men retreated in unison to the conference room leaving Adolf and the receptionist alone.

"Well, that was something," Adolf said, hoping for the slightest of response, or any gesture that would let him know that she was not a robot.

"Looks like we'll be seeing more of each other..." the words seemed to trail off with the receptionist continuing to look through a calendar she had on her desk.

"Professor Sauerbraun is available on Friday at 10:00 am, will that work for you Herr Hitler?"

"Sure...and then maybe we could grab a drink afterward?" Adolf said with the most confident smile he could muster.

"I'm sorry...what did you say?"

"I was just wondering if you would like to have some lunch with me after I meet with Professor Sauerbraun?"

"Herr Hitler, I do not go on lunch dates with students at the institute..."

"How about a dinner date then?" Adolf said with a devious smile. He could tell that the receptionist was mulling it over, perhaps thinking seriously about the request?

"No, I'm sorry. I make it my policy not to mix business and pleasure."

"Well, that's not a good outlook on life. Let me ask you, how many hours a day do you work here?"

"Eight."

"How many hours a night do you sleep?"

"Eight."

"So two thirds of your day is spent completely eliminating pleasure?"

The receptionist finally let out a small smile and shook her head. *She was human!* Adolf exclaimed to himself.

"Well, I will let you ponder that for a while. Get back to me if you change your mind."

Adolf turned with a large grin on his face and stepped confidently toward the front entryway. The receptionist eyed him as he seemed to burst through the door.

Adolf was truly in heaven. His dream of becoming a world class artist or architect was going to come true. As long as he applied himself at the institute the world would be his.

As Adolf headed over to the hofbrauhaus to let his friends know the good news, he was greeted by a tall stranger in a trench coat coming from the nearby alley.

"Saw you coming out of the art institute…you a student there?" The man asked with a demanding tone.

"Yes. Yes, I was just accepted."

"You know that place is run by Jews don't you?"

"I guess I never really thought about it."

"Well, think about it. Jews run everything, the banks, the courts, you name it and they run it."

"Well, if that is true, then it just shows they are an intelligent and industrious people – we can learn a lot from them."

"You're just fooling yourself." The man then turned and walked across the street narrowly avoiding a tram. Adolf a little shaken by the terse conversation stood and watched him as he passed to the alleyway on the other side of the street. *Who in the hell was that?* For Adolf that question easily answered. It had to be one of the thugs from the mayor's office. The mayor was anti-Semitic and he made his philosophies quite clear.

Shaking his mind of the encounter, Adolf proceeded to the hofbrauhaus where Josef and Siegfried were waiting. The two men greeted Adolf with giddy excitement, barely able to hold in their exuberance. When Adolf had announced he had been accepted to the art institute the two men almost exploded with celebration. The rest of the hofbrauhaus' occupants were soon made aware of the news and all began to applaud Adolf. The pub owner offered Adolf several free rounds of beer and the party was on!

Adolf was again aloft, somewhere where few dare to be – somewhere in the mind where few found that elation or pure joy. Adolf felt he could do no wrong and felt as if he had been nominated the King of Austria.

CHAPTER 3

For the next several years, Adolf's career began to thrive. While studying architecture at the art institute, he continued to paint. His paintings were all selling well and were being exhibited in most of the major art centers of Europe; Amsterdam, Brussels, Berlin, London, Prague and Budapest.

And while Adolf was thriving, a dark shadow was being cast over the political world of Europe. Tensions in Europe had been growing for decades since the Franco-Prussian War, and now in 1913, the Balkans were again in the midst of another war, with Bulgaria fighting their old enemies of Greece and Serbia. Many thought that Germany was again stirring the fan of war, working with the Ottoman Empire to help them expand their influence in Southeastern Europe. With the defeat of Bulgaria in the second Balkan War, The Austro-Hungarian Empire, was becoming concerned with the growing power of Serbia.

In the summer of 1914, as Adolf was finishing his studies at the art institute, he was spending a warm Saturday afternoon alone at his favorite outdoor café. As he fondled a cup of good Turkish espresso, he poured over several articles in the local newspaper suggesting that war between the Austro-Hungarian Empire and Serbia seemed all but inevitable. Adolf had no time for war, he only had time for art. His creativity was at an all-time high and the money he was earning was providing him a life-style he never imagined.

As of late, Adolf's close friend Kurt Walter Bachstitz would join him for an afternoon coffee. Bachstitz was now representing Adolf in Vienna and Berlin and was arranging a trip for Adolf to have a showing in Paris. The two men began to talk over the details of the trip.

"So, we arrive in Paris at 3pm on Thursday…Adolf, you seem far away. What's troubling you?"

"Oh, I just keep reading the newspaper. Seems like war is inevitable."

"You can't dwell on the negative. What will be will be. For now, you have to prepare yourself for your show on the 16th."

"Yes, you're right. Please continue."

The two men finished their plans and then headed over to the *Esterházykeller* for dinner. Adolf adored the *Esterházykeller*, and especially the fine wines they housed. He dined on liptauer, a spicey cheese spread and vegetable soup and then for his main course a specially prepared "Palatschinke" or crepe that had potato, cheese and spinach with a cream sauce. Mr. Bachstitz had the *Selchfleisch* with Sauerkraut. *Selchfleisch* was smoked meat. Adolf had recently decided to forgo meat. After a hunting trip with his uncle, the thought of eating anything that had been alive seemed wrong to him. And while he did not preach about his new found vegetarianism, he privately disdained those who did eat meat. The truth of the matter however was that he would sometimes stumble when it came to a strict adherence.

******

The following Thursday, the two men arrived in Paris for Adolf's art show. They checked in at a nearby hotel and then spent the rest of the evening over at the gallery, preparing everything for the next day's show. Adolf was nervous. He knew the critics in Paris would be difficult to please. He knew though to be a great artist he would need to be successful in France.

The next morning, Adolf arose early and had breakfast in the hotel restaurant on the top floor. He tried to distract his mind from the art show by reading the newspaper. He wasn't sure what was more distressful, his pending art show or the continuing situation in the Balkans. It was rumored that the Astro-Hungarian Empire was looking for any excuse to start a war with Serbia. Once Serbia was engaged, their ally Russia would soon be involved in which case, all the other major European powers would choose sides.

Rather than continuing with the depressing news, Adolf forced down a roll with jam, and a couple sips of expresso and hurried off to the art gallery. As he entered into the streets, the early morning hustle and bustle was just starting. The various vendors were opening up shop as the early morning twilight was turning to a brighter yellow-ish orange hue. Adolf tipped his hat to a large man who was arranging the produce on a table arrayed with various fruits and vegetables. A worker across the street was pulling out various boxes of produce from the back of a truck and rushing over to lay them at the feet of the large man.

Several blocks later, Adolf was at the entrance to the art gallery. The building was a converted hotel and was one of the up and coming art venues in town. Adolf had already sold two of his paintings to a rich Parisian patron and word was starting to get out about Adolf's talent. As Adolf fumbled around for the key to the front door in his pocket, he looked up and could see the sun rising over the Champs-Elysees. He began to nod his head and smile, *this is where I belong,* he said to himself triumphantly and then practically burst through the front door.

The art gallery was divided into three floors. On the first floor were classical art work from the likes of Rembrandt, Degas and Rodin. On the second floor were the late Nineteenth Century artists; Van Gogh, Gaugin and Matisse. The third floor was reserved for up and coming artists as well as events that would host their work. For Adolf the gallery was hallowed ground. He wandered through the first floor looking at the work of the masters; examining them up close to note the brush strokes and then stepping back further to digest the scenes in their entirety. He quickly sped up the stairwell to the second floor again applying his usual technique of observation. He had always admired Van Gogh and would sit mesmerized by his works. Adolf was transfixed and in another world. It was as if he could see the brush strokes being applied; tormented globs of paint gleaming from the bright sun above the Arles landscape. He imagined the distressed painter infusing his soul with the canvass. The artist simply did not exist, only the spirit, only the brush and paint for *no human could possibly paint like this?* Adolf mused to himself.

Finally, Adolf found himself on the third floor. He examined the work he and Kurt had done the night before, it was even better than he had hoped. All of his latest works were hung tightly to the walls, all with large type labels beneath them; it looked perfect. All they needed were some hors d'oeuvres from the local restaurant nearby and everything would be set. He examined the flower displays that would greet the various patrons and critics.

Still feeling the effects of the hard work he had put in the night before, Adolf decided to have another expresso at a shop across the street. The art show would start at 11am and there was little he could do now to prepare – it was make or break time for his career in Paris.

Adolf sat nervously in the café across the street, sipping on his expresso and trying his best to concentrate on the articles in the newspaper he was reading. He could hardly keep his mind from flying off. He would read a sentence or two about the brewing turmoil about to engulf Eastern Europe before the images in his mind would segue to triumphant Parisian parties where Adolf's art and genius were being celebrated. It was during one of these phantom festivals that the voice of Kurt brought Adolf crashing down to harsh reality.

"C'mon Adolf!"

Adolf looked up from his paper with a dazed look.

"Your show is starting in five minutes."

As the news registered in Adolf's mind, he quickly dropped the paper, threw a few francs on the table and then sprang to his feet. Kurt was taken aback at the expression on Adolf's face. He looked like a man possessed. His eyes seemed transfixed on the front door of the café as he began a march toward it.

The two men bounded into the street and quickly made their way to the bottom entrance of the gallery. Adolf became nervous as he could hear voices on the third level. As they arrived on the third floor they were greeted by the gallery owner; Gilles Mingnolet, his wife Zelda and the gallery manager Marta von Hauptman. Adolf nervously shook each person's hand hoping his hand was not too sweaty. For Adolf this was an important day. Was he going to tremble at the feet of the critics, or was he going to show some backbone and let his confidence as an artist rule the day? He realized that he had nothing to fear. He wouldn't be there unless there was some interest in his work. He was making a living as an artist in Vienna, one of the top capitals for art. What did he have to fear?

After several minutes of positive self-talk and observing the layout of the hors d'oeuvres, Adolf turned to hear the booming voice of Baron Waldheim of Westphalia. The Baron often came to Paris to visit the art galleries and he had been a patron of Adolf's most recent avant-garde work.

"Dearest Adolf, so glad I could make your opening here in Paris." The rotund individual practically enveloped Adolf with a bear hug.

"Baron always a pleasure. I really appreciate you coming to my art exhibit."

"My pleasure my boy. I can already see you've been holding out on me with some of these pieces…they're wonderful…"

"Yes, Baron come look at these recent works of Adolf," Marta said as she grabbed the Baron by the arm. Adolf smiled as Marta gave him an approving wink. So far so good.

As the morning turned into afternoon, the showing was going well. Later in the day, a very sophisticated looking man, with the air of a diplomat walked into the gallery. On his arm was a very elegantly dressed woman. These were clearly people of distinction. Adolf began to take notice when Mingnolet, his wife and Marta literally dropped everything they were doing and made a direct line for the couple.

"Ah my dear Baron Rothschild, how nice of you to come today."

As Adolf watched Mingnolet gush over the gentleman, he began to think about the name "Rothschild". *Could this be one of the famous Rothschilds?* He contemplated. If it were, a patron like that could make

Adolf a wealthy man. Adolf was soon keeping an eye on the gentleman's every move.

The Rothschilds, escorted by Mingnolet, his wife and Marta began to peruse each of Adolf's paintings. He nodded at some, and seemed to shake his head at others. Upon returning to the greeting area, a confident Adolf waited to be introduced to the noble couple.

"Adolf, this is Baron and Madame Rothschild…very influential people here in our little burg of Paris," Mingnolet said with a nervous laugh.

"Yes, an honor to meet you Baron, Madame Rothschild."

"So what did you think Baron?" Marta asked. The man began to think and with a seeming glee in his eye began his discourse.

"Well, all in all, not bad, some interesting pieces. I think his efforts are admirable." There was an uncomfortable pause as Baron Rothschild made his way over to the table, grabbing a plate and placing some hors d'oeuvres on it. He then turned and continued.

"However, I don't think this work can really compare to the works produced by French painters and even some of the Dutch."

"Would the Baron like to expound on that?" A slightly trembling Adolf said.

"I'm not exactly sure…maybe it's the color, the clarity. You know, it's like a well-aged French wine, you cannot compare anything from Austria with that of France!" He began to laugh a hearty laugh, his wife giggling beside him. Mingnolet was not sure how to respond. He wanted to stand up for Adolf but Rothschild was also one of his biggest supporters whom he could not afford to offend.

"You seem to have a narrow point of view Baron," Adolf retorted.

"Maybe so, but I know what I like and I know what I don't like."

"I see." Adolf said, looking the Baron and his wife up and down. *Cretans!* He screamed to himself. He made a slight bow to the Baron and his wife, he then turned and bowed to Mingnolet, his wife, Marta and Kurt. He then walked out of the gallery and down the stairs toward the streets. Completely numb, he then walked down the street toward his hotel. Upon arrival he asked the clerk for his room key. He then bounded up the stairs, trembling as he did so.

A distraught Adolf quickly ran into the bathroom and slammed the door behind him. In a completely unnecessary action he locked the door. He walked toward the mirror that was over the sink and began to examine his face. "Is this the face of an artist?" He said with clenched teeth. He walked to the sink and looked at a nearby bowl with fresh water. He began to dip his fingers into the bowl noting how the image of the tips of his fingers were distorted. He again looked at the image of himself in the mirror and began to wonder how distorted was he or how deluded?

He looked to the table at the right of the sink and stared long and hard at the razor blade that he would use to shave himself. Before he could think another thought, he could hear someone beating on the door. He threw some water from the nearby bowl onto his face, grabbed a towel and headed for the front door.

"Adolf, why did you leave like that?" Kurt said with a perplex look on his face.

"Sorry, I guess that wasn't the best thing to do."

"Look Adolf, there are going to be ups and downs as you progress as an artist. Not everyone is going to love your work," Kurt continued as he pushed past Adolf and into the hotel room.

"Yes, but Rothschild holds a lot of sway in the world of art, at least here in Paris. If I cannot gain his support I will not be able to survive here!"

"Look, it's true you do not have him on your side, but you can win him over. You can have other supporters, Monsieur Ligard clearly liked your work and if we can have him as a patron you can get your foot in the door."

Adolf stopped for a moment and nodded his head.

"C'mon, let's get a bite to eat and get an early night. We've have a long day tomorrow."

Again Adolf silently nodded.

******

The next day, after cleaning up the gallery from the previous day's art show, the two men drove to the Gare d'Austerlitz to catch their train to Vienna. Before boarding the train, Adolf went to a nearby newspaper stand to acquire the latest news. As he approached he could see a large crowd gathered with people talking loudly. A young impoverished looking boy wearing a sandwich board was crying out the day's headlines. Adolf looked at the crowd in front of him and then the boy. He pondered from which he should get his news – the boy looked like he had just emerged from the sewer or a chimney as he had soot all over his face and clothes. Not willing to wait, Adolf opted for the young boy's offering. As he tossed him a franc, the boy presented Adolf with the somewhat soiled paper. Adolf could not believe the headline. Archduke Franz

Ferdinand had been assassinated in Sarajevo. Adolf showed the headline to Kurt as the two men boarded their first class car bound for Vienna.

******

When Adolf and Kurt arrived into Vienna the next morning, the city was abuzz with the latest news. No one was talking of anything other than the declaration of war that Austria had made against Serbia. The latest news was that Russia would side with Serbia on the conflict and both Germany and Turkey would side with Austro-Hungary. The streets of Vienna seemed to be bursting at the seams with army transport trucks and vehicles hauling various equipment and armaments that would be used for what appeared to be the unstoppable course toward conflict.

As the taxi Adolf and Kurt rode in was stuck in traffic, Adolf nervously fondled his hat, trying to absorb what the meaning of all this meant. *Will I now have to join the military?* He thought to himself, hoping his concern was not so visible on his face. After what seemed like hours, the two men finally arrived at Adolf's apartment. Fraulein Gerta greeted the two men with a tray of tea and cookies.

"Thank you Fraulein," a troubled Adolf offered.

"How was your trip Herr Hitler?"

Adolf thought for a moment, trying to assess the results of his art show.

"Ah fine, just fine."

Kurt could see that Adolf was not fine. His mind looked to be a million miles away. As the two men began to walk toward the balcony, a knock came on the door.

"I'll get it," Kurt pointed for Adolf to continue to the balcony. Kurt slowly pulled open the door. A man in a uniform presented himself.

"Greetings Herr Hitler?"

"No, I'm not Herr Hitler, but how can I help you?"

"Yes sir, I am from the Imperial Royal State Railways – I have your cargo down in a truck downstairs."

"Oh, yes, thank you. Here let me come down with you so I can have you load the paintings into the basement downstairs."

Adolf, sitting on the balcony, paid little notice to the two men's departure. Instead his eyes quietly studied the Eastern Alps. Somewhere over those majestic mountains lay the "Serbian Menace", poised to destroy all that was beloved of the Austrian people, or so those in political power would have the population believe. Still in a stupor, a knock came on the door. Fraulein Gerta opened the door.

"Greetings Fraulein. My name is Herman Schmidt, I am a friend of Adolf's, may I see him?"

"One moment please."

Fraulein Gerta hurriedly walked toward the balcony.

"Herr Hitler, there's a Herman Schmidt to see you. Shall I show him in?"

Adolf nodded in silence. Fraulein Gerta smiled and hurried back to the front door.

"Yes, please come in Herr Schmidt. Herr Hitler is taking tea on the balcony.

"Thank you Fraulein."

Herman Schmidt made his way to the balcony and greeted Adolf like he was his long lost brother. Adolf tried to muster a smile and shook his hand.

"Can I get you some tea Herman?"

"Oh no thank you Adolf. I am in somewhat of a hurry. Heading to a meeting of Georg Schönerer. I wanted to see if you were interested in coming with me?"

"Thank you Herman, but I don't share Herr Schönerer's ideas."

"Really? You seemed to be interested when you came with me a year ago to one of his rallies?"

"Yes, I know, but things have changed."

"What has changed Adolf? Surely you can't hide your eyes from the plight of our country? How the Jews have turned Austria into a haven for all Middle-Eastern riff-raff; gypsies, Arabs, Africans…this place has become a zoo!"

Adolf ignored Herman and continued to look toward the Alps, hoping to find an answer.

"The Jews have taken over this place; the banks, the courts, the businesses…all controlled by Jews."

Adolf began to think to himself about that comment. Rothschild was a Jew. The Rothschild family had been bankers both in England and France…was what Herman saying the truth? It couldn't be. After all, it was the Jewish professors that had approved his entrance into the art institute.

"You remember what happened to my uncle don't you?"

Adolf gave Herman a cold stare. He again turned away, this time attentively stirring his cup of tea.

"My uncle was in need of money. He sold that plot of land on the outskirts of Vienna. That Jew Feldman would only offer him an amount that was well below the value of that property, but because he conspired with all the other local realtors, who were Jewish, he had no other option! They swindled him Adolf!"

Adolf again continued to look disinterested. But his mind was going over what Herman was saying like a clock ticking over and over. *Could he be right?* Before he could respond, Kurt returned.

"Well we got all the paintings into the basement, I'm sure Herr Vandenburg will purchase..." Kurt soon realized that Herman Schmidt was in the room. He knew Schmidt was anti-Semitic and his hatred for Kurt was well-known.

"Well, I should be leaving. Please contact me when you can Adolf." Herman picked up his hat that he had left on a nearby coffee-table and quickly departed.

"Adolf, you're not listening to that clown are you?"

Adolf wanting to say that he wasn't, but the face of Edmond James de Rothschild was filling his mind, filling his mind with his laughter, with his condemnation and his proclamation that artists from Austria could not compete with artists from France.

"Adolf, that man spreads poison, you cannot continue to be-friend him."

Adolf looked at the concern in Kurt's face and nodded.

"Kurt, don't worry. I tolerate him because he gave me a loan once. His ideas are clearly that of a Neanderthal. Come, I'll pour you some tea."

Kurt, trying to allay his fears that Adolf was listening to Schmidt, sat down with a sigh and plopped his hat on a nearby chair.

"That man is dangerous Adolf!"

"I know, I know."

CHAPTER 4

On July 28th, 1914, the Austro-Hungarian army invaded Serbia. Soon after, Germany invaded Belgium and Luxembourg in a preemptive strike against France. Several weeks later, on an unusually cold and rainy day for August, a young messenger sent from the nearby recruitment center, ran up the two flights of stairs to Adolf's apartment.

"Herr Hitler?"

"Yes."

"A telegram from the Ministry of War."

"Thank you."

Adolf closed the door, and walked toward the balcony. He didn't have to imagine what the telegram contained as he tore off the cover. His darting eyes quickly scanned the letter's contents. He was to report the next day to the recruitment center to enlist in the Austrian army.

Adolf was numb. What did this mean for his career? What did this mean for his life? He considered himself an Austrian patriot but that didn't mean he wanted to kill to maintain his patriotism. Besides, what had this country done for him? It was now the safe haven for all of Eastern European and Middle-Eastern criminals, or at least that's what some of his old friends maintained. It was times like these that he really missed his mother. She would always help steer him in the right direction. Maybe he should do it for her? Or maybe he should just hop the next train for Paris?

Paris? Paris was where he had failed, or at least in the eyes of Baron Rothschild.

"Maybe a pint will help!" Adolf grabbed his hat and headed downstairs and out into the streets of Vienna. After walking for twenty minutes he came upon one of his favorite beerhalls "The Boar's Mouth". The "Boar's Mouth" was in a semi-seedy part of town. A part of town where he wouldn't run into his artist crowd or school colleagues. Here at "The Boar's Mouth", he could be himself.

"A pint of lager, Miss!" He yelled to a busty barmaid who was cleaning up the next table. The barmaid met his gaze, smiled and turned. Within in a minute she was back with a frothy mug of lager.

"What's your name?"

"Adolf."

"Hi Adolf. I'm Gretchen."

"Thank you Gretchen."

The barmaid smiled a bright smile and then turned. The usually shy and reserved Adolf was immediately smitten. He began to chug down the lager hoping that the power of alcohol would help him to forget his current plight. A couple of lagers later he was engaged in a political conversation with two men next to the bar. They argued about how Germany was a much better country – "a pure Germanic" country with no Slavs, no Gypsies…

"But plenty of Jews!" Adolf cried lifting his stein. All three men began to laugh. Adolf was starting to like these hard-working, "earthy" types as he like to refer to the tradesmen.

The three later stumbled over to play snooker. After a fairly uneventful game, Adolf suggested darts. While continuing to extinguish more lagers the three men began a highly competitive game of darts. Toward the end, Adolf's aim became a little impaired and he accidently hit a burly truck driver in his cap. The truck driver, also keenly intoxicated took this as an insult and a fight quickly broke out. Well, not so much a fight as the truck driver decking Adolf with one hard punch of his large, weathered hand.

Several minutes after receiving his first punch, Adolf woke up to water being splashed into his face by Gretchen.

"Sorry Adolf but we're closing."

Adolf's vision was blurry but soon cleared up with the smiling Teutonic beauty beaming a bright smile.

"Ah, if you like, I can take you upstairs and help clean you up a bit."

Adolf nodded, knowing he was in no shape to try and make it home on his own.

"What happened to Hans and Ludwig?"

"Oh, left about an hour ago."

"You mean I've was lying in that puddle of beer for an hour?"

"Probably two."

Adolf, somewhat proud that he could display such decadence, gave the barmaid a smile and a wink. She helped Adolf slowly climb the stairs to the second level. On the second level she led him to a room at the end of the hall. Inside was a small bed and a closet with what appeared to be feminine attire. There was a chest of drawers with a mirror on top and a night stand with a lamp – pretty sparse décor. Adolf looked himself over in the mirror on top of the chest of drawers and could see a large cut across his cheek.

"Here, you rest on the side of the bed here and I'll get a bandage and some rubbing alcohol."

Adolf smiled at Gretchen. Adolf was not wise in the ways of love. He had a few awkward encounters when he was younger, but because of his Catholicism and how his mother conducted her life, he had come to believe that sex was reserved for marriage. Tonight though, he was willing to make an exception.

As Gretchen sat next to him, tending his wound with tender hands, Adolf soon reached out and held her hand as she applied the alcohol. The two looked into each other's eyes and then Gretchen offered Adolf a soft kiss on his lips. He smiled and then returned the kiss. As they began to kiss more passionately, Adolf moved her hand away from his cheek and the cotton swab full of alcohol fell to the ground. Adolf wrapped his arms around the shoulder and waist of the ample barmaid and they fell backwards onto the bed. Adolf got on top of her and began to wrestle with the buttons on the back of her dress. As he pulled the top of her dress down, he stood over her like a lion catching his prey. She lay still, with a look of awe – awe of his power or awe that he could figure out how to unbutton the back of her dress. Her breasts glistened in the light of the lamp. *This was truly the work of God!!!* Adolf screamed to himself.

"What are you waiting for Adolf?"

"Sorry…you just look, so beautiful."

The barmaid smiled, giving a coy look. With that Adolf savagely removed the rest of her dress, her bra and undergarments in what seemed to the barmaid one swift move. She soon helped Adolf out of his garments and the two made passionate love…at least until Adolf passed out.

The next morning, Gretchen surprised Adolf with breakfast in bed.

"Good morning, you savage!"

Adolf's eyes slowly flickered to life.

"Where am I?"

"You're in 'The Boar's Mouth'…well so-to-speak".

"How did I get here?"

"You don't remember anything?"

"Not a thing."

"Well, you were quite the wild man last night…" Gretchen continued as she opened the blind to the nearby window, sending in a flood of sunlight that practically blinded Adolf.

"…you got drunk, got into a fight and then I helped you up here to fix the wound you obtained in said fight."

Adolf began to feel the pain in his cheek. He shook his head and then suddenly remembered the source of his inspiration to get drunk the previous evening.

"What time is it?"

"Ah, about 10:30am."

"Oh no!" Adolf exclaimed as he looked around the room for his clothes.

"What's the matter?"

"I have to be at the recruitment center at 11am!"

"For what?"

"For what? I'm joining the army you twit!"

"You don't have to talk to me like that."

"Well, what other reason would one go to a recruitment center?"

"I don't know, there are numerous reasons why someone might be recruited…could be recruited for an executive positon at a company…maybe be recruited for a cult…"

Adolf began to shake his head.

"Anyway, can you please hand me my clothes."

With the same savagery in which he had removed Gretchen from her clothes, Adolf applied the same swiftness in getting his clothes back on. He asked Gretchen for some shaving cream and a razor, did a quick touch up on his already visible stubble, applied some tonic to his hair which now he was coming over and then quickly dashed out the door.

"When will I see you again?" Gretchen yelled, hearing no response.

******

"Adolf Hitler reporting for duty sir!" Adolf said to a young man behind a table who had been processing a large procession of men.

"Where are your orders?" the young man said, not acknowledging Adolf's presence.

"Orders?"

"Yes, you should have received a telegram. I need that to process you."

"I don't have it sir…I mean I have it but left it at my apartment."

"Well I cannot process you unless I see your orders."

"I can get the paper but I would have to run all the way back to my apartment – it would probably take twenty, thirty minutes."

The young man behind the table squinched up his nose and began to wave his hand back and forth.

"Have you been drinking Herr Hitler?"

"I just had a couple of beers last night…you know…last night of freedom and all that." Adolf offered a bright smile.

"Okay Hitler, you better hurry. The Colonel will be here at noon to inspect the inductees."

With that Hitler turned and vanished out of the building, running down the Ringstrasse as fast as he could.

He debated taking the tram but decided it would make too many stops. With his head throbbing he continued his mad dash to his apartment. Fifteen minutes later he arrived. He darted upstairs, fiddled with his key, finally got it into the keyhole and then pushed through the door. He looked through all the papers that had piled up on his desk and finally found the orders. As he turned, Kurt appeared at the door.

"Adolf, what's going on?"

"I've been drafted Kurt!" Adolf said triumphantly holding up the orders.

"Drafted…that's impossible!"

"Why is it impossible? I'm a young, strong man, ready to do his patriotic duty."

"Yes, but you're an up and coming artist, about to take the world by storm!"

"Not according to Baron Rothschild."

"C'mon, are you going to allow one critic, one man derail your career?"

"Maybe he's right. Maybe I'm just fooling myself!"

"You're not fooling yourself. I just sold every one of your paintings that are down in the basement."

"Really?"

"Really. Herr Gellman bought two, Vandenburg bought ten, Klaus bought twelve…you have a serious career going on here!"

"Well, that might be the case but I'm going to have to put that on hold for a while. Anyway, I need a break from the art world. I need to do something adventurous, something more manly."

"Getting shot at is manly?"

"I don't know…I need something different in my life…anyway, I've got to go. I appreciate everything you have done for me but I need to go."

With that, Adolf marched out of the door leaving Kurt to ponder what this all meant. Adolf had become one of the most important artists that he was representing and helped provide him a solid income. That was now all going away. He shook his head, looked around Adolf's apartment, noting the canvasses, the paint brushes, tubes of oil and acrylic paints that would now not have any use – *at least until this silly war is over*, Kurt mused.

Before leaving, Kurt took the opportunity to use Adolf's telephone.

"Herr Spielman? Yes, it's Kurt. Say I just wanted to let you know that Adolf has been drafted into the army…yes, preposterous I know. Anyway, if you have any contacts in the military, perhaps you can get him moved to some desk job…something safe? I need Adolf back in one piece when this stupid war ends…Yes…yes…well I appreciate that. Thank you Herr Spielman."

Kurt put down the phone and began to smile. He then grabbed a couple of Adolf's paintings and headed out of the apartment.

******

After two long weeks of boot-camp, Adolf was assigned to the 7th Infantry Division of the Austro-Hungarian 2nd Army. Initially he was going to be sent to the Serbian front, but when the Russians mobilized their military to support Serbia, the 2nd Army was sent to Galicia.

While boot-camp had been unbearable, the train ride to Galicia proved even more daunting. The men he was traveling with were rag-tag to say the least. They did not appear to be ethnic Austrians – mainly Czechs, Slavs and Romanians. None of them seemed to speak German. How he wished he had been drafted by the German army! He tried to sleep as much as he could, his newly forged rifle was his only source of security, although he would confess he hardly knew how to fire the damn thing. As the train arrived in Galicia the next morning, he was greeted with a bowl of what appeared to be oatmeal. It was cold and dry and now more than ever he wished he had escaped to Paris; the pâté de foie gras, the consume, the broiled duck in orange sauce and crème brulee…what the hell had he gotten himself into?!!!

After consuming something that resembled maggots rather than oatmeal, the men were herded into columns and then addressed by General Conrad von Hatzendorf. The General harangued the troops for what felt like an hour; telling the men about their honorable quest and that it was similar to the knights of the crusades. Adolf was trying to convince himself more and more of the nobleness of what he was about to do.

After the general's speech, the men were instructed to march. What they were not told was that it was a two-hour march to their destination. The trains had been backed up in the Przemys'l train station and so the train Adolf had been on was a couple of hours away. Adolf began to tire about an hour through their march; the backpack he had was over 60 pounds and was making the going rough to say the least.

When they finally arrived in Przemys'l, Adolf was impressed with the picturesque setting. Everything was green with many bushes and trees lining the road they were marching on. There was a large river which was the San River on one side and rolling hills and mountains on the other. As they neared the city he could see great walls lining the main entrance.

"Welcome to the Fortress Przemys'l men," yelled the sergeant who was leading their column.

"This is where we are going to hold off those Ruskie bastards!"

The men marched through a large brick gate that had guards on either side. Once through they were then marched in front of several large barracks.

"Alright men, you may now rest. Please go to your assigned barracks. You may then go to the mess tent for dinner. Lights out will be at 2100 hours."

"What's 2100 hours?" Adolf asked a be-spectled man next to him. He was hoping the glasses were an indication of the young man's education.

"Oh that's military time, instead of having 1 o'clock which could be confused for either 1 o'clock in the morning or 1 o'clock in the afternoon, there is only one number for each hour of the day. So after 1200, you don't' go to 1 o'clock you go to 1300 hours."

"I guess that's military intelligence for you?" Adolf said with a smile. The young man just stared at him with a confused look.

"Ah…anyway, my name is Adolf Hitler."

"Hi, I'm Hugo Gutman," the young man said brightly.

"Are you a Hebrew Hugo?"

Hugo studied Adolf's face, trying to ascertain why he was asking such a question, although the question had been asked of him many times, especially of late.

"Yes, I am Jewish."

Adolf nodded as they continued to walk toward their barracks. Each man handed a paper to an officer that was standing at the doorway of the barracks.

"Gutman, bed 18…Hitler bed 19," the officer yelled into their ears. The two men then hurried into the barracks.

"That twit must think we have a hearing problem," Adolf said as he held his hand to his ear. The two men put their backpacks and rifles against the wall near their beds.

"Join me for dinner Gutman?" Adolf queried. Hugo nodded and the two men headed out into the fortress courtyard. They walked silently looking around at the medieval architecture around them.

"Boy, Otto Wagner, would have loved this place!"

"You know Otto Wagner?"

"Yes, he was a mentor of mine when I was at the Academy of Fine Arts in Vienna."

"Wow really! I tried to get into that place. I was rejected twice; once in 1907 and again in 1908. They cited my rejection for the school as 'unfitness for painting'."

"Wow, that's harsh. What did you end up doing?"

"Well, I spent a couple of years at the University of Economics and Business, but got bored and left. I think I'd like to get into politics."

"Really?"

The two men entered the dining hall and could see many officers enjoying what looked to be a giant feast. There was pheasant, various potato and pasta dishes, all covered with cream sauce or gravy. Large bowls of salad or fruit and at the very end of the table, cakes, pastries and pies. There were also multiple cups of what appeared to be custard. The two men's mouths began to salivate.

"Hey you two, that's the officer's dining hall, the enlisted men are over here," their sergeant, as usual being helpful, pointed to the other end of the building where there was another dining hall. The two men scampered like mice being attacked by a ravenous cat.

Once inside the dining hall of the enlisted men, Adolf and Hugo became instantly depressed. There was no beautiful table lined with gourmet food here, only a few metal bins of what looked like broiled mutton, some creamed corn and green beans. The men sneered as they could see a large man behind the bins slapping the contents into a man's metal tray. This did not look appealing at all. But the men had to eat and so they did their best to tolerate the setting.

"So politics eh? So you want to become the almighty chancellor of Austro-Hungary. I hear that job is open?" Adolf again laughed hoping for a response out of Hugo. Hugo's expression remained the same however.

"Well, I've been looking at running for a district representative…"

"Oh which district?"

"Leopoldstadt…the 2nd District."

"Well, I don't know about the 2nd District but welcome to the 2nd Army Hugo!" a mound of cream corn was slapped onto Adolf's tray as he made his proclamation.

After their trays had been desecrated, the two men made their way to an open area of tables. The two educated men sensed that the other inhabitants were there due to a lack of anything resembling sophistication. They soon became labeled the "Snobs of Przemys'l" for their perceived isolationism.

"So what was it like at the academy Adolf?"

"Oh it was wonderful. I had the greatest teachers, mentors available. My painting technique grew by leaps and bounds there. I was making good money, both for my illustrations and paintings."

"You also did some architectural work?"

"A little bit – that's what the school thought I would be most successful at. And I worked for a couple of firms on a free-lance basis."

"Did you make much money?"

"Yes, I did, but I learned that architecture was not my passion. I just wanted to paint."

"What do you like to paint?"

"Anything really…landscapes, urban settings, people…nude women…" Adolf hoped to get a rise out of Hugo but again was unsuccessful.

"As of late though I've just tried to be experimental…kind of hybrid between Impressionism and my own style. Anyway, a lot of people seem to like it. I've sold enough paintings to pay my rent for the next two years."

"Wow that's incredible…and now you are here…here in the midst of war."

The two men became quiet as they meditated on their situations.

After a somber remainder of the evening, the two men retired to their barracks and quickly went to bed, both wondering what the next day had in store for them.

For the next several weeks the men did little other than drill and run. Adolf began to enjoy his daily two mile run through the town of Przemys'l. He could smell the incredible bread being baked at a nearby bakery, the scent of savory dishes being cooked at a local restaurant, and fresh expresso being brewed at a local café, it was all too intoxicating. Despite how dark and dreary the sky had been lately, Adolf was feeling bright and chipper, he was starting to feel pride – he felt like he was accomplishing something. If he had been back in his apartment in Vienna, he might have started drinking. The thoughts of Rothschild's laughter booming in his head.

But for now, he was renewing himself. After the war he would become a truly great artist, assuming he survived.

******

In Mid-September, the Russians made their attack on the fortress at Przemys'l. The earth shook as Russian mortar and cannons began to blast the old city. The Austro-Hungarian Army answered back and for the first few days there was the non-stop bombardment of each army's position. Adolf and the rest of the troops who were not involved in artillery were hunkered down in trenches that were just on the outside of the fortress. For Adolf, and for many of the green troops, this was all new. The volume of each explosion seem to split his ear drum. It was if the earth was becoming unhinged…soon to crumble to pieces. As he looked down the line of men in the trenches, he could see some reading the Bible, some were reading the Koran, others were praying. He recalled the English saying that "there are no atheists in foxholes."

Did Adolf believe in a deity? Adolf had been trying to come to terms with his beliefs for the last several years. He had been raised Catholic by his mother. He was not sure what belief system his father held except that a sound thrashing of his son was required every now and again. He had detested his father. His father had wanted him to go into the civil servant business like he had done, but there was nothing attractive to Adolf about being a clerk in an office. Adolf had despised his father, and because of it despised his name. He wanted to change his name. "Adolf Hitler" did not sound like the name of an artist. He needed something like "Gaugin", "Renoir" or "Van Gogh". Or maybe he could make some amalgam of his name? "Adolf Hit", or "Adolf Ler"? He liked the work of Pablo Picasso, whom everyone referred to as "Picasso", but "Hitler", that did not seem to roll off the tongue. Perhaps the thing to do was change his first name? A lot of his friends, especially his Jewish friends had called him "Adi", that was it! Once the war was over he would become "Adi". Like the phoenix springing from the ashes, "Adi" would rise in the world of art.

******

"Hello Captain Hauptman?"

"Yes?"

"Hello, Captain this is professor Spielman from the Academy of Fine Arts in Vienna?"

"Yes, professor, how can I help you?"

"Well, I believe you have a young private in your army there by the name of Adolf Hitler?"

"That name sounds familiar."

"Well anyway, I know this is an unusual request but can you move Adolf to a non-combatant position? You see, Adolf is a tremendous artist and it would be a shame if something happened to him. He has so much potential and we feel here at the academy that he will be a major contributor to the art world especially here in Austria."

"Well, I'm not sure what can be done, but I'm open to suggestions."

Basically what Captain Haptman was referring to was a bribe which Professor Spielman was clear on that point.

******

In late September, the Russians advanced to the River San and laid siege to the fortress. Hermann Kusmanek von Burgneustädten, the Commandant for the fortress tried his best to rally the troops, but the Russian force opposing them was significant. For several days the Russians bombarded the fortress city causing chaos and confusion among the civilians who then fled the city en masse. As the Austrian artillery returned fire, there was little Adolf and the other infantrymen could do other than either support the artillery men or hide in a trench. For Adolf, he decided to make himself useful and be available to the sergeant for anything he wanted. Typically, the sergeant would use Adolf to run messages back and forth to the artillery sites.

On the fourth day of the siege, Adolf was running a message up the hill to where the artillery battery was when a Russian shell came screaming near him, blowing up the mound of dirt he was climbing and a nearby fence. It seemed like the earth had been blown away from his feet as he tumbled down the large hill, through the fence and down toward the city center below. As Adolf came to a rest at the bottom of the hill, he began to stare back up at the fortress. The entire fort seemed to be ablaze. The Russians must have hit an armory setting off a massive explosion.

As Adolf stood he could see there was no way to get back up the hill. To go around to the front of the fort would be suicide as not only was their Russian cannon firing but sharp shooters picking off any lone soul who was stupid enough to get within their sites. Looking to the right, he could see the main village through some trees and decided to head in that direction. As he moved through the forest, stray Russian shells began to explode near him. He picked up the pace and soon arrived at one of the city streets. He looked around – the town was deserted. Adolf sought refuge in a nearby café. As he walked through the front door he was greeted by an elderly woman. Her presence caught him by surprise – he assumed that all civilians had fled the city. The angry woman tried to tell him to leave, but Adolf could not understand the woman. Seeing that her commands were being ignored she started to swipe at him with a broom. She pushed and prodded Adolf out of the café and the two began to argue at the entry way to the café.

As the two argued, a bullet came careering through the air and struck the woman in the head, her head exploding in front of Adolf. Blood, cerebral fluid and tissue landed all over his face and chest. *This could not be happening; this could not be real?* Adolf fell to the ground in shock, vomiting profusely. He could feel himself losing consciousness. Not knowing whether he was in a dream or not, he looked over at the woman on the ground. Blood was everywhere – it seemed to be continually gushing from her neck, filling the street. Soon the only thing he could see was a vision of red, a depth of red he had never seen in his life. He felt himself starting to choke.

He woke up several minutes later realizing he had passed out. He picked himself up and ran back into the café, jumping over the elderly woman's body as he did so. He did everything in his power to not look at her. The thought of what he had just seen brought him to near vomit. He closed the door behind him and sat down at a table. The café was empty and dark. There was one stream of light coming through a nearby window shade. He could see large quantities of dust in the beam of light. Tired and hungry, he lay his head in his arms on the table and closed his eyes. The only thing he could hear was the shelling from the Russian artillery in the distance.

After an hour or so of trying to nod off, Adolf got up and headed toward the kitchen, looking for something to eat. He found some bread that was laying out; good pumpernickel and some gouda cheese. He began to rip away pieces of bread and force into his mouth. He produced a knife and quickly cut the cheese into multiple pieces that he also then thrust into his mouth. He was like a man possessed, but it was necessary. Given the situation he didn't know when he would eat again. As he continued to eat, he noticed a mirror above the kitchen sink. He walked closer and began to look at his reflection. He could tell he had changed. What changed exactly he couldn't quite tell. Was he more mature? More aware of the realities of life? He ran his hand through his greasy hair and looked at the palm of his hand. He hadn't showered or shaved in a week. His hand was covered with hair tonic and grease. The stubble on his face gave him the appearance of someone living on the streets. At that moment he did feel homeless, he felt there may never be a home for him ever again.

After finishing the bread and cheese, he found a half bottle of brandy and began to gulp down its contents. Upon completion, he noticed a small cot near the back of the kitchen. He immediately plopped himself down and after several minutes of listening to the continued bombardment of the city, slowly went to sleep.

As Adolf drifted into a deep sleep, he began to dream. He began to dream of a summers day in Vienna. The barmaid was with him on a hill just outside of the city. They were having a picnic, both enjoying each other's company. As they completed their lunch, the barmaid began to take off her clothes. As she completed her strip-tease, she began to swing the sheer white dress she had been wearing.

"Where do you want me Adolf?"

The smiling Adolf took the blanket they had been lying on and moved it to a nearby tree. He instructed her to lay on the blanket while he retrieved a canvass and paints from his car. He began to set up his easel, all the while feeling more and more aroused by the beautiful barmaid. He began to paint the canvas but all he could seem to do was throw wild blobs of paint across its surface. He became frustrated not knowing how to paint. The barmaid whispered for Adolf to not get so frustrated but it made him even more angry. The barmaid got up and walked over to Adolf trying to calm him. The two began to enjoy a sensual kiss when a loud noise caught the two lovers by surprise. Coming over the hill was a large contingent of Russian soldiers firing away at the two. Rifles and cannon were firing away at them with loud pounding explosions overhead.

Adolf quickly awoke from his erotic dream to the sound of a man pounding on the door of the café. He quickly got up and opened the door.

"Herr Hitler?"

"Yes?"

"Hello, I'm sergeant Hanz Gruber. I've been trying to locate you. You have orders to return to Vienna!" the young officer said with a bright smile.

"You're kidding? Aren't we in the middle of a battle?"

"Well there has been a break in the fighting. The Germans arrived from Poland last night and broke the siege – the Russians have pulled back."

Adolf could not believe it. He was still trying to comprehend the elderly woman's death. He could not shake the image of her exploding head from his mind. He began to shake his head and then looked up at the sergeant.

"I guess we have to thank the Germans for bailing out us Austrians again eh?"

"Yeah, I guess so. Anyway, there is a car waiting outside for you to take you to the train station."

Adolf was puzzled. How did he rate a transfer like this to Vienna? Why him? He was soon about to find out.

******

The next morning when Adolf's train arrived into Vienna, an officer greeted him from the Ministry of War.

"Herr Hitler?"

"Yes."

"I'm Fritz Schneider from the Communications Office. We hear you are an excellent artist?"

Adolf raised an eyebrow and shrugged his shoulders.

"Ah, modesty. Yes, you must be a true artist. Anyway, please come with me."

The officer showed Adolf to a car that was parked just outside the station and they were soon heading down

Rhienhardtplatz at a good pace. Within a few minutes they were at the Ministry of War and the young officer was guiding Adolf up the stairs to the Communications Office. Adolf was then introduced to the head of communications in the Austro-Hungarian Empire, Randolf Eichman.

"Ah Hitler, good to meet you."

A still somewhat dazed Adolf returned the handshake.

"I've heard a lot about you from Professor Spielman at the Academy of Fine Arts…"

Spielman? Ah, that explains it – that crafty Jew. Adolf began to smile as he realized what was happening. He was now in Professor Spielmans debt for eternity. He knew it was Spielman who was the one behind getting him into the academy and now he knew it was Spielman who had saved him from the war.

Eichman motioned for Adolf to follow him down a long hallway.

"Anyway, I'd like you to head up our graphic arts department. We know how important good communications and public relations are in a war effort. So you will be helping us put together post cards, posters, graphics for newspapers and so on. Here is the graphic arts department."

Adolf was duly impressed. It wasn't a large room but it held some of the latest in high production printing presses and page setting tables. There were three men hard at work. One appeared to be working on a newspaper layout while the other two were hovering over one of the printing presses.

"Thank you Herr Eichman but I really do not know anything about printing presses…"

"No, but you have an eye for what is eye-catching. These three lads are just going to put into print your ideas. You will direct them on how you want everything to look. We have confidence in you Adolf. We need someone who can convey a sense of nationalism, convey the Austrian spirit if you will!"

"Not the Austro-Hungarian spirit?"

Eichman just smiled and shook his head. He then introduced Adolf to the three other men.

And so it was that Adolf spent the rest of the war, conceiving, creating and designing posters and other advertisements for the Austro-Hungarian Empire. He enjoyed the work, although tended not to believe in the messages he was creating. The proud Astro-Hungarian Empire was shrinking with each passing year. The only admirable empire he could see was that of Germany. The Germans were really the only power in Europe to be reckoned with. And likewise, the Americans, French and English agreed with that assessment, later assigning full blame for the conflagration on the Germans in the Treaty of Versailles in 1918.

CHAPTER 5

With the conclusion of the war, the Austro-Hungarian Empire was slowly broken up; many provinces were ceded to the new Czechoslovakia, or to Poland and Romania. The states of Slovenia, Dalmatia, Croatia joined Serbia and soon became Yugoslavia. The treaty also called for the dissolution of the Habsburg family and Austria and Hungary were separated into their own countries.

For Adolf all of this meant very little with the exception that now his country was rid of the Eastern European ethnicities, and Austria might join Germany in partnership. During his time in the graphics arts department of the war ministry, Adolf had learned much about Austria's neighbor to the north. There had always been ties between Austria and Germany, they shared similar culture and language, but for Adolf he had been an Austrian first. Now though, with much of the Central Powers in tatters, Adolf started to long for a country he could be proud of. And although he desired to have national pride, for now it was time to develop himself again – to become the artist he wanted to be.

In the following December and January, Adolf became prolific as a painter; creating over hundred new pieces. Kurt of course was always there to lend a hand and the two men quickly regained some of the wealth they had lost because of the war.

******

The year 1919 would be an important one for Adolf. Once again he had become one of the most celebrated artists of Vienna. He had been invited to the most high-profile events, dined with actors and dignitaries, despite the economic woes of most people in Europe, Adolf had not been affected.

And for Kurt the sky was now the limit. He continued to watch Adolf grow as an artist. His work had become more mature. There was a new expression to his work – clearly it had been forged in the heat of battle, but it was a new force in his life. While war had brought a somber tone to the work of many artists like Picasso, Adolf's work seemed to be lifted to a new level. Maybe after such a traumatic experience, his mind was trying to create a better world – whatever it was he had a renewed energy and the art brokers of Vienna liked what they were seeing.

Kurt had broached the idea of going back to Paris, but Adolf insisted he was not ready. Adolf did suggest a possible move to Berlin. While the economy in Germany laid in ruins, many of the residents of Berlin prospered. Berlin had become a mecca for artists all over Europe. The film industry of Berlin was exploding and performance and visual artists were also gaining notoriety. Kurt agreed and two weeks later, the two men boarded a train for Berlin.

******

The train ride through Germany had been a depressing one. It was clear the war had rendered most of the population to poverty. Inflation had sky-rocketed and there was little employment for the average German. Unless highly-skilled, there was little opportunity for one to advance.

As the two got off the train in Berlin they were greeted by one of Kurt's old friends, Horace Goldman, a well-known art-dealer. They were also greeted by several beggars.

"I apologize gentlemen, please ignore them." Goldman quickly ushered the men over to a nearby car that was waiting for them. Adolf could tell Goldman was a wealthy man; expensive suit and overcoat, top of the line derby hat, neatly polished shoes and a gold pocket watch that he kept pulling out of his suit pocket every five minutes or so. He began to think the action was just for Adolf's benefit.

"Adolf, I'm so glad you have chosen to come to Berlin. I think you will find it a refreshing break from Austria. Artists here have influence and a freedom unimagined in any other part of Europe."

Adolf smiled and nodded, noting the lines for soup kitchens as they made their way down the Friedrichstrasse. As they drove further the views began to improve and clearly they were going through a more affluent part of Berlin. Goldman asked the chauffer to pull over near a street-side café. As the three men got out they were immediately received by the maître d' and were marched to a table in a secluded part of the outside patio.

"Gentlemen, what can I get you to drink?"

"I'll have a gin and tonic please Franz." Franz nodded while in one motion took Goldman's hat and coat.

"And for you gentlemen?"

"Scotch and soda please," Kurt volunteered.

"And for you sir?"

Adolf had to stop and think. He had been on a beer diet for the last several years and had never really had any cocktail before. Given the company he was now keeping perhaps it was time to change his outlook.

"How about a cognac?"

"Adolf, that's an after dinner drink, why don't you try a martini? The bartender here makes an excellent martini."

"Very well, a martini then." Adolf smiled but was embarrassed by his blunder. He could see Goldman smiling like he was amused by Adolf.

"Sorry Herr Goldman, I've pretty much lived out of beerhalls for most of my life."

"Understandable dear boy, nothing to fret over, and please call me 'Horace'. Now down to business. Adolf, we are going to have an exhibit of your work at a local dealer in town; one of the finest galleries in Berlin. I work with the owner very closely – Hyman Friedman. The show will be on Monday so we'll need to start setting up tomorrow."

Adolf nodded while Franz dropped off each drink and then immediately, seemingly out of nowhere, handed each man a menu – Franz was truly a magician.

"That sounds perfect Horace, Adolf and I will get down to the gallery early tomorrow and set-up. The paintings should be delivered later tonight. I am having a truck meet the train tonight. They then take the paintings over to the storage house over at Potsdamer Platz."

"Perfect! Franz, I'll have the usual."

"Yes sir, and for you gentlemen?"

"I'll try the Coq au vin, please." Kurt said as he snapped the menu shut and handed it to Franz.

"Excellent choice Kurt. This is the only place in town which can make French food."

Everyone then turned to Adolf who nervously eyed the contents. He could feel the attention was on him and he needed to make a decision quickly.

"I'll have the same as my colleague here."

"Very good sir."

As the three men handed back their menus, Goldman continued.

"I think you will really like it here Adolf, it's the perfect environment for an artist of your stature."

"Yes, I hope you are right, Horace."

"Of course he's right Adolf, you seem to have some doubts?"

Adolf looked around and shook his head.

"I just don't know. The world has changed. The once 'Mighty German Empire' hardly looks mighty anymore."

"Well it was ridiculous of us to get into that war," Goldman said matter-of-fact.

"That was really the Austrians and the Hungarians fight. If they wanted to hold on to their crumbling empire it was up to them to do it, not us."

"I think the Germans are loyal and honorable, they keep their word."

"Well, look what it got them…"

"What do you mean them?"

"I mean Hindenburg and the like. This country was heading toward prosperity, and now look at it – it's a shambles, a complete mess!"

"Yes, but you seem none the worse for wear."

"Well, me and my family have worked hard for what we have. Just because there was a war on didn't mean we had to drop everything we were doing. We built some really nice shops, some great galleries and invested in art."

"Did any of your family fight in the war?'

Goldman gave Adolf a scowl. The tenseness of the moment was lessened as the waiter brought the men their food.

"Herr Goldman, I apologize if I offended you. I was just a little discouraged with what I have seen and heard. I think the Treaty of Versailles is the greatest travesty the world has known. To throw 100% of the blame on the Germans for the war is an atrocity. How will this country ever recover?"

"I know Adolf, I know. But what can we do about it? The best thing is to keep working hard and hope the country can return to its former greatness. One way we can contribute to that is by putting on a great show of your works. What do you say Adolf?"

Goldman raised a glass of wine that seemed to have been secretly inserted on the table. Adolf noticed a glass of wine near his right hand – it was true, Franz was a magician.

"Perhaps your right Horace, let's put on a good show."

"That's the spirit Adolf," Kurt added as he clinked his glass with the other two men.

The afternoon continued with a bright haziness to the sky that relaxed Adolf. Along with the fermented beverages his mood soon changed. The men began to enjoy small talk, enjoying cigars and watching the street life pass before them. They quickly became enchanted with a street mime. Apart from his white face, his skin was very dark – Adolf assumed he was a Turk. Whatever he was he was hysterical. As various people walked by, he would walk right behind them mimicking their posture, their gait, their stride. It left the men, including Adolf in stitches. It had become a perfect day.

******

Adolf continued to flourish as an artist. His version of expressionism had a look and feel all its own. He was one of the few bright lights in an otherwise depressing era for Germany. He even took on a new moniker – "Adi". One of his fellow artists decided to call him that one evening while they mused in a nearby biergarten. Remembering the nickname from his early years in Vienna, the name stuck in Adolf's head and he soon started signing his work with his characteristic "Adi" that sometimes resembled more of a swoosh than a signature.

Life in Berlin for Adolf had become quite pleasant. His work had given him enough money to afford one of the nicest apartments in a wealthy section of the city. He hobnobbed with artists like Ernst Ludwig and George Grosz, musicians like Bertolt Brecht and Kurt Weill. He had also become an admirer of film producer and director Fritz Lang and was impressed by his advances in film. Adolf's circle also included many outside of the artistic world, like Carl Jung, Walter Benjamin. His work had also been noticed by one of the greatest minds the world has ever known. On several occasions he had met with and discussed art with the Director of the Kaiser Wilhelm Institute for Physics; Albert Einstein.

And while Adolf found his life to be very stimulating in Berlin, there seemed to be something else he was driven to but didn't know exactly what. There seemed that there must be something more to life than just art. He felt as an artist he was not in touch with the common man. In some ways he acknowledged that was a good thing. The common man in Germany was not doing so well. Kurt and Horace would often argue with him that his art was helping the "common man". But there was a restlessness, a void in

Adolf that he didn't know how to fill. The question he kept asking himself was *what do I believe in?*

What did Adolf believe in? He was raised by his mother as a Catholic. While he had stopped going to mass, he still felt some ties to the Church. What were his politics? He had felt for the German people after the war and wished he could help, but he had been focused on his art. Was it right however that he should be flourishing while the rest of Germany lay in ruins?

It was that thought that led him to start reading more about politics. He had become interested in the Communist Party of Germany. He began to read the writings of one of the party's earliest leaders – Rosa Luxemburg. He enjoyed her speeches and was introduced to her after a party meeting. The two soon grew close and Rosa became an admirer of Adolf's work. They were soon closely linked and it was known that they were lovers.

Adolf soon became infatuated with Rosa. She was a strong woman and knew what she wanted. Adolf had never been around a woman of such strength and intelligence. Rosa was a force, both politically and in bed. Adolf often wondered however if Rosa was just using him for his connections and notoriety. Whether she was or wasn't he soon didn't care, he was mesmerized by her.

Adolf would often attend her rallies or speeches. She was a wonderful speaker – he wished he could captivate an audience like she could. For a woman, she took no guff from any male. With her intellectual prowess she could put any man in his place. Adolf wanted to learn from her. She had seen a lot in her time and maybe such experiences could help him not only with his own politics but with his art.

Adolf truly admired Rosa. He had only known her since the previous November when she had been released from prison. It was like meeting a whirlwind. She was either meeting with fellow communists, writing speeches and propaganda or making love to Adolf – the woman was passionate. Adolf tried his best to keep up, but Rosa was a bright light and was going to be a prominent fixture in the new KPD or Communist Party of Germany. Her colleague Karl Liebnecht tried to warn Adolf off, but he wouldn't listen. He adored Rosa and tried to help her as much as he could. Sometimes he would lend her money which he knew went straight into the coffers of the KPD.

Not knowing all that was happening, Adolf sensed that there was trouble on the horizon. Rosa and Leibnecht were up to their necks in work. They had reorganized something called the "Spartacus League". Adolf had no clue what the league was about other than possibly being something related to Ancient Sparta. Rosa was also spending time on the party's new newspaper called Die Rote Fahne or Red Flag. Rosa employed Adolf as an illustrator to which he happily agreed and came up with any rendering she desired. It was later in January of 1919 that Adolf started to get a little nervous with some of Rosa's rhetoric. In a speech that seemed to invite intellectuals, politicians and Weimar thugs, Rosa cried for a new roll for the KPD,

"Today we can seriously set about destroying capitalism once and for all. Nay, more; not merely are we today in a position to perform this task, nor merely is its performance a duty toward the proletariat, but our solution offers the only means of saving human society from destruction."

Along with some inflammatory articles in the Red Flag, Rosa and Leibnecht were soon on the run again and this time it was Adolf who would save Rosa's life. As the Social Democratic Party of Friedrich Ebert came to power, Rosa was his target and the Friekorps were sent to remove her. When they came to her apartment to arrest her, she was not there but was in Adolf's bed. Her associate Karl Liebknecht called Adolf to warn he and Rosa of the pending purge. Rosa and Adolf decided that it was best for her to flee the country and so Adolf made arrangement with Horace Goldman to get Rosa and Karl Liebknecht out of the country. They found refuge in the South of France. Adolf and Rosa were unable to continue their relationship. Later she would flee to Poland where she seemed to vanish without a trace.

As the 1920's forged on, Adolf had to disassociate himself with Rosa Luxemburg. He half-heartedly pledged himself to Friedrich Ebert and his successor Paul von Hindenburg. Adolf looked fondly upon von Hindenburg, secretly admiring him for his military service and particularly for his defeat of two Russian armies in the Battle of Tannenberg. As an artist however, it seemed incongruous to be aligned with the military. For the current socio-economic situation in Germany, Adolf preferred a strong military presence to hopefully guide Germany out of its current plight. To utter such sentiments though with his artistic inner-circle would not look good.

Frustrated by living a "secret political life" Adolf decided to write down his memoirs; "Mein Kampf", or *My Struggle*. In the book he wrote down his struggles of trying to be an artist and at the same time keep his Catholic sensibilities. It was during this period that he decided to align himself with the German Workers Party, who was led by Anton Drexler. He would often listen to Drexler's speeches and was soon, employed by the party to create graphics and posters for the movement.

As the Worker's Party grew Adolf soon began to meet some of the most prominent members of the party; Drexler himself, Joseph Goebles and Ernst Rohm. Rohm ran the violent *Bund Reichskriegsflagge* who were often employed to keep the peace at various union protests and rallies. Rohm was somewhat of a hero to Adolf, being one of the many arrested at the November 9th, 1923 Beer Hall Putsch. Adolf felt with such men in the leadership that the Worker's Party couldn't help but be successful.

Wanting to learn more about Rohm, Adolf invited him to dinner one evening at his Berlin apartment. The unsuspecting Adolf sent his valet home early after setting the table and leaving several silver trays of vegetables, salad and duck l'orange.

At 8o'clock, Adolf invited the scared-faced Rohm into his apartment. The two men dined on duck and Adolf served a nice Chardonnay wine to compliment. The two men talked for several hours about politics and the changes they hoped would occur in Germany. Around 11:30, after consuming two bottles of vintage Chardonnay. Ernst seemed to get a little close to Adolf as they continued to talk on a nearby couch. Adolf noticed that Rohm began to look at him funny; his face seeming to blush.

"Adolf, I really appreciate everything you are doing for the Worker's Party," Rohm said as he moved closer.

"Thank you Herr Rohm, but why do you keep moving closer to me?"

Rohm then put his arm around Adolf's shoulder.

"I just feel very close to you Adolf, can I call you Adi?"

"Please move away."

"C'mon Adi, you must know how I feel about you?"

"What are you talking about?"

"And inviting me here to this intimate dinner? Are you just teasing me Adi?"

"What, do you think me homosexual?"

"C'mon, you're a renowned artist. Everyone knows that artists like to experiment, eh Adi?"

Rohm wrapped his other arm around Adolf's other shoulder and tried to kiss him.

"Get off me you oaf!!!"

Adolf broke free of Rohm's embrace.

"Get out of here you bizarre freak!"

"Look, I'm sorry. I thought you knew. And given who you are friends with, I figured you were sympathetic to our situation."

"What do you mean?"

"I mean your patron?

"Goldman?"

"Yes, Goldman. Didn't you know he's homosexual?"

"Impossible. He's married...has children."

"That's what he wants you to believe. He has been running in gay circles in Berlin since I can remember."

"That's sick!!!"

"Well, I can see you're upset. I'll take my leave. And again, I am sorry Adolf. I wouldn't have taken such liberties if I had known how you feel."

Adolf just sat on the couch, shivering with anger as Rohm let himself out. Adolf could not believe what he had heard. How could that be? His biggest patron was homosexual? This was too incredible of a story. Adolf had often dined with the family. Goldman's wife Hilda was very attractive and a doting wife; his children wonderful. Adolf would often play with them and bring them presents. How could someone live such a dual life?

******

The next morning, Adolf met Goldman for breakfast at the nearby café.

"Adolf, sold another three of your paintings last night!"

"That's great Horace, but I want to speak to you about something rather sensitive."

"Please go ahead Adolf..." the two men waited as the waiter set down two cups of expresso.

"I had a visitor last night."

"Oh, who?"

"Ernst Rohm."

Goldman looked up from his expresso cup as he was taking a sip. He became very quiet as he set his cup down.

"You know who Rohm is don't you Horace?"

"He's the chap from the Worker's Party you have been involved with?"

"Yes, Horace he is. He enlightened me on a few things last night."

"Oh yes, and what was that?"

"He mentioned that you had a fondness for your fellow man."

Again Goldman became quiet as he took another sip of his expresso. He finished and then wiped his mouth with a napkin.

"Adolf, what can I say. It's something that I have hidden for many years. I cannot say why I feel this way…it's the way I'm built I suppose. Anyway, I would never hurt Hilda for all the world – she's a terrific woman…"

"But why even bother to be married?"

"Adolf, if you grew up in the family that I did; it was not possible. My father would never have approved. Look Adolf, I'm not going to apologize for who I am, it's the way it is and there is nothing you can do to change it."

Adolf stared at Goldman. He shook his head. A smirk soon appeared on his face.

"I guess as an 'artist', someone living a 'bohemian lifestyle', I'm supposed to accept this?" Adolf said to himself as he began to look around the café.

"Adolf, nothing has changed between you and I. I will represent you as I have always done. You are one of my top artists."

"Not the top?!!!"

Goldman looked at Adolf as a smile began to appear on his face. The two men chuckled and soon burst out into laughter.

"What am I to do with you my dear Horace?"

"There's nothing that can be done I'm afraid."

"So Hilda knows nothing?"

"No, I've never had the heart to tell her. It would destroy her. Luckily it's one of the best kept secrets in Berlin"

Adolf again took a look around the café.

"You know, you've probably ruined my reputation with the women of Berlin."

"I don't think so, again it's really known to only a few…"

"Unfortunately Rohm has a big mouth. You're going to have to be careful Horace."

"I will Adolf, I will."

The two men finished their breakfast and headed over to the gallery to plan out Adolf's next show. He also made plans to make a visit to Madrid and visit another up and coming young artist.

CHAPTER 6

Being afraid to fly, Adolf took the early morning train from Berlin to Madrid. He found the trip exhilarating as the train wove through the Pyrenees Mountains and then into the Spanish plains, arriving in Madrid at 8 am the following morning.

"Adolf Hitler, Ich nehme an?" The man spoke in broken German.

"No, no. Soy 'Adi', senor Picasso!"

"Welcome Adi, my name is Maria Flores, I will be your translator on this trip."

Adolf shook the woman's hand while simultaneously receiving a bear hug from Picasso. Picasso grabbed his suitcase, put his arm around his shoulder and the trio marched off to a nearby car. Picasso instructed the driver to go to a café in the center of town. After a few thrilling minutes of zooming from street to alley and from alley to street, narrowing missing pedestrians, cyclists and various other vehicles, the three emerged from the car and entered the *El Toro*.

"Adi, they make the best expresso coffee in the city here – you'll love it!" It was true Adolf was in love. In the five or so minutes he had known Maria he was already smitten.

After expresso and some of the most excellent rolls Adolf had ever had, the three exited and headed over to Pablo's studio. The two men talked for hours about the art world, the latest works in expressionism. Pablo introduced Adolf to cubism showing some of his recent work. Adolf was pleased with what he was seeing. Picasso was on a level all his own. He knew he could learn a lot from Pablo. The men seemed to be in a trance as they both began painting large canvasses. Maria smiled as she saw the two artists begin to experiment. At various points during the proceedings, Pablo would turn on a record player so the two could listen to various composers. For Adolf he played Mozart, Beethoven and his favorite Wagner. Pablo, a fan of French composers; played Ravel, Debussy and Saint-Saens.

It was to Wagner's *Ride of the Valkyries* that the two men seemed to go into a frenzy; brushes slapping paint everywhere, hands smearing canvass, rags blending colors; it was a hypnotic blur. When done, the two men looked at each other and broke out into uncontrolled laughter, the ridiculousness of what they had done was something reminiscent of two schoolboys gone mad.

"You know, Wagner was an anti-Semite?" Picasso said through Maria as he tried to catch his breath. "But his music is inspired."

As the two men sat at a nearby table to inspect their results, Maria excused herself. She quickly re-appeared with two plates and two sandwiches. She then exited quickly again reappearing shortly with a large bottle of wine. She poured wine into two coffee cups; Adolf's assumption was that the artist did not have time to spend on shopping for wine glasses. The three made a toast to non-convention, and about a half hour later were at it again. This time, with the aid of alcohol they became even more savage with their canvasses, creating mayhem and havoc to a new degree. All the while Maria sat transfixed at what she saw. She believed Adolf a genius and began to have warm feelings for him; but then thought that perhaps it was the just the wine. As the two men continued, Pablo, through Maria, explained to Adolf that he was a Francophile; his dream was to one day live and paint in France. Adolf smiled, recounting to himself the humiliation he had felt in France.

"Now that is a culture, they know what art is. They know what good wine is. That's where I am going to live one day!" Adolf wished he could share Pablo's sentiments, but the memories were too painful.

The two men continued their barrage until 2am when they both slipped into a couple of cots nearby. Maria had left an hour earlier, leaving the two maniacs to themselves.

The next day Pablo and Maria showed Adolf the sights and sounds of Madrid. Adolf loved it. While he had seen the noise and hustle and bustle of large cities, Madrid seemed different. He couldn't quite place why but it was different. Maybe it was the language. Maybe it was the attitudes. Whatever it was he fell in love with Madrid. Later that day they went to one of Pablo's favorite bistros in town. That had civeche, carne asada, various wines and a new favorite of Adolf's flan. The three then made their way back to the studio where they again made wild experiments with paint and canvass. Pablo tired around 11pm and Adolf continued to play with his creations.

It was around midnight when Adolf realized, thanks to a nearby mirror, that Maria had been watching him. He turned and smiled at her, she returning his smile with a bright gleam. Adolf began to joke around and suggested he paint her portrait. Adolf became quite nervous when she agreed, but with one additional caveat; that she be nude. Adolf smiled and nodded. Maria walked over to a nearby couch. She then unzipped the back of her dress. Adolf liked the dress as it had emphasized all of Maria's curves. Now he didn't have to imagine what those curves looked like as she quickly slipped out of her undergarment. Adolf exhaled, trembling slightly. He began to think back to his time at the Vienna Art Institute, when his professor used to criticize him for his inability to paint the human form. Well this was a human form worth painting. Maria sat on the couch and then changed her position, lowering herself onto a large pillow. It was a magical moment for Adolf. Outside the nearby window was a full moon. It reflected onto Maria giving her an almost luminescent appearance. A large lump filled Adolf's throat. Was he dreaming this whole episode?

As Adolf began to mix paint, he wasn't sure if he should paint her as a real-life or use his expressionistic form. He decided to just start painting, hoping God would direct his hand. As he started with large swatches of paint he then decided to use more detail, using a combination of his brush and a small metal trowel he often used. Maria seemed to be transfixed, not allowing one muscle to flinch. Adolf admired Maria; not only for her beauty but her mind. Right now though all he could think of was her beauty.

Adolf became a little self-conscious as he could hear Pablo snoring in a nearby room. Adolf hoped that Pablo would not awake, being surprised by what Adolf and his translator were up to. Adolf did his best to concentrate. He was under pressure. It wasn't just the need to come up with a good image, but he needed to prove to himself that he did in fact know how to paint the human form. But what did he care about those professors back at the art institute?!!! Those men were of no use to him now. Besides, he was a professional artist; making his living in Berlin as one of the best painters.

After doing what he thought was a good job on the room and the couch. Adolf began to concentrate on Maria. He would slap on white, mixing it with some green to create an olive complexion. He would then paint thick black lines to capture her eyes; filling them with blobs of light green to resemble the hazel, with large black pupils and a mark of white to show the gleam she had. He made four small curves that shaped into her nose; her delicate sweet nose and another streak of white to show the light shining off of that adorable nose. Several quick strokes of red later he had her full lips with again a streak of white to show the light. He then applied wild strikes of black paint to show her full mane of hair. Next it was on to her body. Again Adolf began to tremble. While he was pleased with what he had accomplished with her face; how was he going to complete the rest? He took a deep breath and began.

Adolf took the red and white and began to come up with some flesh tones; adding small dabs of yellow. With the right flesh tones, he began to make large sweeps of paint which were her arms. He did the same for her legs and feet. As he began to focus on her breasts; he could feel his heart race. He continued to play with the white, red and yellow paint. He then made sweeping strokes to show the outline of her breasts. He began to meditate on Vincent Van Gogh and his painting of Paris street life. He began to image the sketches of the prostitutes and their forms. He tried to apply the same appearance using shades of black to show the outlines. Before he could apply another stroke, Maria clasped his arm. She winked at him and nodded in the direction of one of the rooms. A large lump grew in his throat. He immediately complied and they walked over to the room.

Maria turned on the light and then walked over to a large cot, where she beckoned Adolf to come sit with her. As he sat, she threw her arms around his neck and planted a passionate kiss on his lips. Adolf grabbed her around the naked waist and pulled her into him. He then kissed her, slowly lowering her back down onto the bed. He paused for a moment, wrestled quickly with his shirt and then threw it to the floor and then continued his assault on the Spaniard. As the two fought for physical ecstasy, Maria loosened the belt around Adolf's pants. Working together they achieved their aim and Adolf was soon sans undergarments.

Adolf mounted Maria like a Valkyrie laying wasted to an Andalusian village. Maria liked how authoritative Adolf was. They were soon in unison rhythm and Adolf began to penetrate Maria. Up and down they went, causing motion-sickness to anyone who would have happened upon them. Maria writhed in glorious pain as Adolf continued the attack. Maria dug her fingers into Adolf's back trying in some way to draw him to her even closer, but it was not possible. Both of them soon rose in simultaneous euphoria with Maria letting out a muffled scream and Adolf a loud groan. The two relaxed their grip on each other and began to look into each other's eyes, smiling brightly. They both began to giggle like school children, Adolf slowly fell to the other side of Maria like a cow that had been tipped.

"Cigarette?" Maria offered Adolf. Adolf, still panting, signaled that he would not be in need of tobacco at the moment. Maria found a lighter in the nearby nightstand and set flame to one end of the cigarette. Slightly out of breath she choked back a large intake of smoke. Adolf got onto one elbow his head resting on his hand as he admired Maria.

"You are beautiful Maria."

"Please Adi, don't ruin the moment."

"What?"

"You artists try to put us women on some romantic pedestal."

"Is that not what you want?"

"I just want to be treated as an equal."

Adolf stopped for a moment and began to contemplate what that meant. Had he been unjust to her in some way?

"What do you mean?"

"I mean that it's a difficult world for women. We do not get the same opportunities as you men."

In a matter of minutes Adolf had gone from ecstasy to the greatest scourge of womankind, or so he felt.

"What issues have you dealt with being a woman?"

"Well, physical inconveniences aside, I would like to be an artist like you and Pablo. But those old men at the academy will not accept me."

"I didn't know you were an artist."

Maria produced a sketch pad from under the bed and handed it to Adolf. Adolf poured over the pages. Maria was a talented artist. She seemed to capture the many streets scenes of Madrid with just pencil and charcoal. If she could bring such life to these media what could she accomplish with paint?

"I'll help you."

"You will?"

"Yes, these are fantastic!"

"You really think so?" Maria said with the glee of a six-year-old on her birthday.

"Yes, you are very talented. I'll just ask Pablo to get some canvass and paints for you…what?"

"Pablo won't do that. He sees me only as his translator."

"Has he seen your work?"

"Yes."

"And he doesn't like it?"

"He doesn't give me any straight answers, no critiques."

Adolf was quiet wondering what Pablo's complaint toward her could be.

"Well, let me talk to him, maybe he will listen to me."

Maria smiled and put her hand on Adolf's cheek. He gave her a kiss on the lips. She got out of bed walked toward the doorway and then turned to him. Adolf was in awe of the image; one of the most beautiful women in the world was standing naked in front of him. He could feel his chest start to beat again and a dryness in his mouth. She flicked the switch to the light and he could she her feminine silhouette in the doorway – he was aroused again. She made her way back to the bed and jumped back in. The two began to hold each other and were soon making love again.

******

The next morning, the three had a quick breakfast in the studio and then Pablo suggested that "vamos a la playa!" Maria and Adolf agreed and the three hastily packed some clothes and headed down to the garage at the bottom of Pablo's studio. Maria hopped into the driver's seat and popped open the passenger side for Adolf. Pablo sat in the back like a king on a throne. They headed into the Madrid streets and soon were out in the country heading down the road for Valencia. Prior to departing from the garage, the phone in Pablo's studio was practically ringing off the hook. It was Horace who had been trying to get ahold of Adolf. He wanted him to return immediately to

Berlin to plan a large scale art show in connection with a newly announced art festival that was going to be produced that summer. But unfortunately for Horace it was going to be awhile before he could contact the newly christened Iberian.

For the next several days the trio lounged by the beach, attended to by several servants from the apartment that Pablo had let. The weather was idyllic and water refreshing. Every afternoon, Pablo would rent a motorboat and the three would find an isolated beach or cove and have a picnic lunch that the chef at the apartment's kitchen would pack for them. Adolf was relaxed and was content; he could not think about going back to cold, dark Berlin.

On one of the beach outings, Adolf with the aid of Maria decided to broach the question of Maria's art. The conversation did not go well. "I hired her as my translator, driver and cook, that is all!" Maria translated to Adolf. Adolf urged Pablo to take another look at her work and to reconsider, but Pablo would have none of it. The ride back in the boat to Valencia was a quiet one.

Later that night, Maria and Adolf walked together to a quiet café near the waterfront. The two dined on the local seafood cuisine.

"I'm sorry I couldn't get Pablo to see it your way."

"Thanks for trying but I had a feeling it would end that way."

"Well don't give up."

Maria planted a long passionate kiss on Adolf's lips. It was a public display of affection Adolf did not exactly feel comfortable with but since he was in Rome or this case Valencia he just relaxed and enjoyed it.

"So tell me about yourself, now that we are lovers."

Lovers. While Adolf liked the sound of that, he doubted whether his mother or the Church would approve of such a moniker.

"Well, I was born in Austria. Went to the Institute of the Arts in Vienna for three years. Was set to become an architect but then found I could make money as a painter. That stopped with the war."

"You served in the war?'

"Yes, a very harrowing experience. Luckily I got sent back to Vienna after several months and got to work in the graphics department. After the war I just painted. People seemed to like my work, well with one exception…"

"Really, who was that?"

"Edmond James de Rothschild."

"Oh him."

"Well, he didn't like my work so well…eventually I would like to go back to Paris but not yet."

Adolf could see Rothschild's face as he shook his head trying to erase the pain of that meeting.

"Anyway, enough of me, what about you?"

"I was born in the small town of Angles in Girona Spain. I was very close to my mother growing up."

"Oh?"

"Yes, she lost a child in childbirth and then when I was born she said it helped her get over that loss tremendously. We were inseparable for a while. By the way, my last name is not Flores."

Adolf pursed his lip in surprise.

"I am Maria de los Remedios Alicia Rodriga Varo."

"Well that is a mouthful!"

Adolf began to look at Maria in a new light, more appreciative of this remarkable, intelligent and beautiful woman.

"So why did you change your name?"

"I wanted something simple yet pretty…like a flower…Flores."

"How did you get mixed up with Pablo?"

"I wanted to become an artist so, what better way to learn than to get hired by the great Pablo Picasso."

"Starting to regret that?"

"No, it brought me to you."

Adolf smiled and began to hold Maria's hand.

After dinner they went to a nearby hotel overlooking the ocean. The two made love listening to the sounds of the ocean outside. Adolf felt himself seeming to rise with ecstasy with each wave crashing on the beach below. As Maria came to orgasm she began to shake and shiver, clutching onto Adolf. The two seemed to melt into non-existence, later crashing to each other's side of the bed. Their hearts pounding, completely out of breath, they began to hold hands, listening to the continued crescendo outside.

"Maria, will you come with me to Berlin?"

Maria was quiet, contemplating the offer.

"Maria, did you hear me?"

"Yes my love…yes, I will come to Berlin with you."

Adolf rolled over on his side clasping her hand in his. He had a bright smile and a glee in his eye.

"Oh this is wonderful. I can get you set up in my studio and we will make wonderful art together!"

Maria smiled, trying to hide her enthusiasm. She did not want to get to get too emotional about the prospect.

She had been used to promising ventures only to be disappointed in the end. She continued to smile and the two tightly embraced.

The next morning the two met with Pablo at the apartment and explained their plans to him. Pablo was clearly unhappy, feeling Maria had taken advantage of her position. The meeting ended on a sour note with Pablo dismissing her from his employ. Adolf tried to smooth over the situation but Pablo would not hear of it. The two left the apartment, taking a taxi to the nearest train station.

CHAPTER 7

The next morning the couple arrived in Berlin. Adolf called Horace from a nearby phone booth.

"Adolf, so glad to hear from you!"

"What's the matter Horace?"

"We've got a festival to attend, I'll be right there!"

Within minutes Horace was at the station and whisked the pair away.

"Maria, I'm sorry about our quick introduction but we have to get Adolf over to the Berlin Arts Festival, it's a big event I've been trying to make Adolf aware of for the past several weeks. I can see though by your skin color Adolf you have been busy?"

Adolf and Maria smiled a knowing smile, almost like two school children hiding a secret. For Horace however it was painfully obvious what that secret was.

As soon as the car came to a stop at the Tiergarten, the three hopped out and began to walk quickly toward the center of the park where they soon encountered multiple booths on either side of the road. The main road through the Tiergarten had been closed and there were a multitude of street vendors with food and beverage of every kind. Most of the booths were occupied by artists who were trying to get their works seen and hopefully sold. Maria and Adolf tried to take a look at the many artistic offerings but Horace kept them going at a strong pace. They eventually came to a larger exhibit with large paneled walls. As they came closer they could see it was Adolf's work.

Next to the large exhibits of Adolf's works was a pavilion with a large orchestra playing what sounded like the works of Wagner. Next to the pavilion was a stage with a microphone in front. Horace ran up onto the stage and began to speak.

"Ladies and gentleman, the artist has finally arrived. Please welcome Adolf Hitler!!!"

Horace motioned for Adolf to join him on the stage. Adolf was stunned and not sure what to make of the scene – there must have been several thousand people milling about. He had never spoken to an audience of this size before. He felt as though he was about to faint. He looked at Maria who offered him a hug and with the expression in her face, motioned him to go to the stage.

There was furious applause as Adolf, slightly trembling, climbed the stairs to the stage. He had no idea that so many people liked his work. As he reached the microphone he shook Horace's hand and Goldman seemed to disappear. The surprised Adolf was hoping for some physical support from Horace but he soon learned he was on his own. He looked up over the grounds – again noting there must have been upwards of three thousand people. He looked over at Maria, hoping to gain some strength.

Was this going to be a key moment in Adolf's life? A moment where he could express his goals, his dreams his philosophies? Would this be the place to express his feelings from his biography in Mein Kampf? Adolf smiled and looked out over the sea of people.

"Thank you for this great honor. The panels look magnificent..."

The crowd began to applaud and cheer. Adolf smiled gaining some courage.

"I hope you enjoy my work..."

Again loud applause and cheering erupted.

"These works I hope symbolize Berlin, symbolize the people of Germany, the hard working, industrious people of Germany."

More cheers and applause.

"I have really come to love Berlin, it's people, it's artistic community. I find the people here in Germany a good humble people who find reward in their imagination, in their originality, in their culture…"

Adolf looked over at Maria who seemed to urge him on with her eyes.

"What a great culture this is. The people seem as family to me. A strong people…a su…" Adolf was about to say superior people as he looked around he felt that might be a little too over the top.

"Anyway, thank you for accepting me as your own. Thank you!" and with that Adolf promptly fainted backward onto the stage. Maria and Horace along with several men standing by rushed the stage to assist Adolf.

"Adolf are you okay?" Horace yelled as he tried to wake Adolf. They were able to revive Adolf with a few soft slaps to the face and some cold water.

"What happened?"

"You passed out," Goldman said as they helped him to his feet.

"Well, that was not very manly," he said to himself shaking his head.

"Oh Adolf, not to worry…you're a big hit!" Maria said. Maria grabbed Adolf's hand and they walked over to the bandstand where the orchestra was playing. The two stood listening to the music, holding each other's hands, smiling as they gazed into each other's eyes. Adolf had arrived in more ways than one.

For the next several weeks, Maria and Adolf remained at his apartment. They were hard at work creating what they hoped would be an art form that would change the world. As they worked they would often break to enjoy a little love-making. Adolf was hopelessly in love with Maria and Maria was quite fond of Adolf.

As their work progressed, they decided to do an art exhibit at one of Horace's galleries. They worked feverishly to put the show together. When the day arrived for the show, the critics and art dealers were not too kind.

"Complete and utter trash," one Berlin critic wrote. "Adolf's new direction is mindless and without any of his previous genius for color and design." The two were broken by the reception. Deep down, Maria blamed herself, or at least thought that secretly that was what the critics were doing, blaming her. Berlin had quickly become a cold and dark place to Maria. She told Adolf she had to return to Madrid. Using school as an excuse she asked Adolf to help her to get into the academy there.

"But why do you have to leave, there are many good schools here Maria?"

"I just need to be back home in Spain, can't you understand?"

"Then I'll come with you."

"Maybe later. I need to focus on my art Adolf and that will be difficult with you there…you understand?"

Maria was feeling the long shadow of Adolf's success and needed to be able to explore her own talents on her own. She had enjoyed being with Adolf but needed some time to be on her own. Adolf understood, but was heartbroken.

The next several days Adolf was in a sort of trauma as Maria packed her things. He had put in a good word for her at The Real Academia de Bellas Artes de San Fernando, and she was accepted immediately. Adolf took her to the train station and kissed her goodbye. Maria for the first time began to cry, thinking of her loss. She knew though to become a great artist she would have to strike out on her own. She hoped that one day "Adi' would be back in her life.

******

For the next several years Adolf had established himself as one of the pre-eminent artists in Berlin. His shows gathered some of the greatest minds and art lovers from all over the world. And while he was the toast of Berlin, he was alone. He missed Maria. He would often write long passionate letters to her. Her responses were often short but he understood. As his wealth continued to grow, he purchased a house outside of the city where he could enjoy nature. As much as he liked Berlin, he now began to seek the solitude of the country.

Adolf would continue to go into Berlin on the weekends, often attending parties that Horace had organized. There Adolf would meet all of the elite artists, writers and actors; he would often dine and drink with Bertold Brecht, Fritz Lang and Marlene Deitrich. He once had an affair with Deitrich but was later told by the actress that she preferred the company of women.

During this period, he would often go to the theatre to see the latest musical or play. He became an ardent admirer of Brecht and his work. The two would often dine together after one of Adolf's visits to one of the writer's plays. And while it was a glorious time for Adolf, being wrapped up in a world of vast cultural experiences, pleasures and exploration, he deep down still felt lonely. He missed Maria and wanted to be with her.

******

In October of 1929, as Adolf continued his climb toward artistic immortality, an event in the United States quickly captured everybody's notice. During a lunch with Horace he broke the news.

"Did you hear about the stock market in New York?" Horace shook his head as he continued to cut through his plate of roast beef.

"No, what happened?"

"Looks like a major sell off."

"Hmmm…that can't be good."

Adolf, who had invested a small amount in the Berlin Stock Exchange wondered what this could mean for his money.

As the 1930's began, Adolf continued to do very well, despite a worldwide economic depression that had started the previous October. Horace Goldman was making him wealthy. All the money did little to fill the inner void he felt. He had met multiple women but none of them had the spark that Maria had. Horace would often try to set him up with various women he thought that Adolf would like, but he often would hardly speak to them during a meal or entertainment of whatever sort, this due to his mind being consumed only by one woman.

"C'mon Adolf, you're starting to get a reputation of being boring. Being a bore will not help with sales."

"I know Horace, I know. It's just that I miss Maria. Hey, what if I moved to Madrid?"

"What, no, never. You need to be here Adolf where you can help promote your work. Just shipping me paintings from Spain will not help promote your work. Your patrons want to meet you…know you."

"Please Horace, I need to be with Maria."

"Does she need to be with you? Does she even write you?"

"Occasionally."

"My boy, she is an artist. She wants to become a famous artist and you'll only stand in her way. Now, let's have no more talk of this, Berlin is your home!"

Adolf reluctantly agreed. This however did not change Adolf's mind about Maria. He continued to write to her on a regular basis, getting a few replies here and there. Maria was a rising artist in Spain and Adolf knew that there was little he could do to rekindle their relationship at that point. He had pleaded with her on several occasions for him just to make short visits, but she refused saying she had to prepare for various art shows, or that there were deadlines she had to meet for her work.

CHAPTER 8

In 1934, with the death of Paul von Hindenburg, a general election was held for the 3rd President of Germany (since the end of the Great War.) and Ernst Thalmann was elected. The KPD or Communist Party came to power in Germany. With the escalation of poverty in certain parts of Germany, many felt that with the election of Thalmann there might be a better distribution of financial resources amongst all the people of the country.

During this period Adolf had continued to be quite political. He wasn't sure if he was doing it for the right reasons as it was mostly just to keep his mind on something other than Maria. Adolf had been enlisted in the KPD to help with posters and pamphlets which he eagerly helped with. Adolf had become familiar with the inner workings of the KPD, being aware that it was heavily influenced and often funded by Josef Stalin.

Adolf had been going to many party rallies during the year to hear all different views. He had listened to Joseph Goebels and Ernst Rohn of the Workers Party, Wilhelm Marx of the Center Party, but the one who swayed him was Ernst Thalmann.

Adolf found that being a KPD member during the 30's also seemed to help his popularity. He was often invited to various KPD functions; dinners, conventions, parliamentary sessions. Adi's star was continuing to rise.

By 1935, Germany was on its way to becoming a world power. Albert Einstein and his colleagues at the newly constructed Berlin Institute of Advanced Physics were doing things that no one had ever imagined. Their work was bringing new ground-breaking inventions related to high-speed transportation in flight and rail. New means of bringing power to the world via a new type of Atomic energy called fission. The work at the institute had far reaching applications for all of humanity. And just down the street from the institute, at the Goddard Center were new experimentation with rocketry by a little know engineer by the name of Wernher von Braun. Von Braun was so bold to say that Germany would be able to place a man on the moon by the early 1980's. Very few people believed it could be done, but von Braun was none-the-less convinced.

Everywhere in Berlin there was visible signs of the city's growing prominence around the world. New stadiums and arenas were being constructed in anticipation of the following year's Olympic games.

For the rest of 1935 Adolf continued to go about life it what he would later refer to as a "malaise". He churned out great works of art, was invited to all the great events that anyone could be invited to. He was making so much money that he now had a luxury apartment in Berlin, a house in the country and now a vacation home in Bavaria in Berchtesgarden. For anyone else it seemed it would be the most idyllic life. But Adolf felt his life was missing something, he assumed it was Maria. He tried going back to church, seeking God. He continued to invest time in politics. For a while he considered applying for membership in the Center Party which was Catholic. He eventually decided against the idea, having to listen to many complaints by Horace Goldman about Catholicism, especially the form it took in 1500's Spain.

Throughout 1935 Adolf continued to write to Maria;

My darling Maria. I hope you are well. I continue to hear about what strides you are making in your artwork. The things you do with color and light are incredible. Your concepts and the spotlight you shine on society are rich and refreshing. You seem so wise beyond your years. Where did this ancient soul come from?

I wish we could be together. I was thinking the other day about our trip to Valencia and how entertaining that was – especially how our dear Pablo fussed about so much. I can still remember the night we spent alone – listening to the waves crashing on the beach. I remember looking into your eyes that night – I could see the endless possibilities.

In any event, I know you are occupied and do not have time for such nonsense. You have many things to attend to and are very busy - I wish only that you could make a little room for your Adi as well.

I recently heard from Pablo and how impressed he has become of your work. He wishes that the two of you can get together soon. In any event my love, I continue to think about you and wish only the best for you. Maybe we can meet soon?

Yours forever,
Adi

A despondent Adi didn't hear from Maria until a month later – it was a short two sentences…

Dearest Adi,

I hope too that we can be together one day. Right now I am too busy with my work, but we will get together soon.

Love Maria

The words were little succor for Adolf – he yearned for Maria and at times was distraught over their separation. He was becoming slightly distracted from Maria when he went to check on his new home in Bavaria one weekend. While meeting with his personal photographer Heinrich Hoffmann, he was introduced to a young woman named Eva Braun. Fraulein Braun was Hoffman's assistant and was learning about photography. Eva was quite nervous meeting the famous artist and Adolf could sense it – he tried to joke with her in an attempt to make her feel more at ease.

The three spent the day together, with Hoffman taking many pictures of Adolf in and around Berchtesgarden. The three then had dinner together and enjoyed a late drink and a long discussion devoted to the works of Bach, Beethoven and Brahms and who was the greater. The mood became light as the three sipped the finest French wine Hoffman could offer. Hoffman could sense that Adolf and Eva were attracted to one another. Excusing himself for the evening as he wanted to retire for the night, Hoffman suggested to Adolf that he walk Eva home to which Eva gleamed at such a suggestion. Adolf too thought it a capital idea and the pair were soon out the door with coats in hand.

As the two strolled the quiet streets of the town, Eva began to pepper Adolf about his background and soon found they were both Catholic. She wanted to know about how he became an artist and Adolf recounted the glorious and mystical events of his acceptance into the Vienna Institute of the Arts.

"A day that marked the turning point of my life. I have no idea what else I would have done had I not been accepted into the Institute."

"I'm sure a man of your stature would have found plenty of things to do."

"Not sure – politics maybe. I am interested in politics. Perhaps would have gone to law school."

The two continued to stroll until they reached the front entry to Eva's apartment.

"I'd invite you in but it's a little late."

Adolf smiled a great smile and doffed his hat to her.

"Understandable my lady. Until another time."

Adolf made sure she locked the door behind her and then began to walk back to his apartment nearby. The Berghof residence he had purchased was still in need of furniture and some clean-up so in the meantime he rented a nearby apartment. This way he could also be close to Hoffman.

Within a couple of days, Adolf had asked Eva to dinner. The two seemed very compatible and he suggested that she come up to the Berghof to help him decorate. She spent several days there helping him with curtains and carpeting and many other touches to the large estate. After spending a long day, working on the house, Adolf took Eva by the hand and led her to the bedroom. She became nervous as he placed his hand on her arm. He then placed another hand on her hip and leaned in for a kiss. He could see her shaking and whispered to her that it was alright. Eva smiled and giggled. He then pulled her tightly to his body and gave her a passionate kiss which was soon returned with equal passion. Adolf then picked her up and placed her into his newly decorated bed, adorned with the down comforter she had suggested.

Adolf stepped back and viewed the beautiful Eva who was beginning to relax. He took his tie and dress shirt off and then moved toward her. She again began to tremble…she hoped that he would rip her dress off and savage her, her heart pounded. He ran his hand through her hair as he sat beside her. She grabbed his hand and kissed it. Adolf moved over her and began to undo the buttons on her dress – Eva was scared yet completely at ease, a dichotomy of emotions. Adolf began to caress her, picking her up in his arms and then moving her toward the center of the bed. He lay her down on the bed and then removed his pants and undergarments. He then removed Eva's bra and undergarments. He began to kiss her neck which soon led to a firm embrace with both participants writhing in ecstasy. Adolf began to rub himself up and down upon her body eventually plunging his erected penis deep inside of her. Eva seemed to give up completely to the artist, letting out a muffled scream. Adolf continued his actions which Eva was completely compliant. The two eventually rose to orgasm and then crashed on either side of the bed in an exhausted heap. Later they both looked at each and embraced, both of them still panting as having just competed in the 100-yard dash.

As they lay in bed, just staring at each other, Adolf stroked her head and then smiled.

"With a woman like you Eva, I could rule the world."

"Let me help you my liege!"

"Sometimes I wish I was more than just an artist, a politician or ruler. This world needs so much help."

"Why don't you run for office Adolf?"

Adolf was quiet. He had never really pondered such a move before. He had always been interested in politics, and now as a member of the KPD, he might be able to serve in the party."

"Maybe you're right Eva, but maybe I'll start in some administrative capacity first, get my feet wet."

"That would be wonderful Adolf, I mean comrade."

She made a mock salute and the two began to laugh. Adolf began to tickle Eva and the two quickly submerged below the sheets.

******

When Adolf returned to Berlin the following day, he was greeted by Horace Goldman at the train station. On Adolf's arm was Eva.

"Horace, please meet Evan Braun."

"A pleasure my dear," Horace said as he kissed Eva on the glove. Secretly saying to himself *here we go again.*

Eva smiled and curtsied like a pre-school girl to which Adolf let out a loud laugh. On the ride back to the apartment, Adolf let Horace know of his plans.

"Well, Adolf you certainly look jubilant."

"I am Horace I am. I've met a wonderful girl in Eva and she has inspired me to reach to new heights."

Horace was hoping she had inspired him to pick up a paint brush. Adolf had not painted anything new in almost a month.

"And what heights are those Adolf?'

"I want to enter politics."

"Politics! Whatever for?" a bemused and startled Horace offered.

"I don't know. I feel like I've been a bit stagnate lately – I need a change."

Horace rubbed his chin and nodded his head. *Maybe a change of pace would inspire Adolf.*

"It might be an idea my boy…as long as you keep at your art."

"Oh yes of course, an artist is always an artist, he never quits – it's a part of him," he smiled at Eva and nodded to which she returned a bright gleam.

"So what plans have you Adolf to secure such a position?'

"Well, I'm going down to the KPD tomorrow and I'll have a word with Thalman about getting a position."

"Sounds ambitious. Well good luck my boy. Now let's get you and your lovely Eva back home."

That evening, Adolf showed Eva the many sights of Berlin. Having been raised strictly a Bavarian girl she was unfamiliar with Berlin, except of course what she had heard from her family which was mostly that it was the next thing to Sodom and Gomorrah. Eva was intrigued with the city and found it stimulating. She was also quite stimulated by Adolf – an artist, a poet, perhaps even a politician. She was enamored.

Later the two retired to Adolf's Berlin apartment where the two could barely contain themselves. Adolf and Eva made love throughout the night, hardly taking a break. They arose early to breakfast at Adolf's favorite pastry shop where they had expresso and croissants. Adolf, with the giddiness of a schoolboy, finished his coffee, grabbed Eva by the hand and were soon at the KPD offices.

Adolf walked past the receptionist, giving a wink and a smile, gave the KPD salute to three guards and was soon through the door of Thalman's office. He found, as expected, an early rising Thalman perched over his desk writing down something – perhaps his next speech Adolf thought.

"Ernst, I've come seeking employment," Adolf said with a bright smile.

"You're already employed here Adolf," Thalman said without raising his head.

"I know, but I want to do more than just posters and graphic work, I want to contribute more."

"Adolf, you can't…oh excuse me, I didn't know you had brought a guest Adolf. That's rude of you not to introduce us."

"Oh sorry, Eva Braun, please meet Ernst Thalman." Thalman offered his hand to shake to which Eva gave a hearty response.

"Mr. Thalman, I've heard so much about you. I am so honored to meet you. To be the leader of our country must be very thrilling." So much for being enamored of Adolf. It was as if Adolf didn't exist. He could see that Eva was mesmerized by the KPD leader and that he had been played. It seemed the blonde Bavarian maid was as power hungry as his dear Ernst.

"Let me take you to breakfast."

"We already ate Ernst."

"Now Adolf don't be rude, Mr. Thalman, the leader of our country has offered to take us to breakfast."

Adolf rolled his eyes and then accompanied the two to "brunch". He began to feel like a restless spirit who had come to haunt the couple, they clearly seemed to think him invisible. Not sure whether it was because he didn't have an offer of employment or that the two would soon be intertwined, Adolf politely excused himself from the pending lovefest.

He shook his head and just smiled. After all, he really didn't know Eva – he hadn't really had time to get emotionally attached. *Perhaps the Worker's Party has a position for me?* He queried himself and was off to Ernst Rohm's office.

Adolf approach the building with a bit of trepidation recalling the last time the two had met. He greeted the receptionist who made a quick inquiry to Herr Rohm. Ernst was through his office door like a shot, all smiles and putting his arm around Adolf. He closed the door behind him and gave him a big hug.

"I knew you'd come back you big lug."

"Please Ernst, I'm not here for that, I just want to see if you might have employment?'

"Employment? Why on earth would you want to be employed by the Workers' Party? Adolf, you're the toast of Berlin – one of our greatest artists, why do you want to bother yourself with politics?"

"I don't know Ernst; I just feel like I need something more. I love art, don't get me wrong, but I feel like I was put on earth to do more – to help my fellow man."

"Hmmm…I thought you were helping out with the Communists?"

"I was but I don't think they really need me anymore…in fact I'm sure of it."

"Well, what were you thinking of?"

Adolf thought for a moment and then began to pace.

"I was thinking that maybe I could run for election…you know like the senate…"

"Well, after the communists took over we have very little in the way of seats in the senate – just three and they are all filled."

"How about as a speech writer – I can write a great speech."

"Well to be honest Adolf, we're not really hiring right now – financially the party is a bit in debt after the election and we're waiting on Thalman to pay our debt off which he pledged but I have no faith he will do it. Anyway, sorry Adolf. You'll just have to go back to your country house, luxury apartments…" Rohm began to laugh uncontrollably. Adolf just nodded and headed out the door.

Adolf was exasperated. How could he have all this wealth and fame and yet feel so unfulfilled?

******

As the summer of 1936 began, Adolf used his membership in the Communist Party to get a free ticket to the opening ceremonies of the Olympic Games. The entire city as well as the rest of the country were excited to host the games – this would show the world that Germany was again great despite everything it had to overcome after the Great War. Adolf enjoyed the pageantry and spectacle – he enjoyed seeing all the athletes and the countries they represented. He also couldn't help noticed that many of his posters and paintings, mostly related to the Communist Party were well displayed.

Adolf was surprised by the Olympic Games and especially about how they changed his views on the Black Athletes. He attended several track and field events featuring the American Jesse Owens. Generally sharing an old prejudice of his Austrian upbringing that blacks were inferior or were "animals" as one of his uncles referred to them, Adolf's views quickly changed. Jesse Owens was not only a superior athlete but a gentleman in every sense of the word. Adolf was even afforded an opportunity to meet with Mr. Owens and Adolf began to see things in a new light. He clearly had been a "racist" and was learning to change his mind. He had refused to submit to being anti-Semitic, and now was the time to throw out his feelings of racism – everyone was truly equal. It was just a lot of hogwash that had been handed down to him over time. It was a revelation to Adolf and it was as if he could see things clearly for the first time in his life. He had unconsciously been harboring feelings of self-superiority and could now see that everyone was completely equal.

How could one be judged based on the color of their skin or the culture they were born in or their ethnicity – none of which anyone has control over? Adolf pondered.

With this new freedom of thought, Adolf poured himself back into his art. He seemed to have an explosion of ideas to which Horace Goldman was especially pleased.

CHAPTER 9

Adolf was triumphant at an art exhibit in Berlin later in the summer of 1936 that saw his prestige grow even more. Letters of congratulations came in from all quarters; Pablo Picasso, Marlene Dietrich, Max Plank, Albert Einstein, Ernst Thalman and his new wife Eva. One letter though was not so congratulatory – it was a letter from Maria. Maria was writing to "Adi", describing a terrible situation that was happening in Spain. A civil war had broken out between the left leaning Republicans who supported the Second Spanish Republic led by Niceto Alcala-Zamora and the fascist National party led by Francisco Franco.

Maria seemed almost hysterical in her letter, asking that her beloved "Adi" speak to his friend Ernst Thalman about helping to supply the Republicans. There were rumors that Thalman would send tanks and airplanes to help support Zamora. This was all news to Adolf – he had read in the paper about changes going on in Spain but didn't imagine it would come to this. For Adolf, Maria's letter was a call for help and he for one would not sit by while she suffered. He immediately packed a bag, hired and taxi and was on his way to the train station. He put a note in the post to Horace Goldman letting him know where he was going.

******

Adolf's train made many stops along the way to Madrid. Once across the border it seemed his coach was stopped at almost every town and city. Boarding the train at various stops were several officers who would inevitably ask for everyone's passports which Adolf would quickly comply with. One particular officer looked over the passport for several minutes and then walked toward the front of the train. Adolf became nervous and concerned for his fate.

The officer returned later and asked him what his business was in Spain. Adolf, in his broken Spanish advised him that he was attending an art exhibit in Madrid. Given the current conditions in Madrid, the officer expressed doubt that such an event would be occurring. As a desperate measure, Adolf advised the officer of his friendship with Pablo Picasso to which the officer, still somewhat suspect conceded to Adolf out of ignorance and the train was soon on its way.

After three days in route, Adolf finally made it to Madrid. He looked up Maria's new address and hailed a taxi. In the distance he could hear air-raid sirens and wondered what was happening. After a ten-minute ride, the cabbie let Adolf off at a two-story apartment building. Adolf drew a deep breath. It had been several years since he had last seen Maria – he wondered how she had changed. He hoped she did not have a new partner. With all the courage he could muster, he mounted the stairs, drew his hand back to knock. Before he could strike the door, it flung open with a smiling Maria almost in shock. She jumped into his arms. Adolf grasped her and pulled her up as she threw her arms around his shoulders. The two embraced in a passionate kiss.

"Oh Adi, I've missed you so," Maria said with a large smile. Adolf carried Maria through the door and gently let her down in the main room of the apartment.

"I haven't stopped thinking about you Maria. Since the day you left Berlin, I've been a mess."

"Oh Adi…" they embraced in a passionate kiss.

"Can we…" Maria smiled and pointed to her bedroom. Adolf picked her up in his arms and in one motion carried her to her bedroom, all the while they continued their passionate kiss. Adolf lay her on her bed gently. Maria was on her back waiting for Adolf to envelop her. He placed his hat on a nearby table and quickly disentangled himself from his jacket and tie. Maria lay frozen in her bed as if some wizard had cast a spell on her. Adolf, now in his vest and undershorts began the Spanish offensive. He sat on the bed next to Maria, placing his firm hands on her hips, she smiled as he examined her. She felt helpless as he removed her blouse and then her dress. He then laid himself on top of her, unbuttoning her bustier from the rear. The light was shining through a small seem in the window blind. The light showed Maria's shoulders – they gleamed. Adolf smiled at her beauty. His heart began to pound as he mounted her. Suddenly the apartment began to shake. Was it a tremor? The lovers looked intently at each other. The apartment began to shake again and again. A faint siren began to become louder and louder. The sound of an explosion could be heard in the distance.

Maria and Adolf quickly redressed themselves and headed to the back balcony of the apartment. Off in the distance they could see smoke and fire. Buildings began exploding.

"What is happening?!!!" Adolf yelled.

"It's happening I'm afraid," Maria said calmly.

"What Maria, what?'

"Franco…the Fascist…he's coming."

"So soon?"

"I'm afraid so."

Maria explained to Adolf that because of her political ties to the Republicans they would not be safe in Spain – they would have to flee to France. She asked Adolf to take a couple of suitcases she had already packed and walk them down to the garage. Adolf found the car as Maria explained and quickly put the suitcases in the back seat. He ran back up the stairs and found Maria staring at some of her paintings.

"I think I was finally getting the hang of it Adi." She said in a somber tone.

Adolf looked at the works. He had not been able to see them when he first arrived – he had been distracted. But now, looking at Maria's work for the first time since they had been together – he was spellbound. He had seen some photos of her work and some lithographs, but to now see her work in their original form…they were incredible. She had become a genius. She had grown beyond what Adolf thought possible. She was on a level even greater than he.

"Maria, these are incredible. Let's take them with us!" he exclaimed. He looked at her – she seemed to be at peace.

"No Adi. We need to leave – we can't be tied down by the past."

Adolf was stunned. Not only at her incredible talent but her complete willingness to let her hard work be destroyed. As he thought and pondered her sacrifice, the apartment began to shake again and they could now hear airplanes flying overhead.

"Adi we have to go!" Maria snapped Adolf out of his trance. She grabbed him by the hand and they seemed to fly down the stairs to the garage. Maria yelled for Adolf to get in the passenger seat while she seemed to jump in and start the car all in one motion. She drove the car through the partially opened garage door, breaking several posts as she did so. The car sprung into life as she accelerated past throngs of people who had flooded the streets. Some were pushing carts while others with looks of horror on their faces just collected what they could and began dashing to and fro. Children cried as they searched for their parents. Other children were collected like a mother cat grabs her young by the scruff of the neck.

Bombs began to explode in the street behind them as Maria and Adolf raced toward the main square. An ambulance was whining toward them almost hitting them square on as he swerved out of Maria's way at the last second. Adolf watched in horror as Maria seemed to be completely out of control – but it was clear she knew what she was doing. She flung the car around the larger street of the square and then immediately swerved onto a dissecting road leading south away from the main square. Adolf was amazed that she had not killed anyone. Everyone was in a panic and looked like lemmings about to throw themselves off a cliff. Only Maria seemed to know what was happening.

As they hurtled down the main road out of the city, they nearly collided with a fire truck as it sped down a perpendicular street. Maria nearly burst into tears, fearing for the mem who would try and engage a useless struggle against irresistible forces. She had to compose herself however and although her world was coming apart, she had to be strong and keep it together.

After about twenty minutes of winding their way through the Madrid streets, they were soon in the country heading on a road toward Valencia. Adolf recognized it as the road they had taken years earlier. Maria explained that in Valencia they would take a boat to the Southern Coast of France. Adolf wondered how long she had planned this excursion. Her timing seemed impeccable.

As they drove through the night, Adolf held on for dear life. They later stopped briefly at a small inn that was slightly off the beaten path. The innkeeper, who knew Maria invited the pair in. The inn looked deserted save for a young girl who was the innkeeper's daughter. He ordered her to bring Maria and Adolf some drinks. She quickly appeared with a tray with glasses and a picture. Maria quickly poured the picture's contents into a glass for herself and Adolf and told him to drink it quickly. It was fruity and slightly bitter with a taste of alcohol – most likely a left over batch of Sangria. After another few command in Spanish from the man, the girl re-appeared from the kitchen, carrying bread and cheese and some fruit. Maria told Adolf to quickly eat so they could get back on the road.

As the pair ate like it was their last meal on earth, the innkeeper gave Maria an update on what was happening. The fascists had organized in the north with tanks and planes that had been donated by Russia and Germany. They were now on the march and hoped to take Madrid shortly. The innkeeper, who had a son loyal to Zamora had just sent him a telegram indicating that he would be marching north to stop Franco. Maria could only hug the poor old man, knowing that his son's fate was almost certainly sealed. She quickly kissed and ordered Adolf to go to the car. The girl presented Maria with a basket full of bread and some dried meat for their journey. Adolf saluted both the innkeeper and his daughter and then was grabbed by the arm by Maria, they rushed back to the car. Like a bat out of hell, Maria flew the car down the country road and then back onto the main highway for Valencia. As it was now completely dark, they could see a yellow-orange glow off in the distance – it was Madrid, and soon to be many other cities that were in Franco's path.

At about 2am in the morning, the pair arrived in Valencia. Maria sped through the deserted streets of the city eventually arriving at a boat dock near the northern outskirts of Valencia. She parked the car, motioned for Adolf to grab the suitcases and they began to walk down the quiet dock where several boat sat bobbing up and down on the water. As they neared the end of the dock, there was a large boat that had its engine already running. Maria quickly jumped up on its side and then was helped into the boat by a man. Adolf quickly followed behind and was helped by the same man. As the light on top of the boat began to shine down on the trio, Adolf could see the man's face.

"Pablo…you're here too!" Adolf said with a yell – Maria asked Adolf to keep it quiet, as she hurried inside. She put their suitcases in a small room in the lower galley of the boat and then motioned for both Adolf and Pablo to follow her. They walked up to the wheelhouse of the boat and Maria greeted a tall gentleman.

"Vamanos Miguel!"

Miguel began to push forward on the throttle and the boat began to move. Maria looked toward the back of the boat seeing that the other deckhand had untied all the ropes that had docked the boat. Adolf felt like he was in a dream, everything had happened so fast.

"Maria, how did you know to prepare all of this?" Adolf said completely perplexed.

"I had been planning it for a couple of weeks. My brother who lives up north was telling me of what was happening. He knew I had to leave. Everyone knew I was a supporter of Zamora. I tried to hold out as long as I could but I had to leave – and what luck, you my love came on that same fateful day – it was fate. She immediately hugged Adolf and they began to kiss. Adolf could not believe what had happened. What he thought would be a nice, peaceful trip to Spain had now become an ocean-going adventure to the South of France.

CHAPTER 10

Late the following afternoon, the boat docked in Marseille. Adolf and Maria had tried to grab whatever sleep they could below deck – it had been cold with only a thin blanket to keep them warm. Pablo had stayed in the wheelhouse, sleeping in a corner where there was a small cot. As the deck hand tied the boat to the dock, the slumbering artists below were being summoned up on deck. The two stirred and submitted to the quick shouts from the captain.

The two emerged blurry-eyed and trying to make out what was happening top-side.

"Greetings my dear guests! I hope the journey was not too long?"

As Adolf's vision became clearer he could not believe his eyes – it was Edmond James de Rothschild. The man who had rejected Adolf years earlier.

"Joseph, please go below and get my guest's things."

Pablo, came down the stairway from the wheelhouse completely disheveled.

"Ah Pablo, so good of you to join us!"

"What's going on?" A confused Adolf asked.

"What going on? Well, I'll tell you what's going on! I am your new patron!"

"Patron? I thought you didn't like my work?"

Rothschild motioned for the three passengers to disembark and follow him and "Joseph" to a nearby car. It was a large Mercedes limousine. He motioned for everyone to get in.

"To answer your question my dear boy, of course I liked your work. But if I had said I liked your work then, would you have been driven to reach the heights that you have now ascended to? You are the talk of Europe and if I have my way, soon to be the talk of the United States! Well you, Maria and Pablo."

Adolf was baffled. If what he was understanding was correct, Rothschild's complete humiliation of him back in Paris was a plan? He began to think back on his career – had that moment of rejection set him off to become an even better artist? He quietly contemplated the thought as Rothschild closed the door, ordered Joseph to drive and then popped a cork on a bottle of champagne.

"Nothing but the best for my new charges!" On a tray sitting on the seat next to Rothschild were empty champagne glasses which he carefully doled out to his guests. He then splashed favorable portions of the bubbly liquid as best as he could while Joseph accelerated through the streets of Marseille.

Could Edmond James de Rothschild have been my biggest benefactor? Adolf mused to himself. Even if ten percent of that were true, he would owe much to Rothschild for as Adolf looked back at it, that event did indeed change his art. He was more driven - he was more focused, and his art did get better. His art had a deeper message – deeper meaning to it after Paris.

Adolf shook his head, laughed and then raised his glass.

"To new business associates!" Rothschild practically cried.

It seemed to be complete serendipity, but as Rothschild later explained, the whole escape from Spain had been previously planned, well not so much with Adolf involved, but as soon as Maria had indicated to Rothschild that Adolf was on his way, he would link the two planned transactions together.

He produced a letter for Adolf that he had written two week earlier that he had planned to send to him in Berlin, inviting him to join forces in Paris. Adolf read it over and gleamed at such a prospect. Now it was happening, just not the way Rothschild had originally planned it.

"And who knows…without this planned escape from Spain maybe you wouldn't have met me in Paris? Maybe the pain of that previous encounter would have been too much – too difficult to forgive?" Rothschild proposed.

Adolf shook his head and remained quiet. He thought again about their previous meeting which brought a smile to his face.

"Well, we don't need to think about if I would have come to Paris or not. I'm here now and I am glad we are partners."

Rothschild burst into laughter and began to shake Adolf's hand.

"That's splendid my boy, just splendid." All four continued to drink and laugh at what they hoped to be a fruitful partnership.

After a short ride across town, the limousine glided to a halt at the Marseille train station. Rothschild presented papers for Maria and Pablo as Adolf gave the clerk his German passport. They were soon assembling themselves in to their first class compartment complete with their own personal steward, chef and porter. They dined on lobster, prawns, escargot, pate, linguini and clams while the champagne continued to flow.

When they arrived in Paris the next morning, the four were greeted by Edmond's chauffer in another Mercedes limousine. They rolled down the busy Parisian streets with so many sights to see. It had seemed that Adolf had not seen much of Paris on his first trip. Now he could see the Arch de Triomphe, the Champ-Elysees and something that seemed to hold a strange fascination for him; Napoleon's Tomb.

As they made their way through Paris, their car stopped at the Palace of Versailles. Edmond asked his guests to step out. He wanted to show them what had become of the Palace and that it was now mostly a museum. The four spent several hours surveying the artwork and were awestruck. While continuing to review the various works, Adolf noticed a doorway which looked rather official. While the others were distracted he took a quick look in. He opened the doors and could see a large hallway – when he looked closer at the chandeliers and mirrors he realized what it was – the Hall of Mirrors. In 1919, this is where the Treaty of Versailles had been signed. A treaty in which many had believed treated Germany unfairly. He meditated for a while on the treaty. While at first angry, he realized now what strides Germany was making – it was becoming a truly remarkable country, offering so much to the world in the way of technology, science, art and literature. *Thank goodness there wasn't a second war to seek revenge on the treaty*, he chuckled to himself. He then closed the doors behind him to rejoin the group.

After a further hour or so of enjoying the museum's delights, Edmond shuttled everyone back to the car where they headed to his home, also in the Versailles area. As they pulled up to the tree-lined driveway, the passengers became in awe of the grounds. The property was immaculate with distinct and detailed landscaping of every bush and blade of grass. As they neared the enormous mansion, the driveway became lined with statues of lions and eagles and various other animals of war. They arrived at a walled-gate where an elderly guard waved the car through.

As they approached the mansion, the structure appeared to go on for miles toward the horizon, it seemed endless. The car wound around a large circle which had what appeared to be a gold-plated fountain. Behind the fountain was a large ceramic wall with cloud shaped patterns carved into it. Large cherubic figures were holding vases which rained down streams of water into the fountain. As the car came to a halt, a well-dressed gentleman in fine spirits greeted the arriving party.

"Antoine, please help our guests to their rooms." Antoine with a smile bordering on a moronic grin, quickly exhumed the suitcases from the car and began to lead the exhausted passengers to their rooms. Edmond followed along guiding Antoine as they made their way up a spiral stairway, the likes none of the guests had ever seen before – to say that it was opulent was an understatement. The railings seemed to be made of gold, the stairs a sparkling marble with a velvet carpet laid on top as if it had been poured.

As they showed Maria and Pablo to their rooms, Edmond joined Adolf in his.

"Adolf, I am so glad you joined us here. I think what we will be able to create with you three geniuses is something that no one will ever be able to match."

"Thank you Baron Rothschild…"

"Please call me Edmond."

"Yes, Edmond, I am most appreciative of your hospitality and generosity, but…"

"But?"

"Well, it's just that I have a home in Berlin."

"But why did you go to Spain then?"

An embarrassed Adolf smiled and looked toward the ground, shuffling his feet.

"You wanted something else my boy. You were lonely and wanted someone in your life…Maria."

Adolf smiled and nodded, embarrassed that Edmond was seemingly seeing right through him.

"Well, there's plenty of time for that my boy and Berlin will always be where Berlin is…it's not going anywhere. So enjoy your new surroundings, be inspired! I want to show you something." Edmond motioned for Adolf to follow him. In a large bay window in the bedroom, was a dressing table. On top of the table was a large book that was opened in the middle.

"See this Adolf, this is the Tanach…" he began to leaf through the large pages that appeared to be brittle.

"You've heard of the Torah?"

"Yes, the Law of Moses." Adolf said timidly, remembering his days in Vienna with the Bachstitz family.

"This book is the law and the prophets as well as the Psalms and Proverbs – this is the history and culture of the Jewish nation and I want you to have it Adolf."

Adolf was astounded. It was one of the most beautiful things he had ever seen. Being raised as a Catholic, he was taught by his mother to revere not only the New Testament but the Old as well. The book looked like it had been the original document that descended with Moses from Mt. Sinai.

"But why Edmond? Don't you want your family to have this? This is remarkable."

"Adolf, I can tell you are an old soul like me. You care about things, you care about people, you care about traditions. I see it, I see it in your work. I've been following you ever since I sent you crashing all those years ago. I've seen your work – God is in your work Adolf and that's why I want you to have this."

Adolf was dumbfounded. The book must have been worth a fortune he thought to himself. How could he ever accept such a gift?

"How old is this Tanach?"

"It was produced in 1650 by Menasseh ben Israel. He had the first Hebrew printing press in Amsterdam. He was of Portuguese descent, but his family had fled from Portugal when he was quite young due to the Inquisition."

Adolf continued to be spellbound by the book – it was as if the spirits of ancient Israel were about to rise up out of it.

"Anyway, enough of history, let's move on to the future my boy. Come down for dinner in fifteen won't you?"

Adolf, still in a daze nodded his head. As Edmond left, a light knock came on the half-opened door. Maria peered in and joined Adolf over at the book.

"What is it Adi?" Maria said with profound wonderment.

"It's the Tanach."

"Wow, it's incredible…such an old printing it appears?"

"Yes, marvelously preserved."

"C'mon, let's join Pablo and Edmond for dinner." Maria tried to yank Adolf along but he hesitated.

"Maria, I find all of this so hard to believe."

"What do you mean?"

"I mean, two days ago I was in Berlin, and now I am here in Paris, after originally stopping in Madrid."

"Yes?"

"Don't you find that a bit fantastic?"

"I do…but God had a plan for us Adi. He brought us together. We wouldn't have survived in Spain and so he has brought us here to France."

The events of the past couple of days didn't seem to add up for Adi. It's like God's hand came crashing through the skies, plucked he, Maria and Pablo up and placed them there in Paris.

"It's our destiny Adi!"

What seemed so easy for Maria to understand and comprehend was not so for Adolf.

"God guides us, he shows us the right paths and the obstacles to go around."

Adolf mulled Maria's thoughts over and over in his mind as he let her lead him from the room and down the stairway to the dining room. There in the dining room was a splendid dinner already prepared and laid out. The four dined on squab, cheese fondue and various other culinary delights, completed with Maria's favorite dessert – flan. After an aperitif and a cigar, which Maria also tried, the four retired to their rooms.

"Ah, Maria, Adolf, if you would like to share a room by all means don't hesitate."

Adolf looked at Maria who shook her head. She smiled and winked at Adolf. She then walked up to him and kissed him on the lips, she then whispered in his ear, "un cuarto despues matrimonio," she then kissed him again and sauntered in a rather provocative walk into her room, closed the door slightly, blew him a kiss and then closed the door.

Adolf smiled and knew what Maria was thinking. He had never thought in terms of marriage but it was clear, she wanted him to go in that direction.

That night in bed was anything but a sound sleep for Adolf. He experienced horrible dreams that left him several times in a state of panic. The first dream was during a dark evening overlooking a cliff – the wind which was initially gentle soon turned into a gale. A flock of sheep, which had been grazing on grass near the cliff were soon whipped up into a panic. Then, like lemmings they began to jump one by one over the cliff. Adolf broke out into a cold sweat as he awoke from the horror. He got up and went to the nearby bathroom where he splashed cold water onto his face. He took a sip of water from a glass and then looked at himself in the mirror. It was if something was possessing him, but what?

He then got back into bed and being completely exhausted, soon was again unconscious. He began to dream of what appeared to be some coastal town. There was a marketplace with many people buying and selling various goods - the language he could not recognize although it sounded like it was Spanish, maybe closer to Italian which he was familiar via his Latin studies as a youth.

Like with the dream of the flock of sheep, in this dream a gentle breeze again turned into a gale. This time, off in the distance, a horde of men dressed in black descended on to the townspeople. The people were in terror as the men in black railed against them with swords, cutting down men, women and children. One woman, trying to escape was forced into a nearby alleyway. She was alone with one of the men coming towards her. He dismounted from his horse, drew his sword and then plunged it into the woman. As the woman fell to the ground, Adolf could see it was Maria. He again awoke and tried to scream, but nothing came out. His heart was pounding in his chest. *What was the meaning of these dreams!* He cried to himself. He again went over to the wash basin to get some water which he again liberally applied to his face. He wiped a towel over his face and began to look deeper into the mirror. It was almost as if he wasn't there – his image almost a faint blur. Was this a part of the same dream?

Shaken he again attempted to go to sleep, but once again dead to the world, the images began to arrive. This time there was a dark room. There was a boy cowering in the corner of the room. He was shaking and holding his arms around himself as if trying to keep warm. He was barefoot and looked like he hadn't bathed in weeks. He was extremely thin and his face appeared hallow. He wore torn trousers and had a woolen jacket that looked like it had been dragged through the mud. On his jacket was the Star of David. Next to the boy, emanating from a window were shouts from people who were looking for him. Before anything else could happen, the dream ended. Although he did not know what had happened to the boy, Adolf had a coldness and a feeling of despair he had never known before in his life. He stood up and walked over to the Tanach. The moonlight lit the pages of the Tanach as he groped in the dark to reach the book.

And afterward,
I will pour out my Spirit on all people.
Your sons and daughters will prophesy,
your old men will dream dreams
your young men will see visions.

Even on my servants, both men and women.
I will pour out my Spirit in those days.

Adolf trembled at the words. He stared out of the bay window watching as the trees bent gently with the breeze. The field behind the grove of trees seemed to go on for eternity. Adolf again shuddered. He turned toward his bed which was now illuminated by the moonlight. The light seemed to calm his nerves as he settled back into bed. The rest of the night would be restlessness with Adolf waking several more times.

The next morning Adolf joined the other three for breakfast. He was quiet and somber and talked little. Maria, while trying to carry conversations with Edmond, his wife and Pablo noticed Adolf's dower countenance. After breakfast, Edmond gave the three a tour of the house and grounds and showed them a temporary art studio – it was garage toward the back of the house that had been converted for the occasion. Pablo and Maria were positively delighted and thanked Edmond for his generosity. Adolf was distant and aloof.

Later in the day, Edmond invited Adolf for coffee on the veranda in the back garden.

"Adolf, I hope you don't mind if we take coffee together alone. Maria and Pablo are going to christen the new art studio."

Edmond poured Adolf a cup of coffee and offered him some biscuits.

"Rough night last night?"

"Oh, to say the least."

"Bad dreams?"

"Yes, nightmares."

"Tell me about them."

"Edmond, are you now my psychoanalyst?"

"Just humor me…I'm an amateur dream interpreter."

Adolf laughed and took a sip of his coffee. For early August the air was a bit crisp and there was a cool breeze running through the trees.

"It was three dreams – all equally disturbing. The first was a flock of sheep that were grazing peacefully by a hill near a cliff. Like the Cliff of Dover in England. All was calm and then slowly, the wind began to blow. The sky turned to a velvety black turmoil of clouds, swirling like they would devour the sheep. They then became disturbed by the wind, but rather than just fleeing in the opposite direction, they all flew off the side of the cliff, just like lemmings."

Adolf looked at Edmond for a response. Edmond merely mumbled something and began to stir his coffee.

"And the next?"

"Yes, the next. It was a crowded marketplace – it looked like it was maybe Spain…I would guess by the clothing and the construction of the building that it was maybe the fourteenth or fifteenth century. Anyway, everyone was enjoying their shopping when there was a loud roar. Soon a rumble and then on the horizon it was a swarm of men in black ridding right for them. They descended upon the town and began to hack everyone in sight – men, women and children. The last scene I remember was of one of the horsemen chasing a woman down an alleyway. When he had cornered her he got off his horse and then killed her. To my ultimate horror it was Maria."

Again Adolf looked at Edmond for some kind of reaction but none was forthcoming. He seemed to be meditating on the dreams.

"And the last?"

"Well for the last…it was a young boy…maybe eight or nine years old. He ran into a room, don't know what room – could have been mine. He was shaking and shivering – he was barefoot and looked very bedraggled. On his jacket was a large yellow Star of David. He was hiding from someone, or something. There were people shouting for him outside the window. Before anything else happened I awoke from the dream."

Edmond was quiet. His eyes were closed. He seemed to be in a different state – a deep state of meditation perhaps. He opened his eyes and then looked square at Adolf.

"You've lived a very good life Adolf. The dreams are telling you…in essence is that you could have gone down a very different road. A road that would have led to destruction."

"How do you mean?"

"The massacre in the village, the Jewish boy hiding in fear, they are signs of thing that have happened to the Jewish people and things that might have happened if it wasn't for some intervention. The massacre in the village is a symbol of the Inquisition…"

"But why was Maria in it?"

"It's related to the recent revolution in Spain. You have had insecure feelings about her. You love her very much and that's why you went to Spain. But sometimes you feel you are not good enough for her… that you might lose her."

Adolf nodded and looked out toward the garage where Maria was working.

"So what about the flock of sheep?"

"Like Jesus Christ, you occasionally see yourself as a savior of sorts. You want to lead people, but sometimes you have no one to lead. Your dream reflects the lost sheep in your life – the lost opportunities to lead."

"I don't know – they are all crazy dreams…seems like I might be in need of a doctor…"

"No, no my boy. There was a specific reason why these dreams came to you. Your life up until now has been somewhat stress free, what these dreams tell you is that for most people, life can be dark and bleak. You needed these dreams to put something more profound into your work – a darker element. Not necessarily negative or demonic – but show people your inner soul, the inner you."

Adolf again nodded, somewhat agreeing with Edmond.

"If I didn't know any better I'd say it had something to do with that Tanach you gave to me."

"Probably does have something to do with it – God moves in mysterious ways my boy. Anyway, don't be alarmed by the dreams – embrace them and think anew!"

With that note, Adolf blew a sigh of relief. He finished his coffee and with Edmond made a trip to the new art studio. Inside they found Maria and Pablo discussing their ideas. They and had made some rough sketches with charcoal and were seeming to really enjoy their new surroundings.

"Ah Adi, you look like some color has returned to your face," Maria said with a wink. Adolf walked over to her and planted a kiss on her cheek.

"Welcome back Herr Hitler. I thought we had lost you to the deep thoughts in your mind – you seemed a bit out of sorts this morning," Pablo began to chuckle.

"Thank you my dear colleagues. Yes, I think I am back to my old self. Had a bit of a rough night."

"Oh really, there weren't any chamber maids in your room were there?" Maria said with an expression of mock anger.

"No my dear, just dealing with some inner conflicts I suppose." He turned and winked at Edmond.

"Well, Adi you are becoming deep. You'll have to get that new Bohemian slant down on canvass!"

******

What Edmond said to Adolf was true, or at least Adolf believed it to be true for his artwork did take on a new brooding tone. It was the era of Jean-Paul Sartre, Simone de Beauvoir, Sigmund Freud and many others who seemed to have a new bent on philosophy and the mind. Adolf, while not sharing many of the current philosophers view of life, he did share a new expressionism that let his mind go free. When Adolf released his new work, you could bet that Freud would have liked to have spent a few hours psychoanalyzing him. Adolf though was working with renewed lust for life. Although the images were darker and more abstract, he felt as though he was cleansing his soul. There was a new freshness and creativity to his work and everyone agreed.

With the beginning of 1937, the three artists moved into their own apartments in Paris. Pablo stayed near Versailles while Maria and Adolf took an apartment in the Latin Quarter near the Seine. Maria demanded her own private room however, again indicating to Adolf that she didn't want to be intimate until they were married. A situation that Adolf quickly remedied by calling on Edmond to find him a ring. A couple of calls to several of his friends in the jewelry business and the item was procured. The following weekend, at one of their favorite restaurants, Adolf slipped the ring onto one of the candles that lit their table while Maria had excused herself. Later when she returned, she began to notice the dark object encircling one of the candles. It kept grabbing her attention until she finally questioned Adolf about it. Adolf, acting surprised by the out-of-place object, blew out the candle and tipped the ring on to the table.

"Hmmm…appears to be a ring of some sort. Here, let me try it on you. As Adolf slipped the ring onto her finger, the large diamond was now in full view and Maria let out a small scream. She looked around to see if anyone had seen her reaction. Before she could do anything else, Adolf was by her side and kneeling on one knee.

"Maria, will be my wife?'

Maria, almost completely frozen did her best to nod. She burst into tears and wrapped her arms around Adolf's neck. Adolf rose to his feet and gave her a long passionate kiss. The rest of the patrons began to applaud and the two emerged from their kiss with mildly reddened faces.

Maria was happy. Most of her life had either been turmoil or tragedy and with the recent events in Spain it had all become too much for her. She knew she should never have separated from Adolf but at the same time knew that for her to flourish as an artist she had to be on her own for some time. But now their reunion had led to something permanent – something firm, something solid.

CHAPTER 11

As Mr. and Mrs. Adolf Hitler completed their honeymoon in the South of France, they moved into their new home in Paris. Their wedding had been the biggest event of the social calendar in Paris – two of the greatest artists the world had seen in some time, coming together to tie the knot of matrimony. All of Adolf's friends from Berlin and Vienna made the trip. Of course, Horace Goldman had used the time to try and entice both Adolf and Maria to come back to Berlin. He claimed he was nearly on the verge of bankruptcy - Adolf not believing a word of it.

The two spent the next three years in an idyllic world of their own creation. Their house was an orgy of art that whenever a visitor would see the couple, there would be some new avant-garde creation – a sculpture, a fountain, a mural…it was all so wonderful. Adolf had even taken to welding – he would create some of the most inventive and talked-about objects one had ever seen. Most had no clue what he was trying to create but applauded him none-the-less. What continued to sell however were the artist's paintings. It seemed Paris could not get enough of them - especially Adolf's newer darker paintings. He continued down the dark path that Edmond had helped him imagine. New images that depicted the Great War, the Communist Revolution and the Spanish Civil War which had just ended.

For Maria, she had entered into a bit of a depression. Franco had won the war in Spain and so there was now no returning back to her homeland in the foreseeable future. And while she was happy to be married to Adolf, there seemed to be some finality regarding whether or not she could return to her true home.

With no return to Spain in her future, Maria made sure that Paris, and her home with "Adi" would be her home away from home. And to add to their home, Maria soon became pregnant. Both she and Adolf were a little startled with the news, especially Adolf who was now forty-nine years old. Maria, being thirty-eight had at that point never expected to have children, but now that she was not going back to Spain, it gave new meaning to her life. Adolf smiled and just would nod his head whenever Maria asked about what he thought. Adolf knew that the baby meant everything to Maria and just quietly went along with her excitement.

As the days went by, Adolf began to think in terms of becoming a father. Although a bit older than normal for a first-time dad, he began to think that maybe part of what he felt had been missing in his life was now going to be fulfilled. Of course, having Maria in his life was the most satisfying event for him, but now, the thought of fatherhood was beginning to grow on him. Adolf set himself to work on new baby furniture and found another creative avenue. He began to read books on woodworking and soon was putting together a crib and a rocking chair for the mother-to-be. With each passing month the couple were becoming more and more excited at the thought of becoming parents.

As Maria's pregnancy progressed, the couple would meet with a local doctor to make sure the baby was developing. The doctor would listen to the baby's heartbeat and all was well. Things took a turn for the worst though as Maria entered the eighth month of her pregnancy. She began to get sick and weak and the doctor ordered her to twenty-four bed rest. Adolf became the dutiful husband and met all of her needs. The doctor, a woman named Sylvia Pasqual would drop by almost every day to see how Maria was doing.

For the next several weeks, while Maria was bedridden, Adolf was in a depressive fog. It seemed the skies were eternally gray and many a day it would rain. He tried to paint to get his mind off the situation but he couldn't. He would often just grab the newspaper and read. It seemed the only way to get his mind off of Maria and the baby was to read.

As the new decade had begun, it seemed that Adolf would read about a new discovery, a new invention or some new technology every day. Albert Einstein and his team at the Berlin Academy of Technology had now perfected nuclear fusion and had already had the first power plant built that would supply Berlin with electrical power. Wernher von Braun continued his work with rocketry which now had translated into rocket propelled aircraft. A new "jet" aircraft that a subsidiary company of his had proven to make great strides. They had even started building a commercial version which promised to fly across the Atlantic in just four to five hours.

In the world of politics, Ernst Thallman and Josef Stalin had formalized and created a Communist Pact. The pact promised that each country would share new technology with the other. Their plans even included joint military exercises with both their armies, navies and air force. There was even talk of one day sending into space satellites. What satellites were Adolf had no idea.

At the United Nations, several appeals had been made to Stalin to stop the repression in his country. It had been widely confirmed by several journalists that to keep in power, Stalin had created a reign of fear, killing any political foe that might stand in his way. Ernst Thallman had tried to intervene and had stated that there was no way that Stalin would use such tactics. For the rest of the world though, it was becoming clear that Stalin was corrupt on many levels.

Because of the pact between Germany and Russia, a declaration was made by the United Nations that they would intervene, if Germany or Russia tried to seize land in Poland or any of the Eastern countries. While Germany complained they only had peaceful aims, no one was really sure what Stalin wanted or how far he would go. One thing for sure however was his military was still recovering from the Great War and probably did not pose any real threat.

With the end of the Spanish Civil War, it looked like Europe had finally stabilized and was now ready for an unprecedented time of peace. New alliances were being formed between various European corporations – it soon looked like there was going to be a common market. Many were proposing a European Union that would help allow Europe to compete with the United States and some of the new booming Asian economies. Adolf liked the sound of that – it probably meant being able to travel more freely through Europe and also easier to sell his work.

As Adolf continued to help Maria the best he could, one of their neighbors came over to help lend a hand. She was a kindly older woman who had recently lost her husband. She helped Adolf with preparing meals, helping to bath and clothe Maria. For Adolf this was a big help. He was starting to become a recluse with Maria being bed-ridden. He had turned down almost all offers from friends to visit. But thanks to his neighbor, she helped him to see some light. Having some company in the house helped him begin to think of other things.

Several days later, Dr. Pasqual visited and began to take Maria's vital signs. She could not hear the baby's heartbeat and decided that Maria should be taken to the hospital. Adolf called for an ambulance and they were soon able to get Maria to the local hospital. Adolf had stayed behind to pack a suitcase for Maria and soon hailed a taxi to go to the hospital.

Upon Adolf's arrival to Maria's hospital room. A doctor came out of the room shaking his head. He momentarily looked at Adolf and then continued down the hall. Adolf thought it a strange look and pushed the door open to Maria's room. Dr. Pasqual turned to see Adolf. She turned and took him by the arm and walked him out of the room.

"Adolf, it's too late. The baby is gone."

Adolf could not comprehend what had happened. He could not think. He could not hear anything after the doctor had explained what had happened. He simply went numb. He went into to see Maria, but the doctor pulled him back and asked him to go to the waiting area. She pointed to a room down the hall. Adolf trembled and staggered – he thought he might faint.

Adolf sat alone in a darkened room – all the blinds were closed. There was no one else in the room. No nervous expectant fathers, no one. He looked over at a stack of magazines, but was unable to acknowledge their existence. Nothing seemed to exist. He waited there for two hours with his arms clutched around each other as if trying to keep warm. A nurse would occasionally peer in but decided not to bother him. Finally, the head nurse walked in and addressed Adolf.

"Monsieur Hitler, please come and see your wife," she said coldly. He picked up his hat he had laid down on the nearby table and began to walk as if to his death. The nurse stopped short of the door and motioned for him to go in. He stood at the door and looked at Maria – she looked like she had been through a war. She lay sleeping, dead to the world. Adolf pulled a chair up to her and laid his hand on hers. Eventually he lowered his head and rested it near Maria. He quietly sobbed as she slept on. It was later that evening when she finally awoke, finding Adolf resting his head next to her. She stroked his head and he awoke. Tears filled each of their eyes. Adolf stood to hug her.

"I thought this baby would solve everything."

"Why did you feel that?"

"I don't know. I feel so lost lately. I never realized how being away from Spain would affect me so much. I thought if I was not going to live in Spain that at least I could have a family."

"You do have a family…you have me."

Maria smiled and hugged Adolf as hard as she could. The night nurse came in and advised Adolf he would have to leave. He hugged Maria again and squeezed her, not wanting to let her go. The despair in her eyes was too much for Adolf to bear. He left reluctantly after being quietly scolded by the night nurse. He slipped his hat and overcoat on, blew Maria a kiss and was out the door. Maria began to stare far off into space…a space that new no bounds or depth.

******

Several weeks after Maria had returned home, the two seemed to be in different worlds. When Adolf took her home from the hospital, she wanted to be left alone in her room to rest. Adolf put an intercom in her room so she could let him know if she needed anything. Apart from a meal or drink here or there, she requested little else. Adolf tried to buoy her spirits but she did not really want to talk. At night he would bring her a meal and the newspaper and offer to read to her, but she refused stating that she wanted to rest.

As the same behavior continued, Adolf consulted a psychiatrist, Dr. Lorraine Duvalle. The doctor told Adolf that it would take some time for Maria to get over the loss. And so Adolf continued to help Maria the best he could. Sometimes, when Madame Gaffette, the neighbor came over to help Maria, Adolf would go to the local café, have an expresso and read the paper.

In the news that day was an article on the current state of Europe and where the continent was heading. Most of the article was self-congratulatory on the achievements of European technology. It also discussed the pending European consolidation into one union. Another aspect looked at the population as well as it's religious and ethnic make-up. A good portion of the article discussed European Jewry and its impact to the European economy.

As of June 1ˢᵗ, 1940, the Jewish population of Europe currently stands at 9.5 million. With the current rise of the European GDP, despite the worldwide depression, a significant cause for the growth is Jewish inventiveness and creativity, especially in the sciences. With the growth of Hebrew Universities, especially those in Germany, Poland and many other Eastern European countries, a significant number of engineers, scientists and doctors are being produced by these institutes.

In the United States, there has been a recent attempt at trying to bribe many Jewish teachers and professors to come to America to help build up various departments; especially in engineering and physics. A few professors have left with a concentration of them working at Bell Labs in Princeton, New Jersey.

Besides the Jewish population, there has also been a large increase in the Arabic and North African populations of Albania and Yugoslavia, with a sizable increase in immigration from the Middle East. These South Eastern European nations are also home to a large Muslim population. Similar to Jewish neighborhoods in Northern Europe, the Muslim neighborhoods are booming with markets and mosques throughout. Most estimates place the Arabic and Muslim population of Europe at about 5 million.

The Romani people have also increased over the past 10 years and there are figures indicating close to 2 million now spread throughout Europe.

As European influence across the globe continues, other factors have come into play in helping the economics. Because of the non-market based economies of Germany and Russia, and the technological advances in Europe in general, it is thought that the depression which began in October 1929, ended in Europe in early 1937. Current data, driven by technology in continental Europe and heavy industry in Germany and Russia, along with large agricultural output, put Europe in the black by 1937, while most other nations were still struggling with the results of the US stock market plunge.

And what are some of those technological advances? At some of the other institutes like the Berlin

*Institute for Technology, major strides are being made in
energy production through Atomic energy, automobile
and aviation production as well as new "maglev"
technology that will cut train travel in half.*

Adolf put the paper down. Took a large sip of his expresso and then sighed. He was at the top of his profession and yet he felt empty. Did he need religion? He thought about starting to attend mass again. He hadn't done so since he was a teenager. Something was missing in his life. He no longer had the chance at fatherhood that had grown on him so well. While at first shocked, he was really keen to be a dad after time, and now the loss was staggering. An even more significant loss he feared was Maria. She seemed to be no longer present. No longer in body form, more like a spirit who had flown. Europe was progressing, but he felt as though he was not.

Maybe what he and Maria needed was a change of venue – maybe the United States? From the newspaper article it seemed they were in need of teachers, maybe he could teach art?

With the thought of getting away, he crumpled up the newspaper in his arm, drank the last of his expresso and triumphantly marched down the street toward the house. He could see a beam of light shining down through one of the gray clouds that seemed to continually grace the Parisian sky.

When Adolf arrived back at the house, he noticed everything still. He called out to Maria but there was no response. There was a quiet he had never heard before – it was deafening. It was so quiet he could hear the buzzing of his inner ear or perhaps his mind. He walked up the stairs to Maria's room. He opened the door to find her gone. A note was pinned to the wall.

My dearest Adi. I am so sorry but I need to be away for a while. Maybe we can be together in the future but not now. My mind is a torrent right now and I have to go.

Love, Maria

Adolf's hand began to tremble. *How could she leave me? After everything we've been through.*

Adolf collapsed onto her bed and began to sob. He lay motionless for a while and then collected himself. He ran down the stairs and out of the house, somehow hoping he could see her. He ran across the street to Madame Gaffette's house. He knocked on the door several times. She finally answered the door.

"Madame Gaffette."

"Yes dear, how can I help you?"

"Maria – have you seen her?"

"No, not since I visited this afternoon."

"When you were over there, how did she seem?"

Madame Gaffette paused and thought for a moment.

"Well, not very talkative. I made her some tea and some lunch and brought it to her."

"Did she say anything?"

"No dear, why?"

"She's gone."

"Gone?"

"Yes, here's her note."

Madame Gaffette took the note and began to read.

"Hmmm, this seems impossible. She was practically catatonic when I last saw her. Maybe she's just confused, maybe gone for a walk?"

Adolf nodded. He was trying to control his emotions, but his red wet eyes betrayed what he was feeling. As if guided by Madame Gaffette, he took her word for it and began to walk the streets of Paris. He walked for hours, going down street after street. He eventually descended down to one of the Metro stations and began to ride the subway. Station after station seemed to go by. As the night wore away, there became less and less passengers in the subway and in and around the stations. He finally got off the Metro and made his way to the street level. Looking at a street lamp he could see an office clock read that it was 1 am. He began to walk the streets with little hope. Had Maria, in a moment of madness just walked off, perhaps getting lost somewhere? Perhaps running into the wrong type of people? Her note did not seem to indicate she was confused and surely the police would interpret it the same way.

Adolf continued to walk the empty streets. Now not only was he not a father, but seemed no longer a husband either. He was not only lost on the Paris streets but lost in life.

For the next several weeks, Adolf was holed up in his house. He would sit for hours listening to the radio but did little else. He would occasionally read the newspaper but seldom found any interesting articles. He seldom answered the door but on one occasion he finally did. At the door was Edmond de Rothschild.

"Adolf my boy, where have you been?"

"Here, Edmond, here. Would you like to come in?"

"Listen Adolf, I know Maria left you but you have to pull yourself together. You have to get back to your painting."

"Why, so you can make more money?"

Edmond rolled his eyes and then patted Adolf on the shoulder.

"How about a cup of tea or coffee?"

Adolf relented and showed Edmond to the kitchen.

"My boy this is atrocious, no wonder Maria left you!"

The kitchen was full of empty boxes – the previous contents having been biscuits or cookies. There were bowls of fruit and vegetables starting to turn color and in some cases were completely moldy.

"My dear boy, what have you been eating all these weeks?"

"Not much, I usually go down to the café and have something."

Edmond went over to the stove, picked up the kettle and then ran some water from the nearby sink. He began to hum the French national anthem and returned back to the stove. He turned the knob on the stove, pulled a singular wood match from his pocket, slide it against the side of the stove and ignited the burner. Once the stove burner was lit he resumed his humming.

"Why don't you come to my synagogue with me later today?"

"Why, I'm not Jewish."

"No, but I am. You'll find it intoxicating – it will pick-up your spirits."

Adolf began to envision himself at a synagogue, thinking that God might strike him dead on the spot for the times he had held Jews in low esteem.

"C'mon let's go, it's just down the street."

"Are you trying to convert me Edmond?"

"Hey you owe it to me. With all the paintings of yours I've sold, you can do me one little favor!" Adolf began to chuckle. It was the first time he had laughed in several months, or so he thought. Edmond made his plea with his head raised as if looking down his nose at the poor ignorant gentile. Adolf smiled and nodded his head. The two finished their cup of tea and then headed out the door.

The two men walked briskly down the street, Adolf having no idea where he was going. A light rain began to fall and Edmond raised his umbrella over their heads. The light rain soon turned into a torrent as the men quickly walked up the stairs to the Versailles Synagogue. Inside, Edmond lowered his umbrella and placed it on a nearby coat rack along with his overcoat. He invited Adolf to do the same.

"What do we do?" Adolf asked Edmond as they walked inside.

"Just follow my lead."

The synagogue was full as the two men slipped into a back pew that was unoccupied. Edmond handed a prayer book or siddur to Adolf. He looked at Edmond as if he were illiterate but began to page through the siddur, trying to mirror Edmond and hoping none of the other congregants noticed him.

The rabbi stood behind a tall lectern and began to read the prayers in Hebrew. The siddur had the prayers in Hebrew as well as in French. Adolf, who was now adept in French began to read them out loud as Edmond did, but mostly only mouthing the words, not really saying them…

Hear, O Israel: The Lord our God, the Lord is one. Love the Lord your God with all your heart and with all your soul and with all your strength.

These commandments that I give you today are to be on your hearts.

Impress them on your children. Talk about them when you sit at home and when you walk along the road, when you lie down and when you get up. Tie them as symbols on our hands and bind them on your foreheads. Write them on the doorframes of your houses and on your gates.

Edmond smiled at Adolf as he feigned participation. Adolf though was starting to feel something warm inside of him. He wasn't sure if it were from the many candles and lights that were illuminating the synagogue.

After several more prayers and chanting, and after Adolf tried to say "amen" during the blessing, everyone began to sit as the Rabbi prepared to speak.

"Thank you all for coming today. If I knew it were going to rain this much I would have brought my other ark…" polite laughter followed the rabbi's attempt at humor.

"In any event, I appreciate you. I appreciate all of our guests that have joined us here today. What I would like to speak to you about today is the topic of forgiveness. Why forgiveness rabbi? You say. Haven't we Jews been through enough? Yes, our history is that of a nomadic tribe. First settling in Southern Europe but then being tossed out of Spain, Portugal and France. All of those horrible pogroms we endured in Russia. We were not welcome. But now, now is a new day for the children of Israel. We have been thriving in Germany, thriving in Scandinavia and other parts of Northern Europe. Our day is here and we need to look to the future, not to the past!"

Adolf looked around as he could see the many shaking heads of the congregants. He noted that the women were seated on one side and the men on the other.

"And now, now comes word from Russia that we are beginning to thrive there again. Despite the harshness of Comrade Stalin, he has been putting Jews in high positions – he recognizes what great things can come from our people, unlike some other European leaders.

With our great leaders, with our great scientists like Albert Einstein, Otto Stern, Eugen Glueckauf and many more like them, we have forged the future of Europe. With our gentile brothers we can achieve almost anything if we put our minds together and work in unity. Can you imagine it, when two great minds like Albert Einstein a Jew and Max Planck raised in a Lutheran family…coming together…imagine the possibilities! Well we don't have to imagine - we know what's happening at the Berlin Institute of Technology. Wonderful things – new sources of power…atomic power that will provide a clean source of electricity until the messiah comes!"

The congregation began to applaud and cheer and Adolf became enraptured of the rabbi.

"But what does all this mean rabbi? What it means my dear brothers and sisters is we need to embrace our fellow man, whether Jew, whether Lutheran, whether

Communist, whether Monarchist…whoever you meet, meet them with a smile, with a hand.

We Jews have often been accused of isolationism, keeping to ourselves, hording…hording goods, hording finances. Well, we had a good reason to. But now, those times are over. We are no longer being persecuted and we Jews of France need to take are rightful place in the courts, in the office, in the government, wherever it is, we need to be like our brothers and sisters in Germany – free to express our gifts!"

With that the rabbi sat down and after the closing prayers, the worship service ended and Edmond and Adolf met with the rabbi and the cantor in the front of the synagogue.

"Rabbi, that was a terrific sermon. I'd like you to meet one of the artists in my care…"

"Ah yes, 'Adi" I believed you are called?" To Edmond's surprise, the rabbi knew of Adolf's work. He reached out to shake Adolf's hand to which Adolf returned his greeting.

"I thought your piece *Madrid at Midnight* was spectacular. I wish I could have purchased that one!" the rabbi said practically frothing at the mouth.

"Rabbi, I didn't know you were such a connoisseur. Had I known I would have sold you some paintings years ago!" Edmond said with a mock laugh.

"Adi, you'll have to come around to my residence some time and have some tea. I would love to learn about what your inspirations are for some of your work."

"Ah sure rabbi, I would be happy to."

"Actually, I think your work *The Death of Society,* is even greater!" The cantor offered.

"Ah, thank you, that's very kind of you."

"What were you trying to portray there with your work in that one Adi?" the cantor quiered.

"Gentleman, I need to get Adi home, it's passed his bedtime, he'll join you for lunch or tea sometime," Edmond said with a mock tone, grabbing Adolf by the arm and ushering him out of the synagogue.

"Why did you get me out of there so fast Edmond?'

"Oh my boy, while I love the rabbi you'll never get out of there alive – they will talk your ear off for hours. Besides, I have some news to tell you."

"Yes, what is it?"

"I've secured you a position as professor of Fine Art at the Berlin Art Institute."

"A professor? Me? Don't I need to have a PhD or something?"

"I've spoken to Thallman and it's all worked out."

"Ernst Thallman? The leader of Germany Thallman?"

"Yes my boy, what other Thallman would I be talking about? Anyway, you start on the 22nd so we'll need to pack up your things right away."

"But I was just beginning to get used to Paris."

"My boy you are languishing in depression. You need to get back to Germany and get a new direction in life."

"So not Judaism?"

"Ah well, you're Catholic right?"

"Yes."

"Close enough, let's go."

"Geez Edmond, I thought you were taking me on a spiritual journey?"

"I am Adolf, I am, there is just going to be some sidetracking here and there."

While Edmond's motives were not entirely pure, he did have Adolf's good at heart. What was really happening was that Edmond wanted to get Adolf out of his depression. He would go back to Germany, work in academia for a while and then start painting again – at least that was Edmond's and Horace Goldman's plan. Adolf would split his time between Berlin and Paris. Adolf would teach and paint, he then would do shows in Berlin for Goldman and then shows in Paris for Edmond when school was out. Unknowing what the exact intention of Edmond was, Adolf just shook his head and raised his hands to heaven.

Self-portrait, 1921

Blood-bath in Przemyśl, 1922

KPD Political Poster, 1922

Saving Klara, 1922

Midnight in Madrid, 1937

Alone in Amsterdam, 1946

CHAPTER 12

After arriving back to a hero's welcome in Berlin, which was basically Horace Goldman's immediate and extended family members, the Goldman's had Adolf over for dinner. Fraulein Goldman made the most delicious meals that Adolf had ever tasted – even compared to the cuisine of some of the top restaurants in Paris and Vienna. He never declined an invitation to the Goldman's for dinner. He admired the Goldman's – he loved both of them and marveled at them. He wondered how Horace could keep such secrets from his wife, but he typically didn't dwell on it too long – after all, all humans hold deep secrets.

At this particular dinner, the typical light conversation took a slight turn.

"I went to a synagogue yesterday." Adolf blurted out. The entire room went silent. Mrs. Goldman looked at Adolf as if he had just announced he had arrived from Mars.

"Why, that's excellent Adi – you'll have to come to temple with us sometime." Gretl Goldman said with a look of innocence only a ten-year-old could endear.

"Yes, Gretl, I would like that."

"Ah, you're Roman Catholic aren't you Adi?" Mrs. Goldman questioned.

"Yes, although I must admit I haven't been to mass since I was a teen. That was probably when I was sixteen to appease my mother."

"Are you thinking of converting Adi?" Horace asked.

"I really haven't thought about it. It was a spare of the moment thing yesterday – Edmond got me to go. I think it was just his way of getting my mind off of Maria."

"Quite, quite," Horace offered in a very pensive tone.

"It might give you a new direction with your artwork." Andre, Horace's brother suggested.

"Yes, you never know. I do think that sometimes I have been in a morally ambiguous place with my work. Sometimes, I wonder if I should really be showing some of things that I show in my work…some of the nudity…some of the graphicness…some of the courser things of life.

When I was very young I once pondered the priesthood. I felt a closeness to God then. That closeness has come and gone at times. When I got accepted into the Vienna Institute of the Arts, I really felt like God was on my side – that he was taking me to new heights."

Adolf paused, thinking back to his time at the institute – a simpler time.

"And you seemed to reach new heights, right?"

"Well, then the war came. When I saw death for the first time, I mean cruel death…well of course my mother's death was cruel…but when you are in a battle zone, you start to question God. Had I been going to mass on a regular basis and involved with the church maybe it wouldn't have hit me so hard, but when you see so much death and destruction it's hard to see the greater good.

And then after the war I got so busy with my art, keeping up with Berlin society, I never took the time to go back to church. Going to the synagogue yesterday was the first time I had been to a religious service in years. And it felt good – I felt I was getting close to God again."

"That's good Adi, that's good. Now you sit here with Horace and I will get you that apple streusel that you always love." Mrs. Goldman patted Adolf on the shoulder as she left for the kitchen. Adolf smiled knowing that his conversation was getting a little too moribund for the Goldman's.

"Anyway, Adi, we have a big meeting tomorrow morning."

"Oh, with whom?"

"Ernst Thallman. He wants to meet with you to discuss the professorship. Also, tomorrow is the first day of a very important conference that he wants you to attend."

"Really, what conference?"

"It's the first International Communist Congressional Committee Conference. All the leaders from Russia, China, Albania and North Korea will be there. Stalin will even be there, and he wants to meet you!"

"Meet me, why?"

"He says your one of his favorite artists."

Adolf shook his head in astonishment. The leader of one of the largest nations in the world is a fan of his work? He couldn't fathom it.

After dessert, Horace had his driver take Adolf home so he could get a good night's sleep. That night was one of the first nights in a long time that he didn't dream of Maria.

******

The next morning, after grabbing a quick expresso and a croissant, Adolf headed up the stairs to the Reich Chancellery building where the conference was being held.

He walked into Ernst Thallman's office and was greeted like a long lost friend.

"Adolf so good to see you." Ernst Thallman offered his hand to Adolf to shake.

"So glad to have you back where you belong."

"It's good to be back Ernst."

"I wanted to talk to you about your new position, but before I do, I'd like you to meet someone. Joseph, Joseph will you come in here."

Appearing from a smaller office off of the main one, a short but bright looking man appeared at the doorway.

"Adi!" It was Joseph Stalin. He was wearing a white uniform that made him look like an admiral in the Russian navy. Following right behind him was his translator. Stalin grabbed Adolf's hand to shake and began shaking it rather emphatically. He held another hand down on Adolf's shoulder and smiled all the while. Stalin reminded Adolf of a small bear which was often used as the national symbol.

"The Premier says he is such a fan of your work." The translator began.

"He is especially fond of what he calls your 'red' period…"

Adolf looked at the translator quizzically.

"You know, the one with all the death and destruction – fires ablaze…"

"Oh yes, now I understand," Adolf said as he continued to shake the hand of the premier. Thallman tried to intervene with the hopes that Adolf would not lose his valuable hand through restrictive blood-flow. Thallman grabbed Stalin by the arm and invited him to sit.

"You see Adolf, the premier is here, along with some of his other colleagues to learn from us. He sees our brand of Communism as the most successful and that is why he wanted to put together this conference. I also wanted him to meet one of our proud sons of Germany, why with other greats of ours, Bach, Beethoven, Brecht it's no wonder why Germany is so revered."

Stalin frowned a bit at the last statement after the translation had settled in.

"I knew he was a big fan of yours and I also wanted him to know about your new status – professor at the Berlin Art Institute. Also you will be serving in an honorary capacity of Minister of the Arts for the KPD and as I have mentioned to Joseph here that you will be available to help with any project he may want to start within the Greater Communist Union."

"Greater Communist Union?"

"Yes, that's also why we are here – we are in discussions to form one of the largest partnerships in the world. A union between Germany, Russia, China, North Korea and Albania. This would be a true Super-Power. A union where we would freely trade with one another, no formal passports or visas would be needed – we would all just take advantage of each other's resources, technology and especially in the case of China – it's man-power."

"But what about the European Union?"

"Oh forget that – this will be one of the greatest unions of all time – it will be the greatest economic and militaristic power in the world. It will make the United States and her European allies look like 3rd world countries."

Adolf began to mull this new idea over and was not exactly excited about it, especially what his contribution might be to such a suspicious scheme.

"You don't seem to be thrilled by this Adolf?" The premier asked via his translator.

"Well, it's just that I really don't know. I suppose it sounds good on paper, but I thought that England and France were better suited, especially being our neighbors – we share a similar culture and history."

Stalin frowned again and looked over at Thallman with a very perturbed look.

"Europe is full of nonsense. I mean look at it with all the Jews and Christians. So many fairy tales and myths. Even your great philosopher Marx said it – 'religion is the opiate of the people,'" the translator said as he tried to quickly interpret the animated speech of Stalin.

"How else do you explain this world? This cannot be all that there is. How do you explain conscious thought? How do you explain these complex minds of ours? Did this just happen, did we just appear out of nothing, just some random chance? I've lived now over fifty years and I am more certain than ever that there is something more to life. There is something more than economic achievement, something more to being famous or ruling a country…" Adolf motioned to Stalin as if citing an example.

"There is more. There is more than just the art I do. More than just the canvass, more than the easel. My art – my paintings – they are just a poor attempt at portraying what is real – God is real. I've learned that. I've learned that from Christians, I've learned that from Jews. All humans strive for one thing – to know what's at the end of this life? It's not about power, it's not about being in charge. It's about knowledge, true knowledge!" Adolf said this last line slapping his hand into his fist. He realized that he may have gotten too animated. Stalin looked at him sadly and then scoffed with an angry spitting sound coming from his mouth and his hand waving off Adolf. Ernst Thallman looked stunned – so much for this great son of Germany. In Thallman's mind, communism was about state control – the government was in control and there was no room for God.

"Sorry Ernst, but maybe this is not a good fit for me. I can't accept your offer." Adolf turned and immediately left the building, walking as fast as he could to his apartment. What he had heard at this meeting made his stomach turn. If everything went as the leaders hoped, it would be chaos and a potential nightmare for the proposed European Union. It would be a nightmare for Germany – the German people might lose their identity in such a bizarre partnership with the East. Thallman had to be stopped!

******

Later that day, Adolf had dinner with Horace Goldman.

"Adolf, how went the conference?"

"Ah, not so well."

"Really, you didn't like that bastard Stalin?"

Adolf could see that Horace was not happy as he struggled to butter a piece of bread.

"What's the matter Horace?"

"Oh, when I think of that man it makes me want to throw-up!"

"Who, Thallman or Stalin?"

"Well both, but more to the point, Joseph Stalin makes my skin crawl."

"I thought you were in favor of me meeting with him?"

"No I was…it's just that I've been thinking about what that devil has been doing to Jewish people – you know he's been destroying synagogues in the Soviet Union?"

"I thought things were getting better there – at least compared to the programs of the late 1800's."

"No Adi, I went along with this meeting because Edmond thought it a good idea, but the more and more I thought about it I just wanted to scream."

"Well, here's something else you'll want to scream about. The main purpose in this conference is to hammer out an accord so that Germany, Russia and China and some other countries can forge a union."

Horace was speechless as he chomped on his piece of bread. He reacted as if he had seen a ghost when the waiter appeared with two bowls of soup. He held on to his heart as if he thought he were about to pass out.

"Thallman is weak. Stalin and Mao would take over the union and Germany would be a pawn for those two imbeciles!"

Adolf nodded as he began to butter a piece of pumpernickel bread. He then took a long sip of his cabbage soup.

"Adi, they have to be stopped. What did you say to them?"

"I told them that I thought I was not a good fit for the regime."

"No you shouldn't have done that. Go back and get your job back."

"Why?"

"We need someone on the inside."

"Who is we?"

"Well, me, you and whoever else we can get onboard. Adi, the freedom of Germany is at stake. Thallman will lead us to ruin. He has to be taken out."

"By 'taken out' you mean killed?"

"Shhhhhh…keep your voice down."

The two men began to cautiously look around for anyone they thought suspicious. Upon the realization that there were not many people in the restaurant at that time, they continued their conversation.

"We have to do something Adi. Thallman must be stopped."

"And what am I going to do as their artist puppet?"

"You'll learn about Thallman's movements and then you can report back and we can figure out something."

"Something like what?"

"A murder plan."

"Hmmm…I don't know."

"What do you mean you don't know! You want Germany to fall into a union with those crackpots? There's a reason they want to align with Germany. Germany is communist in name only. We are still a bustling, industrial nation with many market driven businesses and corporations – that's what makes us so great. We are not a true communist country. Stalin and Mao see that we are a wealthy country – unlike theirs. They will see to it that the agreement is really a means for the them to rob and plunder Germany – it's all a sham!" Horace realized he was speaking too loud, especially when the waiter arrived with their main dishes.

"So you want me to go back after what I said to them and ask for my job back?"

"Yes, you have to. We need you on the inside."

Adolf thought about this throughout his meal and then eventually relented to Horace.

The next morning, he called upon Ernst Thallman at the Reich Chancellery.

"Hello Ernst."

"Hello Adolf, funny seeing you here again so soon…change of heart maybe?"

"Actually yes. I thought about it…about what I said and realized I was being a little unreasonable."

"Really, you now want to take up with us god-less heathens?"

"I realize that I was being overly sensitive and would like to apologize for my behavior."

Thallman thought about what Adolf was saying as he lit a cigarette. Adolf coughed as he blew a stream of smoke into his face. He then smiled and nodded.

"Welcome aboard Adolf. I am sure you will find this new position very stimulating."

"I am sure I will."

"Now, why don't you join us for the rest of the conference."

Adolf nodded and Thallman motioned for him to follow him. As they departed his office, they were joined by Eva his wife.

"Adolf, so good to see you," Eva said with a bright smile. Adolf, still a little hurt from their previous attempted relationship smiled and shook her hand. She then grabbed Thallman by the arm and the two walked together toward the main conference room. As the three entered, Adolf became overwhelmed with what he saw. It was like a vast theatre with spot lights pouring down on the main stage. On the stage were five tables, each with a placard indicating each country. What was amazing to Adolf was the interior of the theatre. The pillars seemed to be made of solid gold - in reality gold leaf. The stairs were of marble with velvet covering them. It had all the makings of a Hollywood awards show. The audience was quiet with various groups mumbling with each other. All of them had earphones on so they could hear the translators. It all had a very surreal feel to it and Adolf wondered if he were dreaming. Thallman asked Adolf to join him on stage behind the German table.

As they arrived, Stalin rose and greeted Adolf. He spoke something in Russian which Adolf could not understand but he nodded his head as if he did. Mao Tse-tung rose from his table and ran over to meet Adolf. He smiled a moronic grin and spoke in Chinese. Adolf had no clue what he was saying but smiled and returned his handshake. Thallman motioned for Adolf to take a seat.

"Ladies and gentleman, it's with great pride that I introduce to you one of our great artists here in Germany, Herr Adolf Hitler!" The audience stood as one applauding feverishly. Adolf bowed and smiled, wondering who in the world all these people were. It seemed like some weird movie-set. He was the actor and everyone else was the director, except they had failed to give him the script.

After the applause subsided, Eva Braun Thallman began passing out pieces of paper like she was a showgirl from a Broadway review. Adolf tried to read the paper but became dizzy and decided to sit down. The paper contained an outline to what appeared to be a speech. As he continued to read, he saw Thallman go to a nearby podium.

"Please lower the lights."

As the lights lowered a large screen descended to the base of the stage behind the five tables. A bright light then began to fill the screen with a projected image. It was a map with the images of Germany, the Soviet Union, China, North Korea and Albania, all highlighted in gold. The rest of the world was an undiscernible gray color.

"My dear comrades, as we continue to form the Great Communist Alliance between our nations, this will inevitable grow. Many of the smaller nations between us will eventually either become a part of our alliance or puppet states of ours." Thallman then pushed a button on his podium.

"So eventually, our world will look like this…"

Various countries within the vicinity of Germany, Russia, China, North Korea and Albania began to turn to gold. Adolf noticed that as they turned to gold, the name of the country disappeared. In a quick succession; Poland, Czechoslovakia, Hungary, Romania, Bulgaria, Turkey, Iran, India, Indo-China, Thailand, the Philippines, Japan and South Korea all became gold. Everyone in the crowd began to cheer wildly, they looked like they would begin to froth at the mouth. Even Eva applauded with a confident smile, probably dreaming of being Miss Communist Alliance. The whole scene was quite unsettling to Adolf and he had no idea of how he was going to be able to conceal his contempt for such a scheme. Thallman looked directly at him. Adolf decided that it might be best if he started to applaud as well. He then looked over at Stalin who was puffing on a large cigar, seeming to wink back at Adolf. Mao was also smiling a grand smile as if he had just swallowed a stray bird and was doing his best to keep it in. *I must be dreaming this*, Adolf said to himself over and over, feigning a smile to anyone who happened to look at him. Adolf was starting to feel warm and began to fan himself with the sheet of paper that Eva had passed out. He immediately stopped when he saw Eva frowning at him.

Adolf was in a daze. The morning and afternoon continued with various speakers coming to the podium and speaking in various languages. Adolf put on the earphones he was given but couldn't hear anything. He didn't complain, just pretended to listen. He later found out that there was an on and off switch and a mute button, but he didn't care, he just wanted to get out of this new version of hell. When it was all over, he thanked Ernst and Eva with a grateful handshake and then headed offstage looking for the nearest exit. When he finally hit daylight he breathed in a great sigh of relief. He then headed over to the restaurant where he agreed to meet Horace.

As the two men had dinner, Adolf relayed the day's events to Horace. Horace was stunned to find out that all of his worst fears had been confirmed. What would their plan be now? Horace explained in the softest tone he could muster that he was working on a plan. He wanted Adolf to meet him in a week at his house for dinner to discuss. Adolf didn't know if he could hold out that long.

******

The following week, Adolf joined Horace at his house for dinner. Also there were Horace's brothers Andre and Petr, the latter had a job as a clerk at the Reich Chancellery, Pier Von Brautten, a fellow art dealer, and Michel Gregorson, a banking friend of Horace.

"Gentlemen, thank you for meeting me. As you are aware, our country is about to become unhinged. That idiot Thallman is going to sell us out to the Bolsheviks which we cannot let happen. Why you are here is because we need to devise a plan to get rid of Thallman so this proposed Communist Union doesn't go through."

"If we get rid of Thallman, who will replace him?" A quizzical Adolf asked.

"Good question – any ideas?"

The group was quiet as they pondered a replacement for Thallman.

"Ludwig Kaas?" Adolf offered.

"Thank you Adi but as most of us are Jews, a priest and politician from the Catholic Centre party is not what we had in mind."

"How about someone from the Worker's Party?" Gregorson asked.

"No, they are morally bankrupt, especially that Ernst Rohm fellow."

Adolf gave Horace a look of surprise, knowing the secret that Horace was hiding. He just shook his head and continued to think.

"Oskar von Hindenburg?" Andre forwarded.

Horace looked at his brother like he had just made the most inane remark uttered by the human mouth. Horace shook his head, and motioned with both hands for the think tank to think again.

"Look, I think we all agree that the current leader needs to be removed. Let's just eliminate him and then hold a general election?" Pier Von Bratten suggested.

The rest of the group mulled the thought over while Mrs. Goldman passed around plates of sauerbraten and potato dumplings. The men's attentions were momentarily distracted by the delicious smell of one of Mrs. Goldman's favorite dishes.

"I think I'm with Pier on this one," Adolf said. "The main threat is Thallman – he has to be stopped. Once stopped, whatever leader takes over will not be so stupid as to hand the keys of Germany over to Stalin."

"But wouldn't one of Thallman's cronies take over and then just do the same thing as what he was planning?"

"No, none of them are bright enough to do anything. I'm sure we could speak to the other leaders in the congress to force an election," Petr said with an emphatic tone. The men seemed to agree with Petr. Petr after all was familiar with the inner-workings of the Reich Chancellery and the political system currently in place. The group commissioned Petr to find out all he could about Thallman's comings and goings. Likewise, Adolf was asked to do the same. Then they would be meet in two weeks to devise a plan to rid themselves of Thallman.

******

Adolf was finding it more and more difficult to go to work each day, knowing what he had to do. Adolf was no actor and he hoped that what he was really planning was not apparent in his demeanor. He started to feel a bit paranoid. He would question the looks that Thallman or Eva would give him. He even started to think that Thallman's secretary Erma was starting to suspect. Adolf did his best to just confine himself to his office.

Each day, Adolf would read over the requests for artwork that Thallman had made. Each day the requests seemed more and more the designs of a madman. At first the requests were simple; coming up with logo designs for the new union to which Adolf began to scribble various prototypes here and there. But then Thallman began to request various posters. One idea was to show a red tidal wave coming from Germany and Russia about to topple onto the rest of Europe. Another idea was for a tidal wave originating from a completely red Europe and landing on the continent of Africa. Similar ideas of tidal waves originating from China and landing on the rest of Asia were also proposed.

The ideas that offended Adolf the most were various rough sketches Thallman made of statutes. He wanted to have three statutes of himself, Stalin and Mao all standing together looking toward the horizon. He also wanted the same image on posters. It was clear that Thallman was a crazed egomaniac, craving complete power. Adolf found that it was becoming almost impossible to continue to work in such a position. He decided that he would spend more time at the University. He was a professor after all and a professor needed to oversee the university he had been charged to lead.

Adolf took a taxi from the Reich Chancellery, for the ten-minute ride over to the Berlin Institute of Art. When he arrived he was greeted by the receptionist Hilda.

"Goodentag Herr Hitler!" Hilda practically yelled as Adolf approached.

"Please Hilda, call me Adolf…or if you please Adi."

"No Herr Hitler, a man of your prominence I cannot call by your first name. I am sorry but I was not trained that way."

"No problem Hilda. Can you show me to my office then?"

"Yes, right this way Herr Hitler."

And on that note, Hilda began to escort Adolf through the main floor. There were various students and faculty milling about – many of them whispering as Adolf walked by. Adolf smiled and bowed his head, sometimes tipping his hat as he did so. The pair eventually arrived at an elevator at the end of the lower floor. Adolf was surprised at the size of the building but continued to follow Hilda. Once inside the elevator, Hilda pressed the button for the seventh floor. The two shared an awkwardly quiet ride to the seventh floor. Adolf listened to the *Ride of the Valkyries* playing in the background as they made their ascent. When they finally arrived at the seventh floor, Hilda immediately began a march toward the hallway. As they made their way through the seventh floor, it almost seemed deserted. On the floor there were various objects covered with cloth, appearing to be covered for some painters to arrive. Every door they passed was closed and not a sole stirred.

Eventually they arrived at the end of the floor and Hilda opened the last door. At the end of the hallway was a large window from which Adolf peered down to look at the street below – he felt a slight sensation of vertigo and decided to follow Hilda into the office.

"As you can see you have your desk with chair. Over there is a file cabinet for your papers and notes. Over by the wall are various shelves you can use as you please. You have a phone. There is also a typewriter if you so choose to use…"

"Ah, is there any way I could partake of your services Hilda if I need something typed?"

"No sir, I was instructed to…" Hilda became quiet and she started to shake her head. She had a very worried look on her face.

"Um…I'll see what I can do if you need some formal correspondence Herr Hitler."

Adolf smiled and bowed his head.

"Oh and is there a list of courses that I am supposed to teach?"

"You'll need to speak with professor Grosz for that, he's the one who is in charge of setting up curriculum and class schedules."

"Very good Hilda. Can you send professor Grosz up to my office when you have a moment?"

Hilda gave Adolf a look of contempt which he did not notice as he turned his back to her. She mumbled something and then quickly vanished from view. Adolf looked around the room. While at first he thought this would be the perfect hiding spot from people over at the Reich Chancellery, he began to think his isolated setting was by design. But why? Why would Thallman want him in such a remote place?

Adolf spent most of the following week making himself scarce. Any artwork requests he received from Thallman he would delegate to his assistant, a high-spirited, be-spectacled young man named Gustav. Gustav acted as if he had consumed half the expresso in Berlin; he was jittery, hyper-active and could not sit still in one place for more than thirty seconds. Despite all of Adolf's requests to try and calm himself, it did little good and Adolf had to content himself that Gustav was just Gustav. One thing for certain, whatever Adolf asked Gustav to do, it was competed in record time. Whether Gustav completed the project or three of the artists in the graphics department, the work seemed to always get done with Gustav nipping at everyone's heels. With Gustav on the job, Adolf knew he could slip away from the Chancellery just about any time he wished to. He would often use the time to slip back to his apartment and try and work on some paintings. Both

Horace and Edmond were constantly badgering him for new work, but with the latest happenings around Berlin, it was difficult for Adolf to put paint to canvass.

******

Two weeks after their first meeting, the group of Thallman dissenters met again, this time at Petr's house – they didn't want to arouse suspicion by always meeting at the Goldmans, even if suspicious neighbors were not really a reality, but some thought they were.

Horace quickly got the meeting started by asking if Petr or Adolf had any ideas about when and where would be a good spot to commit the crime.

"I think I have a good idea," Petr started. "This coming Friday, the 20th of July, there will be a meeting at Thallman's Neuenhagen headquarters *The Lion's Den*. On that day, Thallman will be hosting a meeting with Stalin and Mao to go over their plans for the union – we will be able to get all three of them at once!"

"How do you propose we 'get' them?" Pier Von Bratten asked.

"What I propose is that Adi go there with his art gear and offer to paint 'the masters' while they are at work." A lump began to form in Adolf's throat.

"What we can do is put a few sticks of dynamite or some kind of bomb in one of Adi's paint boxes."

"Yes, but what happens to Adi?" Horace asked, digesting the consequences of his most prized artist.

"Yes, what happens to Adi?" Adolf also asked.

"You excuse yourself. You tell them you forgot something…the right paint brush or the right paint."

"Does that work for you Adi?"

Adolf thought for a moment. He nodded for a moment, but then started shaking his head.

"I don't know. I'm an artist not a murderer. I was trained to paint and sketch…I'm not some terrorist!"

Horace grabbed Adolf by both shoulders and peered into his eyes.

"You wouldn't be a murderer Adi. This is for the good of Germany, for the good of humanity. Do you know how many innocent people will be murdered if this thing becomes a reality? Do you realize how many people are now being murdered in Russia and China?"

Adolf stared into Horace's eyes. He then looked away toward the rest of the group. All eyes were on Adolf and what decision he would make. He turned and walked over to a nearby window. He could see down in the street various people walking by, cars driving by…*if they only realized what we were plotting in this house!* Adolf practically yelled to himself. How could he be involved with such an idea? How in the world did he get this involved in such a crazy plot? He turned back to the group and studied their faces.

"Alright, I'll do it. But what happens to me after the bomb goes off?"

"Well, we can set a timer on it that way you will be long gone."

"Yes, but won't the attendees of the meeting get suspicious of why I am gone so long?"

"I know, say you forgot your canvasses at the art institute and that you'll be back in an hour or so!" Andre said, getting a look of approval from Horace this time.

Adolf nodded and then continued nodding hoping the idea would wear on him.

"Ok, but how do we get a bomb? None of us are bomb-builders." Adolf asked looking around the room.

"I know someone." Everyone turned around to look at Michel Gregorson. Everyone was surprised that of all people, the small in stature, be-spectacled banker would know anyone from the bomb-building world.

"Michel, how do you know anyone who has that knowledge."

"There is a private armaments company that builds weapons. I know the owner. We gave them a massive loan to build all kinds of weapons; bombs, chemical bombs, missiles…of course the loan was at the behest of Thallman, he wants to start building up the military."

"How are you going to get the owner of an armaments company to build a bomb to blow-up Thallman?"

"Quite easy, the owner hates Thallman."

There was a unified scratching of the head from the group.

"If Thallman approved of a massive loan for this guy, why does he hate him?"

"Well, after they got the loan and started building the armaments, Thallman would only purchase the bombs at a lower price, citing economic issues…which there really isn't any. Anyway, the company is about to go bankrupt and as soon as it does the government will seize the factory and everything in it. All in the name of communism."

"So this guy has nothing to lose?"

"And everything to gain."

"Are you positive this guy will go along with this?"

"Why tell him what you're going to do with the bomb?" Andre said then realizing the ridiculousness of his question.

"The guy is on the verge of doing it anyway. Every time I meet with him he is cursing Thallman. I bet I can get him to do it if I explain what our reasons are."

"Okay, so we have the plan, we have the means to carry out the plan. Let's get to work!" Horace cried as he raised his fist into the air.

Adolf smiled at everyone, not wanting to let the group down, but deep down he felt that something was wrong. He guessed it was related to his Catholic upbringing. He was sure his mother wouldn't have approved – his blessed mother.

For the next several days, Adolf kept a low profile and began to work on his end of the plot. He now realized that his isolated office on the seventh floor of the art institute was a godsend – no one would have a clue of what he was working on. He did find a large paint box that if one removed all the contents from the bottom, it could house such a bomb. That evening he walked over to a rendezvous spot at a nearby park. He stopped and sat for several minutes at a park bench. He had placed the box under the bench. Several minutes later he stood, stretched his arms and then walked out of the park. The owner of the armaments company, seeing that Adolf had left the box made his move toward the park bench where he picked up the box and headed back to his office. The paint box would be laden with explosives and a timer which would be returned to Adolf with detailed instructions. The box was sent to Adolf's apartment after it had been set inside of a large package.

The day before the plan was to take effect, a man from the armaments plant delivered the package. Adolf was nervous that a neighbor might be spying on him and looked up and down the street for anyone suspicious. He took the package over to a nearby table and then carefully took out the box. He placed the box on the table and then opened it. At the bottom of the box was a tray cover. When he removed it he could see the explosives and the timing device. His hand trembled for a moment. He picked up the note that contained the instructions and began to read. He again began to tremble and felt his heart beating faster. *This was no a job for an artist*. He kept saying to himself over and over.

Before continuing with the note, he decided to pour himself a glass of brandy. He hoped it would calm his nerves and to some extent it did. With a renewed vigor he continued reading. The device would allow him an hour to get away from the building. He simply needed to press a button at the base of the device and the timer attached would start ticking. The instructions suggested that he press the button as he parked his car, that way no one would be able to see him activating the device.

Adolf sat down in a chair next to the table and began to pour himself another brandy. He stared down at the contents of the glass and began to transfix onto the golden liquid. It looked as if a fire was starting inside the glass, the gold was turning to yellow and orange hues. He felt the heat of the glass against his face like the sifter had become a furnace. He sat back into his chair and began to shake his head. He looked at the glass again and it looked normal. He felt his head and could tell it was getting warmer. He took several swigs of the brandy and then walked over to the sink in his bathroom. He ran the cold water and began to splash his face. He dried his face with a towel and then began to look at himself in the mirror. His face looked red. He began to feel his face – it was rough. He felt around his mustache which he had grown to a length that he now considered growing a goatee to match.

How could this be right? He mumbled to himself. He shook his head and then walked out of the bathroom. He took his glass and bottle of brandy to his bedroom where he set them down on the nightstand. He took his clothes off and then started a hot bath. He got into the bath and then began to drink more brandy. He laid in the tub staring at the ceiling, wondering if he could go through with the plot. He then began to think about Thallman. When he had first met him in the late 1920's he liked him. He wasn't particularly awe-inspired by him but thought he had some good ideas about government. Was he really such a bad guy? He did steal Eva from him, but was that enough reason to kill him?

After about an hour in the tub, he dried himself off, put on a bathrobe and then threw himself on top of his bed. It had been a hot summer in Berlin and so he left the windows open. He went to sleep listening to the murmurs of the city down below.

The next morning Adolf was awoken to the sound of a ringing phone next to his bed. He picked up the phone, it was Horace.

"The plan is on," he said in a muffled tone and the phone went dead. That was Adolf's queue that the plot was beginning. Adolf went to the bathroom where he shaved and washed his face. He threw on some cologne and then got dressed. He decided to wear a white suit with a long thin black necktie. He then walked out of his bedroom and into the kitchen where he looked about for something to eat. He decided he was not hungry but then resisted his thoughts of fasting and took a piece of pumpernickel bread from a nearby bread box. He took a tray of butter from the refrigerator and placed it on the kitchen table. He then turned the stove on to heat the kettle. After nervously pacing the kitchen floor waiting for the kettle to whistle, he remembered that there would be a note with further instructions placed in his mail box earlier in the morning. He walked over to the front door and could see an envelope on the floor and the mail slot slightly stuck open. He opened the envelope and began to read the note. Inside was a train ticket.

The noise of the kettle was starting to irritate him so he went back into the kitchen and turned off the stove. He poured the boiling water into a cup with instant coffee and then began to stir in some milk. He took a bite of a piece of buttered bread and then sat down at the table. As he was about to sit, a large black crow landed in the kitchen windowsill and began to squawk. Adolf grabbed a nearby newspaper and began to swat at it quickly sending it to flight. Adolf peered out of the window and began to wonder if that was a bad omen. He sat down again and began to read the note from Horace.

Adi, I've spoken to Edmond about our plan and he suggests you seek refuge in Amsterdam. He feels that would be safer as everyone will suspect that you have fled to Paris. When you get to the Amsterdam train station, take a taxi to Prinsengracht 263-267, 1016 GV. When you get there – just tell him Edmond sent you.

Good luck and God speed,

Horace

Adolf crumpled up the note. He took a match from his pocket, struck it on the nearby countertop and set the note on fire. He threw the burning paper into the sink and then poured water onto its smoldering remains. He began to recite to himself the address he was to go to, *Prinsengracht 263-267, Prinsengracht 263-267.*

CHAPTER 13

Adolf began to drive his Mercedes down the street, feeling slightly paranoid that one of Thallman's henchmen were somehow following him or watching him. He turned-around to look in his back seat – he could see the paint box that hid the bomb. He had strapped the paint box with several cords to secure it in one place. He hoped he didn't hit a pot hole causing the bomb to detonate.

On the seat next to him he had a map laid out with a red line marking the route to Neuenhagan. He looked at it periodically to confirm he was heading down the correct streets. As he got onto the autobahn he began to enjoy himself a little. He imagined himself in a sports car driving the autobahn up to Bavaria – looking at the pristine scenery as he raced at over 140 kilometers per hour. Before his daydream could end, he found himself already at the exit for Neuenhagan. He pulled off the exit and headed down the country road toward Thallman's headquarters. Upon arriving at the *Lion's Den*, he was greeted by a large gate with a guard in front. Never having been to the *Lion's Den*, he was unaware that there was much security. Given that this was an official building for the president of Germany, he realized that it shouldn't have been so surprising to him.

"Ah, I am Adolf Hitler – the new Minister of the Arts."

The elderly guard just stared at Adolf.

"I'm here to see the president."

The guard seemed to shimmy over to the guard shack and then picked up a clip board. He shimmied back over to Adolf's car.

"Hmmm...I don't see any Himter on my list..."

"No it's Hitler."

The guard seemed to peer down at his clip board for what seemed ages.

"The president is not expecting me – I just came here to do some painting."

The guard nodded his head and then began the journey back to his guard shack. Upon arrival he picked up a phone and began to dial.

"Hello, this is the main entrance. There is a gentleman here named Adolf Hitler who would like to see the president." The guard nodded and grunted several times. He then looked at Adolf and waved for him to go on. Adolf tipped his hat and then accelerated through the gate. The road was now dirt and began to wind up through a small hill. Adolf could see dust being thrown into the air as he made his way up the hill. Upon reaching the apex he could see the headquarters compound in the distance. He accelerated toward the buildings on the horizon, finding himself surprisingly calm. Maybe the fact that his target was now visible, he finally could rest in the knowledge that one way or the other, the plan would be finished soon.

He pulled up to the main entrance and was waved on by a guard. He pulled around to a parking area by a large bungalow. The bungalow was sticking slightly outside of a cave that had been dug into the nearby hillside. Remembering his instructions, he turned to the back seat, pulled the paint box from the cords and then opened the box. He looked around for anyone suspicious. He then pulled up the bottom tray and looked at the device. He could see the red button below the small watch face. With a slightly trembling finger he pushed the button. He raised the box to his face so he could hear the quiet sound of the device ticking. He quickly replaced the tray and then got out of the car. He walked quickly into the bungalow and was greeted by Hilda his receptionist from the art institute.

"Hilda! What on earth are you doing here?"

"I often come here on one or two days of the week to help the president."

"A better question is why are you here Herr Hitler?" a voice came from the far corner of the room. It was Ernst Thallman. As Adolf peered through the bright light emanating from the far corner, he could just make out the images of three men standing over a large map on a table – he could see that the other two were Stalin and Mao.

"Oh, President Thallman. I thought about your meeting and thought what a great opportunity for me to capture your images on a portrait."

Adolf could feel a lump in his throat as he waited for Thallman to respond. Thallman had a look of suspicion on his face as he looked over at Stalin for a moment and then at Mao. He looked back at Adolf and then smiled.

"Sure, why not?!!! I think that a splendid idea! Why don't you come over and set-up?"

"Can I get your paint box for you Herr Hitler?" Hilda asked.

"Ah, no I got it Hilda." Adolf gave Hilda an expression of disbelief, still in shock to see her there. The whole thing threw him off and the confidence he had previously gained on the drive over was now almost depleted. He began to walk toward the map table when he noticed Hilda heading for the front door.

"Where are you going Hilda?" Adolf asked in a strained voice.

"I thought I'd help you with your things…your canvasses, etc…"

"No, there not…ah, I mean ah good idea. Thanks. I will just set down my paint box and come out and help you."

Adolf set the paint box down near Thallman's feet. Adolf took a quick look at the map. It looked like invasion plans – large red arrows pointing to what appeared to be troop movements into Eastern and Southern Europe. He smiled at the three leaders and then immediately walked out to help Hilda.

"Herr Hitler, are your supplies in the trunk?" Hilda asked, unnerving poor Adolf.

"Ah yes, let me open that."

When Adolf opened the trunk he tried to put on his best expression of feigning surprise.

"Damn! How on earth could I have forgotten my canvasses, what a logger head I am."

"Canvasses, there are some canvasses in the bungalow. Chairman Mao is an artist as such as well – he does calligraphy. Maybe he can lend you some?"

"No, I wouldn't want to trouble the chairman. I'll just rush very quickly back to the art institute."

"Don't be silly Herr Hitler, here let's go ask."

Before Adolf could say a word Hilda was gone, having quickly accessed the bungalow. Adolf followed, beginning to sweat and worry – he hoped the device was truly set for an hour. Inside the bungalow, Hilda was asking a diminutive Chinese woman to translate for her. Hilda asked her to see if the chairman would accommodate her canvass request. The woman walked over to the chairman and began to speak quickly in Chinese. Mao looked over at Adolf and nodded his head with a great big grin.

"It would be an honor for the chairman if you would use his canvass." The translator said with a suppressed smile.

"Oops, I just remembered. I didn't bring my brushes."

"Aren't they here in your paint box?" Thallman asked.

"No, it's a special brush that I need."

The translator then whispered something into the chairman's ear. He again smiled and motioned toward a large paint box over by his canvasses.

"The chairman says you are welcome to use any of his supplies – he has a wide variety of paint brushes."

"There, you're all set Adi – paint away!" Thallman said with a seemingly sinister look on his face.

Adolf's mouth seemed to drop to the floor, or so he felt like it had. His mind began to search for any ideas as he navigated his way over to where the canvasses were. He fumbled with the paint box and eventually opened it. The three men were now back to their planning and Hilda began a conversation with the translator. Adolf's mind kept racing for some sort of excuse to leave. This whole episode was eating up time – by his calculation fifteen minutes had gone by. *Think Adolf, think!* He screamed to himself as he continued to fumble through the chairman's paint box. He examined the contents and then began to smile.

"Oh, I know – I need my charcoal – I wanted to do some rough sketches of you all with charcoal pencils before I painted. I'll be right back!" Adolf said as he raced through the door, not waiting for anyone to object this time. He ran over to his car and began to turn the ignition. And of course the car wouldn't start. *Looks like today's the day*

I become a martyr! Before another thought could enter his head, the face of Hilda suddenly appeared.

"What's the problem Herr Hitler?"

"My car won't start – I think it's the battery."

"We have a mechanic up at the other end of the compound – I'll have him take a look."

Adolf pondered if he should just make a run for it. He looked at his watch - twenty minutes had gone by. On the other side of the compound he could see what appeared to be a battalion of soldiers marching, doing their daily exercises he imagined. As he began to look around the compound he could now see that the place was infested with various guards and soldiers patrolling the grounds. He had to get out of there as fast as he could.

After what felt like an hour, but was really only five minutes, a man by the name of Fritz presented himself as the chief mechanic at the compound. He asked Adolf for the car keys and began to try to turn the engine over.

"I think it's the battery," Adolf said as he pointed to the front of the car, hoping the mechanic would stop his incessant car starting and open the hood. The mechanic finally relented and hopped out of the driver's seat and then popped the hood. He began to tinker around, checking various hoses and lines, all the while driving Adolf into a state of emotional imbalance.

"Yeah, looks like the battery. I'll go get a new one. I think I've got one up the road."

"Up the road? How far is that?"

"Ah, it will just take me ten minutes or so."

"Can you hurry it up? The president is expecting me to paint his portrait today and I have to get back to Berlin to pick up some things before I can do that."

"Ok, I'll do my best."

Adolf watched as the man disappeared out of sight. He looked at his watch and realized that thirty minutes had passed. He calculated that if the man returned in ten minutes he would only have another twenty minutes to replace the battery and for Adolf to get out of there. The day was especially hot and Adolf pulled a handkerchief out of his pocket to wipe the sweat and dust from his forehead. He continued to look at the soldiers marching by and noticed that some of them had machine guns. The situation could get complicated quite quickly if he couldn't get out of there soon.

Just as the mechanic had predicted, his return with the much needed part took exactly ten minutes. Adolf exhorted him to try and finish the job as quickly as possible. As if he were related to the front gate guard, the mechanic seemed to suddenly become bereft of speed. The way he removed the battery seemed to require a forklift, the weight of the block seeming to weigh him down immensely. *Must be a union man*, Adolf mumbled to himself.

With the new battery in place and the mechanic turning over the engine, Adolf implored him to vacate the driver's seat so he could take the reins. He immediately placed the gear shift into reverse and accelerated like he was at the Indianapolis 500. He then turned the car around and began to accelerate through the summer dust, leaving the mechanic perplexed.

Adolf kept nervously looking at his watch as he sped onto the autobahn – the bomb would go off in five minutes. He had now secured himself from being blown up but was he far enough away to escape whatever marauding band would soon be in pursuit?

Adolf zoomed down the autobahn hoping to be back in Berlin in fifteen minutes. He looked at his watch as it stuck exactly one hour after he had first activated the bomb. He imagined the carnage at the scene and hoped that the device had done sufficient damage. He began to think about Hilda, an innocent bystander. He also became sad at the thought of the translator. *But it had to be done* he told himself. *There was no other way.*

As Adolf sped through the main center of Berlin, he arrived at the train station. He parked his Mercedes, pulled a suitcase out of the trunk and sprinted over to the main gate. He produced his ticket to Amsterdam from his top jacket pocket and handed it to the conductor standing outside the first-class cabin. As the conductor looked over his ticket, Adolf could hear a woman shriek.

"There's been an assassination attempt on the president," the woman cried. Adolf could see many people gathering and talking to one another in animated voices and expressions. He waited for the conductor to finish scrutinizing his ticket. The conductor, not distracted by the commotion around him, smiled at Adolf and motioned for him to get on the train. Adolf blew a sigh of relief as he quickly found his first class cabin. He threw his bag into the overhead compartment and sat down by the window. He picked up the newspaper that was on the table in front of him and pulled it up over his face. He attempted to read but could not concentrate as he could see many people talking in almost heated discussions.

"Can I get you a drink sir?" a porter asked as he poked his head into Adolf's cabin.

"Yes, your finest brandy please."

The porter smiled and then disappeared around the corner. He re-appeared a minute later with a silver tray containing a bottle of brandy and a snifter. He placed them on the table in front of Adolf. The porter opened the bottle and then filled the snifter with a small amount of the brandy so Adolf could have a taste. Adolf smiled, shook the snifter lightly several times so as to send the liquid into a short rotation around the glass, smelt the aroma with raised nostrils and then consumed a small amount. He let the brandy circulate through his mouth and tongue. He placed the snifter down and then nodded to the porter. The porter added some more of the contents of the bottle to his snifter and then vanished out of the cabin.

Adolf continued to pretend to be engaged in the newspaper he held out in front of him. He would occasionally peer from behind the paper to gaze outside as a large crowd of people began to mill about. Everyone seemed agitated outside and he could only assume it was because of one thing. He looked at his watch and noted that the train should be departing in five minutes. The porter came by and presented Adolf with a lunch menu. He was starting to get his appetite back when he noticed some soldiers walking on to the platform and starting to question the crowd that had been milling about. The conductor poked his head into Adolf's cabin.

"Sir, sorry for the delay but I'll share some quick news. There was an attempt made on the president's life…"

"Really, what happened?" Adolf said in his best surprised voice.

"Well apparently a bomb went off at his headquarters in Neuenhagen."

"Is he alright?"

"Yes, apparently the map table he was working over protected he and his party from injury. Apparently Chairman Mao was taken to the hospital for some stitches to his abdomen, but both President Thallman and Comrade Stalin are in good shape."

Adolf was stunned. How in the world could anyone have survived that? What he would later find out is that Thallman had accidently kicked Adolf's paint box so that it was directly under the center of the table. The table was made of solid oak and it shielded the leaders from the explosion. They were all sent flying to the floor – but no one was seriously injured.

Now more than ever, Adolf had to get out of the country. With Thallman alive, Adolf would have little time to flee. The train pulled out of the station just as a wire had been sent to all airports and train stations to hold all travel until everyone could be searched. Luckily, Adolf had been booked passage on an express train that would not make any stops until it arrived in Amsterdam.

CHAPTER 14

The next morning, when Adolf's train arrived in Amsterdam, he gingerly disembarked, holding his suitcase and wearing his overcoat with the lapel collar flapped upwards to try and conceal his identity. As he walked past a newsstand, he could see the morning headlines…

FAMOUS ARTIST SOUGHT IN ATTEMPT ON GERMAN PRESIDENT'S LIFE

Adolf started to panic when he saw the headline. He then debated as to whether or not he should take a taxi to the hideout – *should I just walk?* The problem was he had no idea where the house was. He had no choice. He hailed a cab pulling is lapel collar as high as he could pull it over his face. He lowered his hat to the point that he could barely see through a thin opening between the hat and the overcoat.

"Where to sir?"

"Prinsengracht 263-267."

"I'm sorry sir, but I'm having trouble understanding you."

"Prinsengracht 263-267."

"Very good sir, we are on our way."

Adolf sat back in the large seat of the car, noting that the cabbie kept looking up to the rearview mirror.

"You here on business sir?"

"Ah yes."

"Where do you hail from?"

Adolf stopped to think – he dare not say Germany.

"Vienna," Adolf said with confidence as that was a true statement.

"Ah, great city Vienna – I love the pastries. Are you okay sir – you look like you're all bundled up back there."

"Yes, bit of a summer cold – if you don't mind my throat is quite sore and it's difficult to speak."

The cabbie nodded and waved his hand as if he had suddenly become mute. Ten minutes later they arrived at their destination.

"That will be twenty guilders' sir."

Adolf quickly handed the man the money – Horace had sent Adolf some Dutch currency as part of his escape plan out of Germany. Adolf grabbed his suitcase and rushed out to the sidewalk as quickly as he could. He stopped and looked up at the tall building – there appeared to be three stories. Not wanting to tarry further he quickly ran the doorbell.

"Adi?" A tall gentleman asked.

Adolf nodded his head and the man quickly ushered him, not before taking a quick perusal of the surrounding for anyone looking suspicious.

"Adi, my name is Otto and welcome to our house – our house is your house."

"Thank you Otto, you are very kind."

"Believe me, it's an honor to have you in our house – I am a big fan of your work."

"That's very nice of you."

"Please don't mind the mess down here, the first floor is the company warehouse where we keep all of our spices and grinding implements."

Adolf looked around surveying the ground floor as they made their way up the stairs. They arrived at an area that appeared to be a dining room or kitchen area.

"Adolf this is my wife Edith, my eldest daughter Margot and my youngest daughter Anne." The three ladies smiled and offered various greetings.

"Thank you ladies, it is nice to meet you."

"Would you like to join us for breakfast Herr Hitler?" Edith asked.

"Thank you very much, but if I could maybe rest a bit – It was a very stressful journey."

"Yes, no problem Adolf, let me show you to your room. Now this is going to be a little odd to you, but we have an annex built on to the back of the house. I think it best that you hide there. We have a room for you on the top floor back there where there shouldn't be anyone able to see you. I'll help you with your things."

Adolf tipped his hat to the ladies and then followed Otto up another stairway. Otto led Adolf to the annex toward the back of the house and then climbed another flight of stairs to his room. There was a large room with a nearby sink and bathroom with a shower. A nice bed had been prepared by Edith with flowers in a vase on the nightstand. There was a small desk with paper and pen and a few volumes of various forms of literature.

"Adi, it's not much but I think you will find it safe. Now I've inserted an intercom which you can just press the button down here to call any of us. You of course are welcome to wander the house as you choose, you are certainly not a prisoner, but in case for whatever reason the house is searched, your best chance not to be found will be here. I don't know if you noticed there was a bookshelf by the door leading to this annex. I put it there so if we do get searched we can use it to cover up the door leading here – no one will know."

"Do you think there will be a time when I can go outside?"

"Well not for the foreseeable future – the assassination attempt is Europe's worst kept secret. We heard about it yesterday – we thought for sure you had been captured. Anyway, if you must go outside, I think the best thing would be to go out at night. Let's wait a few weeks for things to calm down a bit."

Otto smiled and patted Adolf on the shoulder. Adolf smiled and nodded in agreement with his host's suggestion. Otto turned and departed. Adolf was profoundly impressed with the family's hospitality. He hoped that he could repay them for such kindness. Adolf unpacked his suitcase, hanging up several shirts, jackets and slacks. He then pulled out a smaller version of the Torah that Edmond had given him and laid it on his bed. He removed his dress shirt and tie, removed his shoes and then plopped onto the bed. He took a quick peak outside pulling the drapes back just enough to look. He could see a long backyard with a garden and then some trees and another row of houses – he felt it would be very difficult for anyone to find him there. His fears somewhat allayed, he began to read from the Torah but then passed out from shear nervous exhaustion.

Adolf slept most of the day away, not waking up until six pm that evening. He pressed the button on the intercom and asked if it was okay to come down. A bright young female voice said "sure!" Adolf put on his dress shirt and shoes and then began his odyssey back to the front of the house.

Upon his arrival he could see all three family members gathered around the table with Edith presiding over a large pot which she had been stirring.

"Join us for some dinner Adi?" Otto said with a large smile motioning for him to sit.

"That would be very nice, thank you."

"Herr Hitler, I am a big fan of yours," Anne said with a bright smile.

"Oh really, I didn't think I had such young fans," he said with a chuckle looking at Otto and Edith.

"Oh yes, your paintings of the early 40's are breath-taking, I think they were mostly completed when you lived in Paris?"

"Well, you are quite well-versed on my history young lady."

"Yes you will find that our Anne is quite the chatter-box. Margot is our quiet one – she's a deep thinker and only some time lets you into her inner being."

"Oh papa be quiet," Margot said blushing.

"They look like fine young ladies."

"Thank you Herr Hitler. If you don't mind me asking, what were you thinking about when you painted the *Driving Hoard*? It's an incredible work – it looks like a sea of humanity fleeing from tyranny like they are caught up in tornado or storm of some kind."

Adolf smiled, trying to remember his inspiration.

"Well, Anne, I tend to have a lot of dreams – and you can tell they are quite disturbed," he began to laugh with Otto and Edith joining him. Anne just looked at him with a look of quiet amazement.

"Sometimes, I really don't know. I just start splashing paint on a canvass, I leave it for a day or two and then I start looking into what I've done. I then take that chaos and turn it into something resembling human experience – that one came to me when I was looking through a book about Russia, specifically Stalingrad, what used to be Volgograd. It was like some sort of great battle took place there – I don't know, maybe in earlier times like back when the Tartars existed. Anyway it was like a vision – a horrible vision in many ways. I saw people fleeing for their lives – they were being swept away by anger, pain, discrimination – almost anything and everything.

"It's intoxicating," Anne said with her chin on her folded hands, looking up as if Adolf was her favorite singer or movie star.

"Enough chatter, I am sure our guest is starved," Otto said as he started serving bowls of cabbage soup. There were large pieces of bread with butter. Adolf enjoyed the meal very much, especially the attention he was receiving from Anne. After a slice of apple pie and a cup of coffee, Adolf excused himself to go to bed. All the while he was climbing the stairs he kept remarking to himself, *what an intelligent young girl. She could be somebody great one day.*

Adolf shaved, showered and put on his pajamas. While feeling somewhat rested, the trauma of the previous day was still wearing on him so he slowly drifted off to sleep. Before he knew it the sun was up and someone was knocking at his door.

"Herr Hitler, good morning!" It was Anne.

"Yes?"

"I've brought you some breakfast."

"One moment please Anne."

Adolf put on his robe, ran a comb across his greasy hair and then opened the door. Anne marched into his room with a tray and put it down on his desk.

"Anne, you shouldn't have."

"Well, I like to be hospitable when we have guests. It seems the right thing to do. I made you coffee is that alright? Some people prefer tea."

"No, no, that's fine. This looks wonderful."

"Yes, there are eggs scrambled, some kippers, toast with jam – it's a breakfast worthy of a king!" she said with a bright smile.

"I also took the liberty to bring you the morning newspaper – I'm sure you will want to catch up on the latest events?"

"Why thank you Anne, it is very much appreciated."

"You're welcome." And like that, the young lady was gone.

Adolf wondered for a moment if Anne knew the real reason why he was there. He would have thought Otto might have left the young ladies in the dark so as not to frighten them. But there straight across the headlines, was an update about the attempt on Thallman's life;

SEARCH CONTINUES FOR ADI HITLER

Adolf decided to forget about the headline and focus on his breakfast. He enjoyed a first-class meal – he hadn't had kippers in ages. Being close to the Atlantic he assumed them to be as fresh as could be. After a satisfying breakfast he then decided to shave and shower again, this time deciding on a long hot bath. While relaxing in the warm soapy water, he gave into curiosity and began to read a long statement made by Ernst Thallman.

Yesterday, an attempt was made on my life. Luckily for myself and for Germany, it was unsuccessful. I will not let crackpots like these try to ruin what we in the KPD have accomplished. All that we have done. We have pulled this great country out of the mire that it was in after the Great War.

We have helped modernize Germany with great roads like the Autobahn, atomic power to provide electricity to all our cities, maglev trains that can race at 200 kilometers an hour, getting our citizens to anywhere in Germany in a couple of hours at the most.

Despite everything that the KPD had done, there are still those who are jealous – jealous of what we have done. They are small minded individuals – some of them call themselves artists. Well, they are idiots, idiots who want to return this country back to the years of the Great War. Well I will not let it happen!

We are making great strides with our partners in the East. Our new partnership will create great wealth and prosperity, almost completely wiping out unemployment. We will have access to the great lands of Russia and China and participate in the use of their resources – oil, wheat and other grains. It's a partnership that is in our favor and we stand to gain the most.

Now, as for this assassination plot. Those who are responsible will be brought to justice quickly. Even now we have various police personnel on the ground arresting those who are responsible. I will not rest until everyone of them are found and dealt with. One of those men you know – Adolf "Adi" Hitler. One of our great sons, one of our great artists. But even one of our own can go down the wrong path – unfortunately for Adolf, he went down that wrong path. The only way to deal with this is swiftly and we will find him and bring him back from wherever he has fled – whether we have to go to the ends of the earth to bring him back, we will!

But above everything else. Please know that I am well, I am healthy and I am still strong and in control. Likewise, Chairman Stalin is also fine. Chairman Mao is in the hospital with minor injuries but will be released soon.

To all the good people of Germany, I wish you all the best as we look forward to the next 1,000 years!!!

> *-Ernst Thallman, Chairman of the KPD and President of Germany*

Slightly shaken at the prospect of 1,000 years of the KPD, as well as the manhunt that was on, Adolf sank into the hot water, flinging the newspaper to the floor. He lay in the tub looking at the ceiling. His ears were submerged so he couldn't hear anything except the inner-workings of his head. *Perhaps the best thing would be to just slip beneath the water and slowly go to sleep, forever?* Adolf finally rose, stood up in the water and was greeted with a stimulating gust of cool air that came in via a nearby slightly opened window. It felt so good. He immediately wrapped himself in a towel, put on his slippers and then walked back to his room.

He decided to wear a nice suit, and although he wasn't' going anywhere, he thought it a good way of making him feel less confined. He polished his black shoes, put his pocket watch into his tweed jacket and then proceeded down stairs. When he reached the floor beneath his he could see Otto speaking with Anne in a whisper. Otto, then seeing Adolf coming down the ladder stopped speaking.

"Please do not let me interrupt your conversation," Adolf said with a bright smile.

"Adolf, I have some bad news."

Adolf could see that Otto had a very stern expression, one that could not mean anything good. As Adolf arrived at the bottom of the stairs he turned and faced Otto for the news.

"I'm afraid that the KPD found out about Petr."

"How?"

"I'm not sure, but someone pointed him out as someone who knew something about the plot. They tortured poor Petr and murdered him. Not before finding out however that Horace and Andre were also involved…"

"Not Horace!"

Otto was silent, he just shook his head. Adolf turned and went back upstairs – it seemed his world was coming apart.

CHAPTER 15

For the next couple of days, Adolf just kept to his room. He couldn't help but dwell on Horace. He remembered everything that Horace had done for him. If it hadn't been for Horace, there was no way that he would have ever become the artist that he did. In many ways, Horace had been his best friend, and like an older brother. It seemed he had always been looking out for him, guiding him. How could he ever repay him?

The next morning, Anne greeted Adolf at his door with another tray of eggs, kippers and toast…along with the day's newspaper. Adolf smiled and accepted the token. He again shaved and showered but this time only sported a dress shirt – no jacket or tie. He shined his shoes and then proceeded down to return his tray. As he arrived on the next floor. He looked down the hallway toward Anne's room. He could hear her listening to a radio, or at least someone was listening to a radio. He walked down the hallway and stopped at the doorway.

Inside her room, Anne was laying on her bed, listening to the latest pop tunes; it sounded like Glenn Miller. She was whistling with her chin supported by her two hands as she poured over some magazine. Adolf looked around the room and smiled. Anne had made an homage to all of the Hollywood greats.

"Well, this is quite a room." Adolf smiled as Anne turned toward him.

"Oh, Herr Hitler, please come in."

Adolf smiled and paused for a moment as he laid the tray on the floor near the doorway.

"You like my pictures do you? They're all Hollywood's greats; Jimmy Stewart, Cary Grant, Katharine Hepburn, Clark Gable…"

"Yes, this is quite a shrine you have created here."

"Oh, it could be much bigger. I have stacks of books and magazines I haven't finished yet."

"You like these Hollywood people do you?"

"Yes, they're the greatest. One day, I dream that I could be like them, starring in some wonderful movie, going to premiers, winning awards, dining in all the fancy restaurants…it would be magic!!!"

Adolf took a chair by her desk and swung it around so he could face her.

"What do you like about acting?"

"I like the idea of being able to be anyone you want to be – a princess, a pirate, a mermaid…anything!"

"How about being Anne?"

"Excuse me for saying so Herr Hitler but blachhh!!!"

"What's wrong with being Anne?"

"Well for starters, I'm stuck here all day."

"Your parents don't let you go out?"

"They do, but I usually have to hang out with Margot and her friends. Otherwise I have to go to some party and dress up or go see relatives before I can go anywhere. My dad also likes me to help him with the warehouse sometimes."

"Don't you go to school?'

"Yes, but we're on break right now."

Adolf looked deeply into Anne's eyes. She was the brightest, most intelligent young lady he had ever met. She seemed to have an old soul. The way she could speak, the words she would use and the imagery she could create.

"You're no actress, I see you more as a writer."

"Really?" Anne perked up again.

"How 'bout a Hollywood script writer?"

"Sure, anything. You are very intelligent Anne. You can use your mind to do anything. Acting, that's a nice job…assuming you can get it, but writing now that's a real profession…"

"You don't think I'd make a great actress?" Anne seemed to pounce off her bed. She pulled a feather boa that had been laying on her night stand and wrapped it around her neck. She then placed a plastic tiara that was laying on her desk on top of her head. Then she grabbed a pencil from a nearby pencil box and pretended to smoke it like a cigarette.

"Darling, how could you say that to me?" She said in a mock deep voice. Adolf broke out laughing.

"I'm sorry Anne…maybe you were made for the stage after all!" Anne laughed and then flopped back on to her bed.

"I guess what I am saying is that of course you can be anything you want to be. But as a writer, you can really impact lives. Who are some of your favorite authors?"

It took Anne no time to respond;

"Emily Dickenson, oh I adore Elizabeth Barrett Browning;

How do I love thee? Let me count the ways.
I love thee to the depth and breadth and height
My soul can reach, when feeling out of sight
For the ends of being and ideal grace.
I love thee to the level of every day's
Most quiet need, by sun and candle-light.
I love thee freely, as men strive for right.

I love thee purely, as they turn from praise.
I love thee with the passion put to use
In my old griefs, and with my childhood's faith.
I love thee with a love I seemed to lose
With my lost saints. I love thee with the breath,
Smiles, tears, of all my life; and if God choose,
I shall but love thee better after death.

Tah-dah!" Anne said with a curtsey.

"Well done, Anne, you have the soul of a poetess!" Adolf said as he clapped. Adolf then picked up his breakfast tray, looked over at Anne and gave her a smile and a wink.

"You have much potential miss Anne!"

"Thank you Herr Hitler," Anne said and blushed.

Adolf departed the room and then headed downstairs to the kitchen. He thanked Otto and Edith for the breakfast and hospitality. They invited Adolf to stay downstairs with them and play some cards and listen to the radio. While the adults played cards, Anne was at the top of the stairs listening to their conversations.

"Are you doing okay Herr Hitler?" Edith asked as she set a cup of coffee in front of him.

"Very well – it would be nice to take a stroll outside."

"Just wait a while Adi, I'm sure with time it will become safe for you to go outside."

"It's funny how you miss the simple things when they are taken away from you - a walk in the park, sitting on a bench, watching as people walk by…"

"Yes, given all the parties you had once attended, all the celebrities you once hob-knobbed with, being stuck in a house in Amsterdam cannot be all that exciting?"

"Yes, I miss Berlin and the socializing was nice, but nowadays I just like reading a paper, having a good cup of coffee like Edith has made and just go for a stroll."

Anne listening intently decided to go back upstairs and meditate on the situation. She went to her bedroom and looking out of the back window came up with an idea. She would spring it on Adolf after dinner that evening.

Later that evening, the entire family including Adolf dined on lamb stew with mash potatoes and fresh peas. Edith also baked fresh biscuits and for desert an apple pie. Adolf was for the time being content – he had Edith continually plying him with lamb stew and he enjoyed the company of a true family. He looked around and realized how much he had wanted such a family. He had hoped that with Maria that would have become a reality. Unfortunately, having a family was not in the works he had figured. It might have explained why he had been a little melancholy of late. While he had been sanguine about his role in the attempted assassination of Thallman, he had been up and down emotionally of late and seeing this family made him realize why. He had missed Maria.

"Father, are we going to watch the stars tonight?" Margot asked.

"Ah, well possibly."

"You like to stargaze do you Margot?" Adolf asked.

"Well, normally we do not get the opportunity, but tonight will be exceptionally clear so I thought we could go to the park and take out my telescope."

Otto looked at Adolf a little uncomfortably, given the fact that Adolf was somewhat confined at the moment. Adolf sensing the awkward moment spoke up.

"Please, do not feel you have to stay behind with me here – please go and enjoy yourselves. I insist." A relived Otto told Margot to get her telescope and to get ready. He invited Anne but she declined, much to everyone's surprise. Edith decided to stay back and do some knitting.

As the sun set and Otto and Margot made for the nearby park, Anne knocked on Adolf's door.

"Oh hello Anne, how are you?"

"Very well, Herr Hitler. I thought you and I could do a little star gazing ourselves..." Anne pulled a blanket out from behind her back.

"I don't understand? Didn't you want to go with your father and sister?"

"Well, I was feeling sorry for you. You know, not being able to go outside, but I have an idea, follow me."

Adolf followed Anne down the various stairways and hallways until they reached a door to the backyard. Anne opened the door and walked out onto the porch.

"Don't worry, no one will know you are here – it's mostly woods back there."

Adolf stared into the dark, seeing only faint lights from the neighboring houses nearby. He followed Anne into the backyard, noting the sizable bushes and plants as well as the very fragrant flowers – the tulips were still in bloom.

Walking slowly, Anne grabbed Adolf by the hand and tried to quicken his pace. They came to the back fence were Anne pulled up one of the planks that made up the fence. It was still nailed to the top but the nails at the bottom had been removed so the plank could pivot up and down.

"Follow me," Anne said in a whisper.

The gap between planks was narrow but Adolf somehow forced his way through.

It was a rare, clear night in Amsterdam. The combination of dry air and high pressure had cleared the skies over the city. A bright moon shone down on the pair as Anne laid out the blanket.

"I thought we could look at the stars – I brought my astronomy book."

Adolf nodded and sat down with Anne. The two peered up to the heavens and Anne opened her book. Each page had a detailed picture of the various constellations.

"Oooh, there it is…the constellation Orion!" Anne practically screamed and then pointed for Adolf to see. It was truly a brilliant night and the stars seemed to be beaming down on them.

"Oh, there's Aquarius."

Adolf just nodded and smiled. He really enjoyed watching Anne as she turned the pages to study the next constellation. She was truly a special child he thought.

"Ew and there's Aries…Aries the Ram!" She almost yelled into Adolf's ear.

"How about that star on the horizon there – what is that?" Adolf asked.

"Oh that's Venus. It's the brightest thing you can see in the sky."

Adolf nodded and smiled. After a half hour or so of identifying constellations and stars, Anne closed the book. She laid down next to Adolf who had, several minutes earlier, decided to lay down and rest his head on his hands.

"Isn't that incredible Herr Hitler?"

"It certainly is Anne."

"Can you imagine the endlessness of space?"

"No. I get a headache if I think about it too long."

"I know what you mean. Do you believe in God Herr Hitler?"

Adolf paused for a moment.

"I do, at least I think I do. I mean, something or someone must have created all of this. I don't think it could have come from nothing."

"Me too. When I go to synagogue I talk to the teachers there about creation…they usually get bogged down with it."

"I can imagine. You are a bright girl Anne – it's difficult to explain a lot of things to you."

"Why do you think that is?'

"Oh, I don't know. We adults tend to make things more difficult than we should."

"How do you mean?"

Adolf looked over at Anne and could see her looking up to the sky with her bright eyes – she was a marvel.

"Well, like your question about God. When I was young, I believed in God as if he were lying down beside me like you. But then as you get older, life becomes more difficult and more complicated, that child-like faith goes away. While it's replaced with education and wisdom, you sometimes wish you could go back to that child-like faith."

"Are you Jewish?"

"No, Roman Catholic."

"Do you believe in reincarnation?"

"Well, Catholics believe that you just live one life and that God will judge us in this life as to whether or not we were good or bad. Depending on how he judges us is where we end up – heaven or hell."

"The Hindus believe in reincarnation. If you were good you are reborn as a wealthy merchant, if you were bad you are reborn as a cockroach or something terrible."

"It's an interesting idea."

"You don't believe it then?"

"No. I think that we are born and God gives us a will. We can either choose to follow him or not. Depending on how we deal with each obstacle in life is where we will be led. If we make bad decisions, we will go down the wrong path..."

"You mean like Joseph Stalin?"

"You know about Joseph Stalin?"

"I've read he is a bad man. He has persecuted the Jews in Russia, burned down synagogues. He's as bad as those Czars that did the programs!"

"Yes, I've heard bad things about him too."

"So he must have gone down the wrong path?"

"Well, I think so. I know he was at one time studying for the priesthood. Later on, he became a communist and then I guess he soon acquired a lust for power. Power can do strange things to people."

"So people are not born evil?"

Adolf pondered the question, wondering how such a young girl could ask so many questions, and good ones at that.

"I don't think so. I think it's like with Stalin. He was on the right path at one point, but got distracted..."

"Distracted?"

"Yes, it's like the devil, or some evil spirit distracts you from your goals your purpose and you then end up chasing the wrong goals and purpose. Often those who end up chasing power end up so consumed by obtaining it that everything else becomes disposable. People become things, things to be stepped on or thrown away."

Anne pondered what Adolf was saying and continued to look at the stars.

"Herr Hitler, was Ernst Thallman an evil man?"

"You know about that huh?"

"Yes, I heard from father why you came."

Adolf looked over at Anne. She was laying down with her head on her hand starring at Adolf. Adolf's mouth suddenly became dry. He began to search the heavens for the right words to say.

"I don't' know if Ernst Thallman is evil, but he has changed since he first became president of Germany. Like I said about Stalin. People can lose their focus when they are more interested in power. They become less interested in the country and the people they are governing, more interested in their ambitions and goals."

"Why did you try to kill him?"

Again Adolf paused and searched the night sky. Nothing seemed to come to him as he searched the space within his mind.

"Well, he was devising a plan to unite Germany with Russia and China…"

"That was a bad idea?"

"Well, for the purposes that he wanted. It was going to destroy Germany. He didn't understand the people he was dealing with – Stalin and Mao."

"Is Chairman Mao a bad person?"

"There is a belief that he has been unfair to his own people. He makes them work hard for the country with little thought to their well-being. Terrible working conditions, unjust court system, while he just lives in luxury and expects everyone to serve him."

"So…you're like a hero. You tried to stop these bad people?"

"I don't' know about that. I was just convinced they were doing a bad thing and tried to stop it."

"Well, you're a hero in my book." Anne then laid back and started to look at the stars. Adolf smiled and marveled at such an intelligent and mature girl. She was going to be something great one day.

The two stayed another half hour and then packed up their blanket and then headed back to the house. Adolf looked around nervously hoping that no one had seen them. The other houses seemed too far away and their windows blocked by the rising trees. Still, he had an uneasy feeling.

******

The following morning, a knock came on the front door of the house. Otto opened the door and found a young man in nice suit and hat, looking very distinguished.

"Hello, I am Detective Van Dyke from the Dutch Bureau of Investigations."

"Yes sir, how can I help you?"

"Have you seen this man?" he held out a photo of Adolf. Otto's blood went cold.

"No, no, never seen him before."

"You probably heard about the recent attempt on the German president's life?"

"Yes, yes, it was in all of the papers."

"Well this scumbag is the one they are seeking for the attempted murder of President Thallman. So you haven't seen him?"

"No, no…I know that I've seen his picture in the papers but have not seen him around here. Wouldn't he be in Germany?"

"The Intelligence Department of the KPD believe he may be in Holland. Several witnesses that have recently come forward say that he was on a train bound for Amsterdam."

"I see. Well, I have not seen him. Now if you don't' mind I have some business to…" Before Otto could continue, the detective put his foot in the door as Otto was about to close it.

"There was a report from one of your neighbors…in back of you. A Ms. Van Breckan. She says she saw a man in your backyard last night fitting his description."

Otto was stunned and tried his best to hide it.

"Oh that was grandfather!" Anne came busting through the door.

"Who is this?"

"This is my youngest daughter Anne."

"What are you saying young lady?" the detective said with a sigh.

"That was my grandfather that Ms. Van Breckan saw."

"Has not your grandfather been here before?"

"Yes, but typically not in the backyard, but that is what Ms. Van Breckan saw. I had asked my grandfather to come with me so we could look at the stars last night."

The detective was quiet and was mulling over the story. He began nodding his head noting that Ms. Van Breckan was elderly and perhaps had mis-identified the man that was in the backyard the previous evening.

"Hmmm…well, okay. I'll go talk with Ms. Van Breckan. Maybe she didn't see what she thought she saw."

Otto and Anne nodded their heads in unison. The detective was soon gone and Otto closed the door quickly behind.

"Anne, what happened last night?"

"I took Herr Hitler into the backyard to look at stars."

"Anne, that was not a smart thing to do. You know there are many people looking for Herr Hitler – we have to be more careful."

"Please don't be angry with Anne – it was my own doing. I just had to get outside for a while." Adolf had been listening from the top of the stairs and had come to the aid of Anne.

"No, it's my fault Herr Hitler, I shouldn't have pestered you to come outside with me."

Otto rolled his eyes knowing how persuasive Anne could be.

"Nonsense child – you have nothing to apologize for. I needed to get out. And if I have compromised my well-being so be it."

"Yes, but Adi, you have to remember that we could also be in trouble. If they find that we were harboring a criminal, it could be bad for us as well."

"Otto, I'm sorry. You are correct. I was thinking about myself and I shouldn't. I apologize – it will not happen again."

"Don't worry Adi, let's all just be a little more cautious."

Adolf patted Otto on the shoulder and smiled. He gave Otto a look of confidence as if everything would be alright. A nervous and slightly riled Otto invited Adolf to breakfast. It would take Otto several cups of tea before his nerves returned to their original state.

The following day, detective Van Dyke returned.

"Oh hello detective, how can I help you?" Otto could see that there were several policemen behind him.

"I have a warrant to search your house, please move aside." Before Otto could react, all four men were running up the stairway and into the house. Otto pressed a nearby button which rang up to the annex. The buzzer signaled to Adolf to stay put in his room. The buzzer also sent a message to Anne and Margot in their rooms to push the bookshelf in front of the door leading to the annex. Everyone one received their message loud and clear and responded accordingly. Adolf in his room could hear the men yelling to each other and running up and down the stairs. For the first time he began to fear for his life. Had his little venture to the backyard the previous night cost him his freedom...possibly his life?

For about an hour, Adolf sat on his bed in his room in the annex, clutching his arms together. He would catch himself sometimes holding his breath which he would realize was an unnecessary action. Finally, the men left and Otto sounded the "all clear" with three rings of the buzzer.

The family gathered with Adolf upstairs near the door to the annex.

"Adi, I think we might have to look for a new hiding spot for you. I think that detective is not going to give up."

Adolf was silent but nodded to the suggestion.

"I'll make some contacts and see if there are some alternatives." Otto departed leaving the girls to try and keep Adolf's spirits up. Anne suggested that they give Adolf a disguise and then take him to one of the ferries where he could escape to England. When Margot asked Anne to whom would he live with in England, Anne had no answers. Adolf spent the rest of the day with Anne as she explained to him who were all of the famous celebrities and stars in Hollywood. Adolf, while enjoying Anne's diversion, still couldn't help but worry about the current situation.

The next morning, while Otto had breakfast, he started having a troubled feeling. He walked to the front window and began to look in either direction down the street. He then noticed what appeared to be detective Van Dyke walking down the street – as the man came closer it was in fact the indestructible inspector from the Dutch police. He walked past Otto's residence and then stopped next door at his neighbors. He began pounding on the door. The neighbor opened the door and before much explanation the detective had let himself in.

Otto became curious about what he could be doing – but whatever he was doing could not be good. He had not been able to obtain an alternative hide-out for Adolf and began to fear what the nosey detective was up to. Otto began to mount the stairs to tell Adolf about what was happening when the doorbell rang.

He felt a heart-attack coming on when he found Van Dyke waiting at the door with several police officers.

"We've returned with another warrant. This time I know where you've hidden the criminal!"

Before Otto could respond, Van Dyke and his men burst through and ran up the stairway to the upper rooms. Once there, Van Dyke ran right up to the bookcase that was concealing the door to the annex.

"Johansen, move the bookcase."

A large burley officer began to push the bookcase away from the door.

"Exactly as I thought! Gentlemen, please have your weapons ready."

And with that they pushed through the door. As the four men practically stumbled into Adolf's room, they were flabbergasted by the complete lack of occupants. Van Dyke then ran over to the open window. Looking down he could see a rope that had been tied to a beam near the base of the roof. Adolf had attached it and then slid down to the backyard. Looking toward the back of the garden, Van Dyke could see a panel askew in the backyard fence.

"C'mon men, to the backyard." All four men poured out of the room and began their flight downstairs. Anne and Margot were in hot pursuit hoping that Adolf had gotten away. Adolf had in fact made his way into the back alleyway and was running as fast as he could. He began to feel himself gasping and felt slightly light-headed. It had been years since he had done any physical exercise of any kind – the art world was not conducive to anything related to recreation.

He began to hear sirens and thought he heard people shouting to him. He began to fear for his life, thinking that the police were just down the street or waiting for him down the next alleyway. *How did I get into this predicament?* He yelled to himself as he continued down the alleyway. He then turned down another street only to find a German shepherd dog on the loose. The dog turned toward Adolf and he immediately back-peddled in the direction he had come from.

As Adolf emerged from the alley a bullet came careening off the nearby wall. Up the road he could see Van Dyke and his men. He made a run toward the canal and was about to jump onto a boat when one of Van Dyke's men grabbed him.

"Not so fast Herr Hitler!" Van Dyke yelled as he came scampering behind the henchman who had Adolf by the collar.

"Justice always finds it's criminals Herr Hitler. Do you like that line? I made it up myself." The heavy breathing Van Dyke said, his face completely red and showing the strains of exhaustion. Within a minute, a police car came and the officer pushed Adolf into the backseat. Standing outside were Otto, Edith, Margot and Anne. Anne had tears in her eyes and was yelling at the policemen to not hurt him. Adolf waved and smiled at Anne to let her know he was okay. Within minutes they were at the local police station. They took a mug shot of Adolf, took his fingerprints and then shoved him into the nearest cell, slamming the door closed.

Adolf picked himself up and then sat on a nearby stool. There was one cot but it was currently being occupied by another individual. Looking at the cell, Adolf was somewhat relived that he had been caught. The agony of hiding had been getting to him and he almost preferred being caught to continually hiding in the annex. Although he enjoyed the company, it was the fear he did not enjoy. The fear that someone was always watching him. The fear that something terrible could happen at any moment. While he certainly had no idea what would happen to him next, at least the horrible waiting had ended.

******

Somehow, Adolf had managed to get some sleep. He had moved the stool close to the cell wall and leaned back. He slept somewhat hunched up but slept none-the-less. He continued to watch for any signs of life on the cot next him but could not see any. He just tried to sleep as much as he could – whatever was coming next he would need all his energy and strength.

Bright and early the next morning, a man appeared at the cell door. A guard let him in and he introduced himself as Adolf's attorney.

"Frederich Stauffenberg at your service Herr Hitler!" The man offered his hand to shake to which Adolf offered a cold limp appendage.

"How are they treating you Herr Hitler?"

Adolf offered a look of indecision and a frown.

"Don't worry my friend, I am working on your case right now – I don't think you have anything to worry about."

"Nothing to worry about? The man who I tried to blow up saw me thirty minutes' prior…"

"Keep it down Herr Hitler…don't admit to anything."

Adolf rolled his eyes and shook his head.

"Very well, what do you suggest, an insanity plea?"

The young attorney looked at him with surprise as if Adolf had found out his best kept secret.

"Well…do you have any craziness in your family that we could allude to?"

Adolf shook his head and smiled at the ineptitude of his lawyer. Adolf had thought about studying the law once but then had been distracted by his true love – art. *Where was art now?* he thought to himself. The lawyer explained the next steps and that he was to have a hearing the following Wednesday. At the hearing motions would be made by the prosecution to extradite Adolf back to

CHAPTER 17

With Rosa now in control, the New KPD Party came to power. Rosa was in charge of all the new appointments, and while there were representatives from other parties, it was the KPD and more specifically Rosa who was the clear leader.

With Rosa's split with Stalin, war was again on the horizon. Stalin was furious with Rosa's "betrayal" not to unite with the new Communist Union. What Rosa did not know however was that a large army was set to march on Germany. Over two million men, split mainly between the Soviet Union and the People's Republic of China were on the Polish frontier ready to strike a blow on Germany.

The Russian- Chinese alliance was as strong as ever. Ever since Stalin had sent troops into Northern China in 1931 to neutralize the northern war lords, Chang Kai Shek was on the run when Mao's armies marched from the South and connected with the Russian troops in Peking. Since that day Mao owed a debt to Stalin and would always back him in whatever he did. Now with the break of Germany from the Communist Union, Mao supported Stalin in their invasion of their former ally.

On March 1st, 1946, Operation Sledgehammer went into effect and the sprawling armies of Stalin and Mao poured over the borders of Poland. The Polish Prime Minister immediately notified President Luxemburg of what was transpiring and Rosa called a meeting of her security council. Her security council had been haphazardly put together over the past couple of weeks but was impressive none-the-less.

Germany. The defense would argue that he would not be able to have a fair trial in Germany. He stated that it was probably of no use and that he would be extradited back to Germany.

"Why did you want to use an insanity plead then if you don't think there's much hope Herr Stauffenberg?"

"I don't know, I thought if the judge thought you were insane he would move to have you institutionalized here in Amsterdam."

"What good would that do me – I want to get out of prison, not live in another different kind of cage for the rest of my life."

"Do you have much time left?" the young attorney muttered under his breath.

"Listen young man I am only fifty-five years old. Many people live to be one hundred now-a-days."

"Sorry…what do you suggest then?"

"Well, if they extradite me to Germany then fine. I will be back on home soil. I can probably find an attorney there to represent me."

With that, the defeated young lawyer packed his satchel and asked the guard to let him out. Adolf just shook his head and wondered how Stauffenberg would turn out as a solicitor years from now.

"I've got an idea – let's escape!" Adolf turned to see that his cell mate was indeed alive and sitting up on his cot.

"I beg your pardon?"

"I said, let's escape."

"Escape…escape how?"

"These walls…these walls when you really think about them are just in our imagination. We are the ones who create this prison. We are the ones who created those bars. If we just think hard enough we can make these walls just go away."

Adolf was slightly perplexed by the gentlemen's strange plan. He pursed his lip and then nodded at the gentleman.

"I'm Paul by the way." The man smiled and offered his bandaged hand to shake. As he leaned toward Adolf he could smell the strong scent of vodka on his breath.

"Adolf. What happened to your hand Paul?"

"Oh, got in a bit of a scrape. I was in a fight. I broke a bottle over a counter and got cut on one of the chards."

"What was the fight about?"

Paul scratched his head, looked around and then upwards for apparent enlightenment but just shrugged his shoulders and raised his hands like he had no idea.

"Anyway, it doesn't matter why I am in here – I have no place to go. Do you have a place to go to Adolf?"

Adolf thought for a moment. He had his apartment and country house in Berlin. He had another house in Bavaria. But what else did he have? He had no one to share them with. He had lost Maria. Horace was dead. Who knows what became of Horace's family? Maybe Paul was right – maybe he didn't have anywhere to go?

"You see Adi, many people fear prison. Not me, I love it here. It's when I get out into the streets that I become awkward, out of step. People think I'm ugly and useless. No one wants to give me a job. But in here – I get free food, a place to sleep."

"Did you ever have a job?"

"Years and years ago I used to work on freight ships."

"Oh yeah, what did you do?"

"Ah mostly as a deck hand – someone was always ordering me around to do things. It was a lot of work. I did enjoy though when we would get into a new port; Calcutta, Hong Kong, Java, Singapore – man, those places were something else, especially the ladies." Paul made an ogling expression and elbowed Adolf, seeming to allude to his prowess with the female gender.

"But you know, if you been to one place you've been too them all."

Adolf nodded and smiled at Paul's philosophizing.

"Whether you are in Sydney or San Francisco, people are basically the same. We all have a head with eyes, a nose, a mouth and a brain. They may all look a little different, but basically the same.

Same way with nature. If you look at a sunset from Honolulu, it's just the same as from Okinawa. The waves crash on the beach at San Diego in the same way that they crash in Acapulco. I mean, I think God did a great job and everything, but the one thing that really sets everything apart…you want to know?"

Adolf nodded, wondering to himself if he should really encourage him further. Paul then began to point to his head.

"It's all in here Adi. Yep, right here in our noggins. You know, it's like the great philosopher asked, 'if a tree falls down in the woods and there's no one there to hear it, does it make a sound?'"

Adolf crossed his arms and then put a finger to his lip.

"So I say, if there's no one there to view it, is there really a sunset? See what these great scientists say is everything that is real has to be a fact. But what about consciousness? Is something a fact if there is not a conscious mind to acknowledge it as a fact or discover that it's a fact?"

Adolf was starting to see this man as something other than an ordinary drunkard.

"Did you study philosophy somewhere Paul?"

Paul shook his head to the negative.

"No, it's just stuff I often think about."

"Hey wait a minute. How did you know my nickname was Adi?" It just dawned on Adolf that Paul had called him Adi.

"I like nicknames – I usually will shorten people's names. You know, like 'Willy, 'Mike', etc. etc."

With that thought, it was as if he had used his allotment of brain for the hour and then collapsed back onto his cot. Adolf smiled at the weary cellmate and then began to start thinking about his own future, or if there was going to be one.

CHAPTER 16

Several days later, Adolf was brought into a Dutch courtroom in Amsterdam. He felt as though he was a captured zoological exhibit being sent to his cage, the entirety of the courtroom was gawking at him, cursing him, and a generally in a heated and agitated state. He did see the friendly faces of Otto, Edith, Margot and Anne. Anne, the ever angelic force that melt his heart every time he looked at her.

As for the proceedings themselves, they were over in a half-hour. After reviewing whatever evidence Herr Stauffenburg presented, the judge quickly decided that Adolf would be extradited to Germany. There had been a lot of fanfare for very little in the way of judicial process. The crowd though had been there solely to see the vile, corrupt terrorist who had dare try to assassinate President Thallman.

As Adolf left the courtroom, he smiled and nodded at Otto, Edith and Margot. He then stopped and winked at Anne. He knew she was under a lot of stress seeing him in handcuffs – he just kept smiling at her, hoping she would cheer up, but there was little to console her at that point, she was an emotional fourteen-year-old and the scene was a bit too overwhelming.

As Adolf was led outside of the courtroom he was immediately pushed into a waiting police car. The car, with alarm blaring, whizzed down the streets of Amsterdam heading to the airport. Within minutes they were at a security gate at Schiphol Airport. The guard raised the gate and waved the car through.

A DC-3 cargo plane was parked with its engines running on the tarmac near a cargo hangar.

"Well, Herr Hitler, we have a cargo plane heading to Berlin right now. The interior will be a little Spartan for a man of your taste but it will do the trick," detective Van Dyke said with a roaring laugh.

The car stopped short of the plane and then Van Dyke escorted Adolf to the plane. As Adolf walked up the stairs and into the plane, he could see indeed it was modest in décor – there were several large bins full of mail and packages and then a small bench right next to the cockpit doorway.

"My man Johansen will accompany you to Berlin. Enjoy your trip Herr Hitler?" Again Van Dyke burst into laughter as if he knew something that Adolf didn't.

As Adolf sat down on the bench, the back cargo door was slammed shut and locked tight. The two men waited in silence and then two minutes later the propellers roared into life. The cargo plane began to taxi toward the runway. It seemed an eternity for the plane to become skyward as it would taxi, stop, taxi stop, taxi and then sometimes ground to a complete halt. It felt as if the pilots were lost on the field and had no clue where the runway was. Just as all hope had been lost, the plane seemed to find the runway and the captain applied full throttle. The plane began to vibrate violently at times and seemed to swerve to and fro but finally the plane lift-off and began to soar. Adolf looked out of the window behind him and could see the airport eventually disappear from view.

Sargent Johansen was good enough to remove the handcuffs from Adolf's hand and then produced a brown paper bag. Inside the bag emerged a couple of sandwiches in wax paper which he handed to Adolf to eat. He then pulled out a thermos from the bag he had brought on board and then handed Adolf a hot cup of coffee. It wasn't first class service but Adolf was very grateful still the same.

The flight lasted a little over an hour and a half. The captain pulled back on the throttles and the plane began a quick descent through the Berlin sky. Adolf, having previously feared flight, began to enjoy himself a little. He could see all of Berlin and its various landmarks. He could see some of his old haunts and places he used to live. Sadly, he could also see the Goldman's house. He became very troubled at the prospect of what might become of him given how they had dealt with Horace.

Once the plane had landed, it taxied to a remote spot at the Tempelhof Airport. The plane came to a stop by a large chain-link fence and the engines were quickly powered down. Adolf, again in handcuffs, was led by Sargent Johansen down the back stairway that had been pushed up to the plane. A large truck came roaring up and three men in the back came running for the plane. Adolf was unsure what their intentions were but they soon diverted toward the cargo door on the opposite side of the plane. Another man from the truck wheeled over a large bin and the two men inside the plane began to throw down mail and packages to the other two men with the bin.

As Adolf focused on the work of the men, he then noticed a large limousine approaching from the main building. The limo pulled up and an officer from the KPD sprang from its interior.

"We'll take it from here sergeant," the officer barked. Johansen then disappeared back into the cargo plane. The officer then grabbed Adolf by the arm and pulled him toward the limo. As they arrived at the door, Adolf tried to peer into the dark to see what was in there but before he could inspect it the officer had pushed him face first onto the floor.

"Well, well, if it isn't the Minister for the Arts, Adi Hitler," it was the cold grumbly voice of Ernst Thallman. Adolf quivered at the prospect of having to face the man he almost blew to a thousand pieces.

"Herr Thallman, so good to see you. You look fit," Adolf said in a feigned voice of empathy. He was then dragged up onto a seat facing Thallman.

"Adolf, Adolf, after everything I did for you this is how you treat me?"

Adolf remained silent yet defiant. For the first time in his life he felt as if he had taken the high-road, had taken the risk to help his fellow man and he didn't feel in the least bit ashamed or in fear. It was the first time in his life he had ever felt that way. He felt strong, almost invincible. He just looked Thallman straight in the eye with a steely gaze and smiled. Thallman was not expecting such a display. He thought he would be humiliating Adolf to the point where he would beg for his life, but clearly he never really knew the true Adolf. The car ride turned into a silent twenty-minute staring contest with Thallman the one having to look away or blink. Adolf knew that right was on his side.

"Well, enough games then Adi. I figure you can do us all a favor…avoid a lengthy trial, so here." Thallman handed Adolf a German luger pistol. Adolf again smiled, shook his head and met Thallman's gaze head on.

A thoroughly frustrated Thallman emerged from the back of the limousine as several KPD officers greeted him. He ignored them and they then proceeded to take Adolf to a guarded room in the Reich Chancellery. In the room was a bed, a desk and several bookshelves. On a nearby table was a pen and some papers. The papers were legal documents and they were entitled *The Last Will and Testament of Adolf Hitler*. Adolf, with his new found sense of courage merely laughed and threw the documents onto the floor. He threw his hat onto the desk and then laid down on the bed. Before he knew it he was sound asleep.

******

The next morning, Adolf was awoken by two guards who had marched into his room. For a moment he had to think where he was. The décor quickly reminded him that it was the Reich Chancellery. He was marched down to another building which contained a small courtroom. There were three judges behind a large bench with one stenographer sitting to the side. In a small viewing area were Ernst Thallman, Eva Thallman, Ernst Rohm, Joseph Goebbels, the representatives of the Workers Party, Ludwig Windthorst and Karl Friedrich von Savigny from the Centre Party and Herman Goring, the commander of the military.

It was clear that it was going to be a mock trial. None of the other party or military leaders had enough power to dethrone Thallman so the judges would simply act as his puppets. And that's precisely how they operated. There was a lawyer assigned to Adolf but he never showed up for any of the hearings. It seemed to not matter however for Adolf was clearly resigned to his fate. It was almost as if he didn't care. He would break out into laughter at some of the motions by the prosecutor – the whole affair was just too profane not to laugh. He at one point just yelled out "why don't you just take me out to that courtyard and shoot me now?!!!"

Everyone, although knowing the outcome was very evident were still shocked at Adolf's defiance. It had built up in him over the past year. It had built up in him from the gentleness and courage his mother had faced when he was a young boy. It had built up in him from the right and wrong that his mother had taught him. It had built up in him from the pain of losing his love Maria and it had built up in him in from the spirit of a young girl name Anne. Adolf was a new creature, a confident man that knew he had chosen the righteous path when he had decided that his fellow man's freedom was more important than any fame or wealth he could achieve. And it was his boldness that led to a quick verdict that Thallman had orchestrated…

"It is with some sadness that we come to this decision today," one of the judges began. "For like Bach, like Beethoven, Adolf Hitler was a talented German artist. Someone that we Germans can be proud of. However, being steered away from what is right and wrong, most likely from that same community that molded him, we see that Herr Hitler acted with malice of forethought when he plotted to have our president killed. It was planned out in advance with savagery and cunning. It was only by a miracle that our president was saved. And therefore, with the evidence that has been presented, we find that the defendant Adolf Hitler is guilty of the crimes to which he has been charged. We also find that the only fitting punishment for this terrible crime is the death penalty - to be carried out tomorrow morning at 9 a.m. The court is adjourned." And with that sentence the judge hammered his gavel. Two KPD guards grabbed Adolf by either arm and escorted him back to his room in the Reich Chancellery.

"I think it a fair sentence," Josef Goebbels said as he smiled at the president.

"Yes, very fitting for a swine. I heard he weaseled his way out of the Great War to sit in a pretty little office in Vienna to finger paint and make doodles. He probably dined on caviar and vodka as he did so," a disgusted Herman Goring grunted as he spoke.

"Yes, and I heard he lived a very decadent life – women, prostitutes…the man was depraved!" Ernst Rohm proclaimed.

"Thank you gentlemen for your kind words. For me it's not important. We have to deal with these trouble-makers the best as we can. Now we need to move on to more important matters such as the Communist Union. Thank you all for your help in building this incredible state that will make us the most powerful nation on earth. Good evening gentlemen."

Thallman offered Eva his arm and they were soon out the door and stepping into a waiting limousine that would take them to their favorite restaurant in Berlin. While Herr and Fraulein Thallman dined on pate, caviar and roast leg of lamb, Adolf sat in his room waiting to step into eternity.

Without much fear, Adolf fell asleep – it was a deep, sound rest. And again he was awoken by the same two guards who had previously helped him to rise. They escorted him to a nearby shower where they instructed him to shower and shave. They took his clothes and left him some baggy stripped shirt and pants that looked more like typical prison attire. He was then marched into a kitchen where there was a table. A lone cook was frying some eggs and bacon. He also functioned as waiter, slipping the fried contents on to a plate. He then buttered some toast and poured Adolf a cup of coffee.

Adolf savored the meal for as long as he could even though the eggs were runny, the bacon tough, the toast soggy and the coffee served in a large tin cup. Unable to finish his meal, the guards raced him out to the courtyard of the Reich Chancellery to hastily-constructed gallows. On hand for the event were Thallman, Rohm, Goebbels, and a recently promoted Heinrich Himmler to the post of aid, helping Goebbel's with his seedy activities. A Catholic priest was there to give the last rites and a very corpulent man who was a photographer who would capture the scene for memorial. The two guards walked Adolf up the gallows and presented him to the executioner who quickly laced up the noose around Adolf's neck. The priest then offered a prayer. The executioner then asked Adolf if he had any last words. Adolf staring at Thallman uttered these words.

"To freedom! Something all men should be allowed." Adolf smiled and then moved forward as the executioner motioned him toward the center of the platform. The executioner then put a hood over his head and moved back to the lever. As he placed his hand on the lever, the ground around them began to rumble. It seemed to last several seconds and stop. The executioner looked over at Thallman who then nodded his head to proceed. As he did so the ground began to shake again, this time much more severely. Was Berlin experiencing an earthquake?

As the rumbling sound became louder and louder the attendees began to look around the grounds for an explanation. It quickly became apparent that the sounds were emanating from outside the Chancellery. The sound became even louder as if the courtyard would start to pull apart from the shaking. And like an explosion an armored vehicle broke through the main gate to the Chancellery and drove toward the gallows. The armored car was quickly followed by two other armored cars and then by a tank. They all pulled up to the gallows where the occupant of one of the armored vehicles popped open the hatch, pointed and gun and began to yell…

"Stop what you are doing immediately!" The executioner moved away from the lever and lifted his hands to the air. Several individuals emerged from the back of the armored vehicle and ran toward Thallman and the other men.

"Raise your hands please." Two women with submachine guns pointed them at Thallman and company – they quickly raised their hands.

The woman who initially yelled at the executioner came running out of the armored vehicle and ascended the stairs of the gallows. She pulled the hood off of Adolf and the two began to smile – it was Rosa Luxemburg. She planted a long kiss on Adolf and then pulled away smiling.

"Rosa, what on earth is going on?" Adolf asked in complete shock.

"It's a revolution Adi! We're taking over Germany for a true Communist revolution!" Rosa removed the rope that had bound Adolf's hands behind his back and then escorted him down the stairway. Rosa ordered the two women to march the other men into the Chancellery.

"What is the meaning of this!" Thallman repeated multiple times.

"What it means Thallman is your days are over as the leader of Germany. Take them upstairs!" The two women started to yell at the men and pointed their guns at them. The men huddled together and were herded over to the main building.

"Adi, so glad to see you!"

"I'm so glad to see you Rosa. Where have you been and what is all this?"

"Long story Adi, I'll have to catch you up in a minute. In the meantime, follow me."

Adolf followed Rosa as she joined the two women who had their guns trained on the men. The two women looked like they were dressed in Soviet soldier uniforms. Rosa was a little less formal – she looked like she had just come from the stables of a wealthy horse breeder or showmen. She had on riding boots, riding pants and even a tweed jacket. The three of them looked like they had been on the road for days.

As the men were herded into the building, Rosa turned to one of the drivers of the armored vehicles. "Take the men and secure the building. Radio for more tanks and position them on the streets outside!" A man slipped his head out of the window and gave a thumbs up.

Upon entering the main building, everyone was forced to go up to the president's office. By now a forth woman had joined them and began to shout at the men to start moving more quickly upstairs.

As they arrived in the president's office, Rosa took her place behind the presidential desk.

"As you may now be aware, I have led a coup against the Thallman government..."

"Why you..."

"Quiet!" Rosa barked at Thallman.

"I am now in control of the government. We have a force of over 100,000 men and women with 300 armored vehicles, 400 tanks and 2,000 artillery guns. We have taken over every major German city in a coordinated invasion from the Polish frontier.

"You'll never get away with this!" Thallman yelled.

"Hannah, please bind and gag Herr Thallman."

As Hannah began to tie Thallman's hands behind his back, Adolf realized who she was, it was Hannah Hock, the great Weimar artist who apparently had turned into a communist activist. When she had finished binding Thallman's hands, she took a scarf from around her neck and then gagged him with it.

"Now, my dear Thallman, the country is no longer yours. You practically ruined the country and thank goodness we have taken it back. You are an imbecile, and idiot who almost gave away Germany."

Thallman tried to respond but was unable to with the scarf tied over his mouth.

"You'll be tried for crimes against the German people and most likely receive a life sentence, depending on what an investigation finds."

Just then, Eva Thallman walked into the office.

"What is going on here? Ernst?"

"Mrs. Thallman, please join us. We were just telling your husband that the country is no longer his. I have led a coup and have taken over the government. The real KPD will rise and rule over Germany."

"But what about the Worker's Party?" Rohm asked.

"The Worker's Party will still have representation, just not by you."

"What, this is an outrage!" Goebbels cried.

"Bertha, Liesolotte, please show these men to their new quarters in the basement prison."

The two women began waving their guns at the men who then turned to go downstairs.

"What are you doing with my husband?" Eva asked.

"Your husband will be put on trial. Hannah, please also show Herr Thallman to his cell downstairs. Fraulien Thallman you are welcome to accompanying your husband downstairs, but you will have to leave by 2pm." Eva with a look of complete confusion looked at Adolf for answers. Adolf just looked down at the ground while she reluctantly followed her husband downstairs.

At that moment, two men dressed in the same Soviet uniforms entered the office.

"The streets are secured President Luxemburg!"

"Thank you Franz. Please stand guard outside." The man saluted Rosa and then left the office, positioning himself and the other men to guard the office. As the men left, Rosa turned and looked out of the large bay window. She could see ten tanks lining the streets outside. Troops were lined up and down either side of the street. She could see several of the soldiers at a nearby police station ordering men to raise their hands in surrender. They were then marched over to the Chancellery were the were interned at a nearby prison complex. Rosa smiled and then turned to Adolf.

"Adi, you will never believe what has happened since we last saw each other!"

"Yes, I'm dumbfounded…I had no idea where you ended up."

Rosa went on to explain that after escaping from the Freikorps, she was able to flee to Poland. She had family in Zamosc. There she was able to find work as well as start a communist newspaper. After rising up within the Polish Communist Party, she became a member of Parliament and later met Joseph Stalin at a party meeting in Moscow in

1940. She began to correspond with Stalin on a regular basis and discussed with him the possibility of helping her organize an army to overthrow the German government.

Ever since the embarrassment of the Great War, Russia was looking for revenge against Germany. Stalin thought that providing arms and weapons to a band of rogues in Poland, wouldn't hurt and that perhaps they could support such an operation with Russian troops. For the next several years, Russia began transporting armaments to Zamosc and the stage was set for a coup. Stalin sent military advisors and offices to help train Rosa's fledgling force. With volunteers from Germany, Poland, Hungary, Romania and Russia, she built a force of over 100,000. Knowing that Germany's military had been critically reduced because of the Treaty of Versailles, the idea of a coup did not seem like such a crazy idea.

Because of the support that Stalin had lent her, he wanted guarantees that they would form an alliance once the coup was over. Rosa told Adolf in confidence that the alliance would not happen. She would not give Stalin a free hand in Germany.

"The prisoners are secure, Madame Luxemburg!" One of the women had returned.

"Adi, I'd like you to meet Liesolotte Lehman."

"My pleasure," Adolf offered her his hand to shake.

"The pleasure is mine Herr Hitler. You are a hero to many of us."

Rosa could see that Adolf was blushing a little.

"You'll have to forgive Herr Hitler, he's a little modest."

At that point the two other women joined the triumvirate in the presidential office.

"Oh you probably already know Hannah Hoch…"

"Yes, I am a big fan of your work."

"And I yours Herr Hitler," Hannah offered her hand to Adolf.

"And this is my right hand lady Bertha Braunthal. She has been working hard in Feminist politics. She was elected to the party executive and took over leadership of its Women's Secretariat. She worked with one of our great pioneers of freedom Clara Zetkin. When Thallman became a little too overbearing, I had her join me in Poland. And you might like to know that she is also of Viennese stock! These three women have been indispensable to me Adi!"

Adolf was duly impressed. These were strong women who knew what they wanted. If it wasn't for them he would have been dead by now. Rosa suggested that Adolf join her for dinner at one of their old local haunts. He accepted and over a bottle of champagne to celebrate the take-over, the two decided to rekindle their romance. Adolf invited her to his apartment where they consummated the renewed relationship. One thing that Adolf had to get used to however was twenty-four hour armed guards surrounding the pair. At that point in his life he no longer cared. Just to have a stable partner was enough. Whether she happened to be the leader of Germany didn't really matter to him.

At the meeting were Admiral Karl Donitz, head of the navy, Georg Lindemann, head of the German army, who had secret negotiations with Rosa Luxemburg during the early stages of the coup, Adolf Galland, head of the German Air Force, physicists Kurt Diebner, Abraham Esau, Walter Gerlach, Erich Schumann, Otto Frisch, Hans Bethe and Albert Einstein – all leaders in Germany's nuclear power programs. Wernher von Braun, in charge of the rocketry program, and Ernst Heinkel, aircraft manufacturer.

"Gentlemen, thank you for joining me on such short notice," Madam Luxemburg began. "We have a grave situation which I am sure you all are aware of. A combined Soviet-Chinese force has launched an attack on Poland. Given the fact that I double-crossed Stalin, the real destination of this attack is Germany. We need to pull together some quick ideas of what to do as those armies will be here in two days, three at the most. Please give me your ideas gentlemen."

Albert Einstein rose and was quickly acknowledged by Rosa.

"Madame President, we at the Berlin Institute of Technology have not only been working on nuclear fission as a power source, but as a deterrent as well…"

"Really…who wanted that?"

"Our colleague from the Bundeswehr, General Lindemann thought it might be a good idea for us to study the application of that in the event that Germany were attacked."

"Hmmm…and what have you found?"

"Well, we have already developed a cell for a bomb core but it has not been tested. We have been in discussions with Wernher von Braun on the possibility of it being delivered via one of his rockets."

"What are your thoughts Herr von Braun?"

"Madame President, it has not been tested. We have made great progress in our rocket vehicles. I think it could work but again it has not been tested."

"Unfortunately gentlemen we do not have time to test it. We do not have an adequate army or air force to fight this gigantic army…I think this is our only hope. Please do what you can to deter this foe!"

"Yes Madame President." Einstein looked at the men and they quickly made an exit for the institute to try and figure out how they could put together a bomb and deliver it in two days. They had already done a lot of the groundwork, it was now just the ability to assemble the necessary elements and work with von Braun to deliver it.

"How did it go my dear?" A timid Adolf asked when Rosa returned to their apartment.

"It's not good news Adi. This joint Soviet-Chinese force is almost at our doorstep. I do not know how we are going to stop them."

"You've got the greatest minds in Germany working on it, what else can you do?"

Rosa, exhausted from her worries slipped into bed with Adolf. Adolf was happy again. Although the woman in his life was absorbed with great problems, he tried to support her as best as he could.

******

After the second day of the invasion, the joint Soviet and Chinese army was on the outskirts of Poznan. It was clear that their target was Berlin. The Polish army had given little resistance and was more or less getting out of the way of the gathering horde from the East. The only thing slowing down the giant army was its own weight of men and materials.

German reconnaissance flights were feeding information both into Rosa's headquarters and into the Institute of Technology. Einstein was giving Rosa hourly updates on their progress and it was coming down to the wire. The latest update was they had assembled two bombs and they were now being fitted into two rockets of von Braun's. The idea was to target an open area near the Mogielnica River, which was a small tributary of the Bzura River, where there wasn't a large population of people. Once they knew that the Russo-Chinese force was in that area, they would let the rockets fly.

The next day, Rosa and Adolf joined Einstein, Galland, Lehmann and von Braun at the Reich Chancellery. She met them at the quickly prepared "war room". Adolf continued to follow Rosa wherever she went like a confused dog following its master. Once inside the war-room, everyone got down to business.

"Madame President, we have a live electronic feed from one of our aircraft near Poznan. The co-pilot will let us know when the invading army is near out target point."

"Very good General Galland. Is everyone else ready?"

Silently, everyone around the map table began to nod. Von Braun looked the least convinced. Einstein was not much better at allaying the president's concerns. Von Brain moved over to a far wall where there was a large curtain. He quickly grabbed one end of the curtain and walked toward the other end of the room revealing a large screen.

"This is a television feed of the two rockets we have aimed at the tributary near Poznan."

The scene was indeed impressive. On the grounds of the institute was a launch pad. Several men were making last minute adjustments to the large rockets but were soon out of the picture.

"Madame President, if you notice the long red nose cone on the rocket, just below is the atomic cell that will detonate upon contact," Einstein said with much gusto.

"Yes, but let's hope my rockets can get it there, Herr Einstein," a less than convinced von Braun said.

At that moment a buzzer went off and then a nearby teletype began to send a piece of paper into a frenzy of activity. General Galland grabbed the piece of paper and ripped it off of the teletype.

"Our reconnaissance plane has spotted the invading army just coming into target. In three minutes they should be at our target spot."

Everyone began to study von Braun as he moved to a nearby phone. He dialed and waited for someone on the other end to answer.

"Standby Weisburg," von Braun said, looking as if he were slightly trembling. The group began to count the minutes and it was soon zero hour.

"Weisburg, fire both rockets." von Braun slammed down the phone and ran over to gain a better view of the television picture. The rockets began to roar to life, white smoke began to engulf the Launchpad. The rockets began to shake and were soon thrusting skyward.

"Well done von Braun!" Einstein shouted as the rest of those assembled clapped their hands.

"Now it's up to my team!" Einstein said with a smile.

Unfortunately, they had no way of knowing their success except for a report from the reconnaissance plane. As they all waited, another teletype machine came to life. Rosa walked around to the machine and ripped of the message that had been sent.

"Hmmm, it's from our friend in Moscow. It says, 'Dear Rosa, by now you know that our armies are on their way to Germany and will be in Berlin by nightfall. If you wish to avoid bloodshed, then reply to this teletype that you surrender. Sincerely, Joseph Stalin.'"

Rosa looked up toward the men who were assembled and smiled. "I think surrendering will not be necessary eh Albert?" Einstein winked at Rosa and began to fiddle with some papers. Adolf poured himself some ice-water and began to drink it like he had just navigated the Sahara. He was nervous and began to wonder if he might be shipped to Siberia once this was all over. He doubted he would even have that privilege. Once Stalin had found him he would be strung up on a noose and displayed in downtown Moscow. He had just regained his spirits after his horrible near death experience at the hands of Thallman, would he now be shipped back to Moscow to face Stalin?

As everyone waited nervously, they all fixed their gaze on the one teletype. Minute after minute went by with no word.

"What could be happening? The rockets must have hit their targets by now," von Braun said practically in agony. Then the teletype started to print. Rosa ran over to the machine. She ripped off the finished message and began to read.

"The two rockets have hit their target. Two large mushroom clouds were produced. The sky is still burning from the explosions. We are currently thirty-five miles away and will be approaching the scene in about eight minutes."

Everyone was quiet. Einstein and von Braun knew what had taken place. Both tried to imagine the horror visited upon the soldiers and military personnel. Rosa and the others were unsure what a "mushroom cloud" was.

"So is this good gentlemen?" Rosa asked.

"Yes and no," Einstein said with a look of concern. "While the immediate threat to Germany is probably over, this ushers in a new world of destruction. It will only be time before other countries, perhaps the Soviet Union or China will develop their own nuclear devices."

"Maybe we drop a bomb on Moscow and Peking?" Adolf suggested not fully grasping the gravity of the situation.

"I would not be able to support that I'm afraid. While the rockets we used today were for military purposes, I cannot support the use of this on civilian targets."

Rosa was quiet and just nodded her head. Several minutes later another teletype began buzz the machine. Again Rosa quickly grabbed the message and began to read.

"We have made several sweeps of the area and can only find smoldering remains. There are several large craters near the target areas with nothing but chards and fragments of men and machine scattered for miles."

The devastation was complete, and while the citizens of Germany could breathe a sigh of relief, the world as a whole could not believe the horror that had been unleashed. While the Prime Minister of Poland was grateful for the destruction of the massive army that had invaded, he was fearful for the future of humanity – and so was all of those who were apart of the project back in Germany.

Rosa thanked the men but she looked as though she had been given a death sentence. Adolf tried to buoy her spirt but she was in another world. She had spent her entire life building a world in which she hoped for the best in humanity. Her development of her communist philosophy was for the betterment of man and womankind, not for its destruction. It would take her days to recover from what she knew she had unleashed.

The world began to look at Germany in a new light. While no one publicly condemn the Germans, for it was clear they were going to be attacked, they were now looked upon as almost sinister with the destruction they had created. While it was not appropriate for world governments to send condolences to Stalin and Mao, people still felt sympathy for the horrific deaths their soldiers must have endured. While a few politicians in England and France voiced their opinions that Russia and China got what they deserved, there were still an air of concern over their Teutonic neighbors.

The state of relations did quickly change. Britain and France signed agreements and treaties with Germany to partner on many projects and pull resources. One such project was a joint-mission to land a manned space-craft on the moon with Wernher von Braun heading it up.

CHAPTER 18

For the remainder of 1946, a type of Cold War existed between Germany and Russia. Stalin was now living in a paranoid world where much of the country had turned on him after the debacle in Poland. It was rumored than many in the Kremlin were plotting against him and because of that he would often seclude himself at his dacha in Sochi.

Early on Christmas Eve, a coup, which had the backing of the Luxemburg government, successfully overthrew the Stalin regime. The coup was led by Rosa's colleague from the 1920's Karl Leibknecht.

When Rosa had fled Germany in 1919, Leibknecht had gone with her to Poland. While Rosa rose in the ranks of the Polish Communist Party (KPP), Karl met a Russian woman in Warsaw, later moving to Moscow. Luxemburg and Leibknecht continued to correspond and keep each other up to date with their lives. Liebknecht later married the Russian woman; Marietta Shaginyan. Shaginyan was a writer who wrote many works on communism. She experimented in a style known as satirico-fantastic fiction. Such novels as *Miss Mend: Yankees in Petrograd, Three Looms* and *Hydrocentral* had all been very successful. While some in the Russian government found her work "decadent", she was still popular. It was rumored that she was romantically linked to composer Sergei Rachmaninoff. Rachmaninoff referred her as one of his "muses".

Although German, Leibknecht had learned fluent Russian and had ingratiated himself to the locals. Whether in Moscow teaching at the university or resting with his wife in their Crimean get-away home, Leibknecht had become a true Russophile. This had made him the perfect candidate in Rosa's mind to replace Stalin.

When the many German-made tanks and armored vehicles came to support the insurrection, the now battered and tattered Russian army was unable to halt the insurmountable tide. Leibknecht was installed by Luxemburg the next day, and to many Russians it was the greatest day of their lives to be finally free of Stalin.

******

On January 1st, 1947, Rosa made a speech that was broadcast to the entire country. It truly was a new day in Germany as she spoke in the Reich Chancellery to provide details about her government.

"My fellow Germans. It is with great joy that I address you today. While you have been through a lot for the past several years under the Thallman government, we want to make our government transparent and provide you with specific details of what will be happening.

First of all, Hannah Hoch will be my vice-president. Hannah has been with me for the last twenty years as we prepared for this day to overthrow the Thallman government. Bertha Braunthal will be my Secretary of Defense and Sophie Bonner-Leibknecht will be my Secretary of the Interior."

Sophie Bonner-Leibknecht had been married to Karl Leibknecht, but when he had fled to Poland and had been in hiding for multiple years, Sophie had assumed that he had passed away. In his absence she had met a military man, Karl Bonner and had Leibknecht declared legally dead. It wasn't until years later that Leibknecht had heard about the situation. At that point he had already been in a relationship with Marietta Shaginyan.

"There will be more announcements about my cabinet to come shortly. But now I want to speak about how I see the coming years for our great nation. Germany is on the rise. We are a nation of great people, great thinkers, great artists and great innovators. Our innovations are the envy of the entire world. We have harnessed nuclear power. We can provide an endless supply of electricity to all of our cities because of this. Also, we are now able to completely defend ourselves from any invader – we are truly sovereign and fear no one.

Along with this great power, we must not abuse our political power. I have renamed our main political party the New German Communist Party or NGCP. We shall use a flat income tax. Everyone will be taxed 25% of their income, no matter what station in life he or she maybe, everyone will pay 25%.

All resources of my government will be distributed evenly. The 25% that we take in will provide for complete medical care for all Germans. This money will provide for free university education for all Germans. This money will provide for income for all retired Germans upon their 60th birthday.

Now, I know many of you in business who run companies and corporations will not like this ideal. But what I say to you is we in the Luxemburg government will provide incentives for business. Companies will be able to submit their ideas, their inventions and will be able to obtain government grants to see them come to fruition. We do not want to stagnate the German economy but grow it. Just last month, we gave a grant to the German Power Company. They have now been able to build cost effective power plants in Hungary, Poland, France, Austria and soon England. These nuclear plants, which will be powered from Germany, will provide these countries with endless electricity. The revenues from these plants will generate over a billion Deutschmarks annually. There are plans to transport our power over various pipelines and tunnels. Eventually, we will be able to sell our power to nations all over the world; Asia, Africa, the Americas, there is no limit.

Yes, my vision may seem grand to some, but I say that we do not need to dream. The German dream is already here. We have the man and brain power to do great things. We have no limit to the German imagination. Our universities are the greatest in the world and every year we keep turning out great scientists, economists, inventors, business people, and most importantly, great thinkers.

So today my fellow Germans, please rest assured that the NGCP will get things done. We will not be corrupt like the Thallman government. You will have a say in our party. Most of all, there will be even distribution of all of Germany's wealth – every woman, man and child will benefit from our great country.

Thank you!"

Rosa departed the platform and was quickly joined by Adolf, offering her his arm. Although the press was in attendance, she quickly departed the room with Adolf, walking to the front entry and then waving for her personal limousine. The limo was waiting to take her and Adolf to their favorite restaurant.

"So what did you think darling?"

"It was fantastic!"

"Really…you're just saying that Adi."

"No my dear, it was tremendous. It reminds me a little bit of the Rosa I knew back in 1919. You still have the energy, the keen mind. I mean look at you…look at all that you have accomplished."

"And I owe it all to you Adi!"

"To me? How do you mean?"

"You helped me to escape. Without you I would have been murdered by the Freikorps."

Adolf smiled and nodded. She put her hand on his and gave him a wink.

"Adolf Hitler, will you marry me?"

Adolf laughed and squeezed her hand.

"Oh Rosa, you kill me."

"No, I'm serious."

Adolf looked into Rosa's eyes and could see that she was in fact serious. He smiled and nodded. He never dreamed that one day he would be proposed to. Adolf joined her on her side of the limo and the two embraced. He planted a long passionate kiss on her lips and the two began to giggle like they were schoolchildren.

******

By early 1948, Germany had become the world's greatest super power (the United States a distant second), and along with that title also found itself as the world's policeman. Germany had intervened in China's escalating war with Japan, helping to drive the Nipponese army from

Manchuria and Northern China. It also helped the French negotiate a ceasefire in Indo-China as well as aid in potential de-colonization of India from England and various Dutch colonies around the world.

One of Rosa's greatest triumphs in 1948 was the declaration of independence by the newly formed country of Israel. Having been a British Mandate since the Great War, Israel, under the guidance of David Ben-Gurion and the support of Rosa Luxemburg finally became an independent nation again. What Rosa had negotiated was an independent force that would help keep Israel sovereign. A small army of French, German and English would oversee all the main Biblical landmarks that Muslims, Jews and Christians held as sacred. So as to not create tensions, this small army would provide access to all of the religious groups who needed access. Also, various areas in Jerusalem and other parts of Israel would accommodate Muslims and Christians so as to not create tensions.

For Adolf, it was an exciting time as well. Having recently married Rosa and declining her offer of Minister of the Arts, he entered into a whole new career as an animator. He began to write scripts and design art with Lotte Reiniger, Carl Koch and Berthold Bartosch. They soon created an animation film studio calling it *Muse Werks*. Rosa also helped the studio along by channeling funds to it citing that the company was to produce educational films for both schools and government propaganda. To which the company did indeed partake, but it was the full-length films that Adi wanted to create. He wanted to compete with Walt Disney. Although trying to compete with Disney seemed far-fetched for the rest of members of the company, it was Adi's competitive juices that saw the company grow. He took themes from his artwork in earlier days such as *Midnight in Madrid* and turned the films into stark reminders of a time gone by. Although the films were expensive to make and were seen by small audiences, it had rejuvenated Adolf to a new level. He had more or less played house-husband for Rosa over the past couple of years but now he was beginning to create again. Rosa was pleased.

By the 1950's Adolf began to work on live-action films, creating detailed backdrops of street scenes, nature scenes; anything that the films of Heinz Paul required. He had grown bored of animation and sold his rights to *Muse Werks*. Rosa had noticed his seeming to get bored easy and suggested he take a trip to the United States to get a different perspective. Adolf agreed and he began an odyssey to the new world – what it would bring him he had no idea.

******

The next day, Adolf boarded the inaugural flight of the new Heinkel jet aircraft, the H-1000. The aircraft was the first commercial jet to be launched. The Heinkel company had received several grants from the Luxemburg government to produce the first commercial jet aircraft. Heinkel had been working on a prototype for years but finally had enough money to do the testing and get the necessary approvals from the civil aviation board. This was going to be the first flight of the new craft, a non-stop journey from Berlin to Washington D.C.

There was a huge crowd out at the airport to see off the new jet. The sleek aluminum airframe would be powered by six Diamler-Benz jet engines. The plane seated 120 passengers in coach class with 20 seats in first class.

There was a three-man crew with 10 flight attendants. Adolf was oblivious to all the attention the flight was getting. He just settled into his first class seat, ordered a bottle of champagne and began to read *A Tale of Two Cities* by Charles Dickens.

By having the first commercial jet ready for take-off on June 1st, 1952, many in the aerospace industry said that Heikel was ahead of its time by eight or nine years. No other company in the world had anything close to the aircraft that Heikel had produced. Everyone was chalking it up to another German triumph and another glowing review of the Luxemburg government. Again, Adolf didn't care about all the commotion that was being generated. He drunk himself to sleep, waking up just in time for the flight to arrive at Dulles International Airport, five minutes early. A valet from the airline grabbed Adolf's bag and escorted him to a waiting limousine outside. The president's husband was then whisked over to the Mayflower hotel where Adolf slept the rest of the day.

The following afternoon, after several attempts to awaken him by the hotel manager, a hung-over Adolf, showered and shaved and presented himself to the front desk. There the manager arranged for a limousine to take Adolf to the White House. Adolf was to be the guest of President Thomas E. Dewey.

Dewey had succeeded FDR, in 1944. After years of The New Deal and various other economic programs, the initial success of those programs began to lose steam and the American people had become impatient. Since the major economic loses of 1929, it wasn't until 1935 that the US economy had gained back all of those loses and started to grow again. Unemployment in 1942 had risen back up to 15 percent and FDR's popularity had started to wane.

Dewey's ideas to stimulate the economy by giving tax breaks to corporations to increase staffing was about the only new idea the country would respond too and so, out of a lack of a better alternative, the voters turned out FDR and looked to Dewey. In 1948, in a complete surprise, Dewey won re-election mostly on the fact that his opponent Harry Truman had little to offer other than FDR leftovers.

By late 1951, Dewey had been desperate to turn the country around and looking for anything that might help him to have a positive legacy after he had gone. He had corresponded often with Rosa Luxemburg, wanting desperately to sign a partnership, but Luxemburg had been busy building the new Germany. She finally agreed that she would meet with him in late 1952. Dewey was concerned that it would be too late to put together a deal with Germany, given that he would be out of office by January 1953. So when Adolf arrived, he wanted to do his best to try and bring the German president to America much earlier.

Upon his arrival into the Oval Office, Adolf was enthusiastically greeted by Dewey and his staff. They showed him several artifacts to which Adolf was not overly impressed. The president then invited Adolf to sit near his desk for a chat and a coffee. Adolf's head was still feeling the effects of the altitude and alcohol and cheerfully agreed to the coffee.

"So Adolf, we are so happy to have you here today at the White House."

"Thank you Mr. President, it's good of you to see me."

Adolf's English was not too bad. He had been corresponding for years with several Germans working in

Hollywood and dreamed someday of possibly working there. To that idea he had started working on his English language studies and had made great progress. He would often speak to Rosa in English as she was wanting to learn to help her with international correspondence. All the world's new common language for things like aviation, international trade, etc. were quickly becoming German. And while there were still affects from the British colonization of much of the world since the sixteenth century, German was now the en vogue language…so to speak.

"So we have been watching all the happenings over there in Germany, you truly have a great nation."

"Thank you Mr. President."

"If you wouldn't mind working on that wife of yours we could really use her insight a little earlier than her proposed arrival in November."

Adolf nodded not sure what the president was asking.

"Do you think you could influence her to come here sooner?"

Adolf thought for a moment.

"I do not think so Mr. President. I believe she has quite a busy schedule this year. She is working with various countries to expand Germany's power grid."

President Dewey stood up and moved over to a nearby bar where he poured himself a scotch.

"Would you like one Adolf?"

Adolf shook his head and smiled, pointing to his head and remembering the plane ride over.

"Let me be frank Mr. Luxemburg…"

"Hitler."

"Hitler?"

"Yes, that's my surname."

"But isn't the president's last name Luxemburg?"

"Yes, that is her surname but not mine."

The president raised his eyebrows and downed a glass of scotch, refiling it quickly.

"Well, let me get to it then. Are you going to let a woman dominate you Herr Hitler?"

"In this case yes. She's a very strong minded woman Mr. President. Rosa Luxemburg is a self-made woman. She narrowly escaped assassination in 1919, fled to Poland and lived on nothing more than her wits. She rose within the Polish Communist Party. Dealt with Joseph Stalin and bringing about a coup against the German government. Took over the government. Destroyed Stalin and is now in charge of one of the greatest countries of all time…do you not agree?"

Dewey nodded his head in agreement. He took another couple of swigs and tried another approach.

"But how does all of this make you feel as a man?"

"Great…I don't have to do anything. I just paint…or I don't paint. It doesn't much matter."

"I don't know Adolf, doesn't sound like you wear the pants in your family…or the lederhosen shall we say?" Dewey laughed while he tapped him on the shoulder several times. Adolf just looked at him with a blank stare. Dewey knew he wasn't going to get anywhere with him by attacking his manhood so he tried another approach.

"Look Adolf, our country is still struggling from the Great Depression. We need help. I need your wife's help."

"Well I don't know if she can help you but you can talk to her in November. It was nice meeting you Mr.

President but I need to get back to the hotel. Thank you for a wonderful time."

President Dewey looked at Adolf with complete confusion. He then got on his knees and begged Adolf to help him. Unsure of what the president was doing, Adolf slowly backed himself out of the oval office and began to run downstairs. The guards looked at him as he raced past them and hopped into the limousine that would take him back to the Mayflower Hotel. Back at the hotel he ordered room service and hoped that he would not hear further from the President of the United States.

The next morning, Adolf rose early to take a taxi over to the airport to get on a flight to New York. He was happy to be out of DC and going to the city he had always wanted to visit. He wanted to see a Broadway play and to eat at one of the best restaurants. When he arrived he took a taxi to Manhattan and spent most of the day at the Guggenheim Museum. The artwork was spectacular and many of the local patrons recognized Adolf or as they called him "Adi". He smiled and waved as various people became in tranced of him. He eventually tired of the museum and walked over to his hotel with suitcase in hand.

Adolf arrived at the Waldorf Astoria Hotel and immediately gained access, writing down his signature on a large ledger and then being handed a key. A bell boy offered to help him with his bag to which he declined. He found the elevators and signaled to the attendant the room number on the key. The attendant closed the door and pushed the button for the penthouse suite. When Rosa's travel planner booked the itinerary for Adolf she spared no expense. Adolf was oblivious to it all, just wanting a clean bed, a bath and access to a bar.

Since their marriage, Rosa had noticed that Adolf was starting to drink more and more. She would often ask him why he needed to drink and his answer was often a trite "I don't know." Subconsciously he was starting to think that maybe he was less a man since he was married to the most powerful person in the world. The conversation with the US president didn't help matters much on that front. With there being really no need to paint for a living, and having felt as though he had progressed as far as he could with his art, he was at a stagnant phase in his life. Coupled with the fact that he was coupled with a giant figure that would one day be one of the most famous people of all time, he was starting to feel a little insignificant.

The next day, Adolf took a taxi to Long Island to pay a visit to the studio of Jackson Pollack. Adolf was a big admirer of Pollack and vice versa. Upon his arrival he was greeted by Pollack's wife Lee Krasner. As he entered into the studio he could see that Pollack was in a frenzy, dripping paint from a can or taking the brush and swirling it around with globs of paint on it. He would also flick the brush in a way to send large amounts of paint across the huge canvass he had laying on the floor. Adolf didn't want to disturb the artist at work so he just admired from a far. He could see that Pollack was in a trance, completely immersed in his work.

After being focused on his work for about twenty minutes he tired and looked up. He began to smile when he recognized Adolf.

"Adi! When did you get here?" he said as he practically ran around the large canvass to greet him.

"Oh, not long. I was just admiring your hard work." Adolf said laughing as the two men embraced.

"What is this you are working on? It's fantastic!"

"I've been playing with titles but I'm thinking about calling it 'Blue Poles'".

Adolf looked at it trying to find the poles but was mesmerized never-the-less.

"I like it. Don't see poles just lines…"

"Hey, it doesn't matter what you see just as long as you like it! Hey let's get a drink!"

Adolf smiled and Jackson grabbed him around the shoulder and led him outside of the studio.

"Just down the road is a little hole-in-the-wall…let's get drunk!"

Adolf smiled and nodded not sure what else to do at that point. The two hopped into Pollack's car and headed down the road, about an hour later they arrived back in New York City, in Greenwich Village and the Cedar Tavern.

"Well, that was quite a ride," Adolf said trying to get his bearings, thinking the bar was just down the road.

"Well, there's not much in the way of real drinking establishments out on Long Island. C'mon, let's go in."

Adolf smiled not really sure what he was getting himself into. The two walked into the tavern and Pollack ordered two whiskies neat.

"What'll you have Adi?" Adolf had assumed that one of the drinks Jackson had ordered was for him.

"I will have a beer. Do you have German beer?" he asked the puzzled bartender.

"Sure, how 'bout Pabst Blue Ribbon?" Adolf smiled having no clue what Pabst Blue Ribbon was. The bartender returned with their drinks and then seemed to dissolve in the darkness of the Tavern.

"Cheers Adi!"

The two men clinked their glasses together. As Jackson downed one of his two whiskies a man staggered next to them.

"Hey Pollack, I saw your paintings the other day…boy they were real shit!"

"Adi, I'd like you to meet a friend of mine Jack Kerouac…probably the most horrible writer you will ever meet." Adolf turned around and extended a hand. Kerouac looked at his hand and then stumbled to a nearby barstool.

"What does your friend do Pollack?"

"He is an artist as well."

"Really, I've never heard of him."

"You've never heard of Adolf 'Adi' Hitler. What have you been hiding under a rock Kerouac?"

"Barkeep, another whiskey if you don't mind."

"Jack, haven't you had enough?" the bartender pleaded.

"I'll let you know when I've had enough."

The bartender shook his head and then poured another glass of whiskey, sliding it toward Kerouac with some disgust.

"Hey Bill, why do you think people come to this joint…not to drink?"

"Hey watch yourself Kerouac you're spilling that on to my lap here!" Pollack yelled.

"Sorry your majesty! Anyway, what's so great about this Hitler character?"

"Do you know that he once tried to blow up Ernst Thallman the president of Germany?"

"Wow man, that must've takin some balls!"

Adolf raised his glass of Pabst and smiled.

"Your friend doesn't talk much."

"He's a little shy with his English, but he's learning."

At that point another man walked by and ordered a drink. It was a colleague of Pollack's Willem de Kooning the Dutch painter.

"Ah, Adi, you might know this gentlemen…"

Adolf turned and smiled. He nodded his head.

"Hey Willem, come meet a friend of mine…Adolf Hitler."

Willem turned and a bright smile appeared on his face.

"Well of course, Adi Hitler! It's great to meet you! Soe emtla, ais Deitscj;amd mocjt wahr?"

The two men began a conversation in German discussing their artwork.

"Hey you krauts, shut up!" a disheveled Allen Ginsberg walked over with a glass of something and began to berate the two.

"Hey if you want to talk like that head back to the Fatherland you bastards!"

Like a flash of lightning de Kooning punched Ginsberg in the face sending him careening into an empty table and chairs. Adolf grabbed de Kooning and told him to settle down. Ginsberg's partner Peter Orlovsky came running over and tried to swing at de Kooning but missed. De Kooning punched him in the stomach and he dropped to his knees. Then Jack Kerouac hit de Kooning with a right cross but it did not land solidly and de Kooning fired back several punches which caused Kerouac to fall to the floor. Mark Rothko then attempted to defend Ginsberg but before he got to de Kooning, he slipped into some spilt whiskey which sent him crashing into a bar stool.

"De Kooning, look what you've done you idiot!!!"

De Kooning smiled and looked at the sprawled bodies on the floor.

"Hey de Kooning, you better get the hell out of here!" the bartender yelled. De Kooning nodded his head and quickly departed the tavern.

"Adi, help me with these Cretans," Pollack asked. Adolf helped Ginsberg, Orlovsky and Kerouac into some nearby chairs while Pollack returned with a tray full of coffee.

"You know if you boys cannot handle your alcohol you should try something else…maybe tea, soda…"

"Oh shut up Pollack," Ginsberg said.

"Something you should know Adi, this tends to happen on Friday nights." Adolf nodded and sat down with the other men.

"So what does your friend do?" Ginsberg asked Pollack.

"He is an artist as well. He's mostly known in Europe but he's had some works exhibited here and there in the states. Actually, he's probably more well known for the attempt he made on President Thallman back in 1944."

Hearing that Ginsberg looked up mesmerized.

"Oh, so you're the guy!" He said with a bright smile, still rubbing his head. Ginsburg offered his hand to shake to which Adolf reciprocated. Kerouac, having downed a couple a cups of coffee began to smile a moronic grin.

"What are you smiling at Jack?" Orlovsky asked.

"I was just thinking how Allen will probably now worship Adi here – Ginsberg is a fan of anarchy…regardless of where it is and who it is perpetrated on." Three of the men burst out laughing. Ginsberg just eyed them with disdain.

"I'm not a fan of all anarchy…just anything that puts the bourgeoisie in its place!" With that Ginsberg vomited and put his head on the table as Orlovsky tried to console him.

"That's it, I want you idiots out of here!" the bartender shouted. Pollack grabbed Kerouac by the scruff of his neck and motioned for Adolf to follow him. They got outside and stepped into the brisk night air. Just down the street, de Kooning was leaning against the wall of the tavern and smoking a cigarette.

"Hey Willem, let's do a road trip!"

De Kooning smiled, nodded his head and then dropped his cigarette and stamped it out. He walked over to Pollack's Oldsmobile and opened the door so he could put the incapacitated Kerouac in the back seat.

"I think we need to go to California boys…who's with me?!!!" Jackson yelled to Adolf and de Kooning. De Kooning smiled and nodded to Adolf, motioning for him to get into the passenger side of the front seat while he ran around to the driver's side back seat. Pollack ran over to the driver's side, turned the ignition and the troupe were on their way.

******

By some miracle the occupants of Pollack's Oldsmobile arrived in Harrisburg, Pennsylvania. They had arrived at 3am. Pollack had pulled over to the side of the road near a large park and the four occupants had passed out. At around 10 am, the sun burst through some clouds and began to shine in Adolf's face, causing him to awaken. He looked around at the other three occupants and could see that they were still passed out. He began to look around for any signs of life. He decided to get out and walked down the street. At the end of the street he could see a small strip mall with several shops. He walked over to a restaurant where he ordered an omelet, pancakes, sausage and some hash-browns along with a cup of coffee. He had no idea where he was until he asked the waitress if he could see a newspaper. He found out that he was in Harrisburg, but that's not all he found out.

PRESIDENT DEWEY INDICTED

The headline read causing Adolf to really wake up. He read the story and was barely able to finish his breakfast. Alfred L. Bennet, a journalist from the Virginia Herald and also a White House correspondent, had been secretly taping conversations of Dewey in the oval office. He would apparently meet with him often to do interviews and when he did he would leave a small tape recorder in the sofa. The next morning, he would drop by to collect the previous day's recordings. What he uncovered would later shock the people of the United States as well as the rest of the world.

Having secured another term in the White House, Dewey knew that he had to bring the United States out of the drudgery of the depression that was still impacting America in 1948. He had been speaking with Secretary of the Treasury who had made a joke about how well the U.S economy had done during the Great War. He said to Dewey that if only we could have another major war it might pull the country out of the current economic depression. While at first not paying attention to the remark, he eventually became desperate enough to turn things around that he actually considered the idea. He not only considered the idea but eventually put a plan in place to make it happen.

Dewey had made several telephone calls to the prime minister of Japan and suggested that the Japanese make a second attempt at attacking China. He had suggested that they create an international incident such as saying that China had attacked Japanese fishing boats prompting an attack from Japan. The Unites States would side with Japan and would need to turn up the economy by producing new weapons, tanks and aircraft for the "under-sized" and "under-manned" Japanese forces. The new war would invigorate the economy by creating new jobs. Dewey had been in contact with the president of Boeing doing some preliminary forecasting of how many jobs the company could generate. He also contacted the U.S Army Ordnance Department, who, with the aid of many private companies, had built the Sherman Tank. Dewey wanted to know how quickly they could get up to speed if they needed to delivery several thousand tanks.

Dewey then began to design, in his mind, what it would take to bring the China-Japan conflict into a world war or at least a very large regional war. There were already tensions in the Korean peninsula so he began to speak with the leaders in both Pyongyang and Seoul. Things were also beginning to heat up in Indochina as well with the rebel Ho Chi Minh trying to free the Democratic Republic of Vietnam from the grip of French colonization. It was phone calls to Ho Chi Minh that later turned out to be what brought Dewey down. At the time, Ho Chi Minh wanted to form an alliance with Germany. What Dewey had divulged to Minh in the way of a proposed alliance against the French was inadvertently leaked by an aid during Minh's talks with the Germans. This was reported to the German newspaper Bild and soon it was clear what was going on. Along with Bennet's tapes and the news from Bild, a picture was painted of an Asian calamity that Dewey wanted to start. It did not look good for Dewey and he was soon indicated by the Justice Department with charges of trying to subvert foreign nations for personal gain.

Adolf was completely shocked at the charges and tried to remember his meeting with the president two days earlier. Was there anything of concern that he had missed? His mind was not really in a good state at the time, still recovering from the effects of champagne and a long trans-Atlantic flight. He shook his head and just chalked it up to the pitfalls of power. He began to think of Rosa but knew that she was impervious to corruption or so he thought.

As he finished his breakfast, he could see out of the window Jackson Pollack's Oldsmobile pulling into the parking lot. The three occupants, looking like they had been dragged through a tornado, entered the restaurant and seeing Adolf already well ensconced, quickly joined him – all three pleaded for the waitress to bring them cups of coffee.

"Boy Adi, you just dropped us chumps in the park and headed out for breakfast?" Kerouac asked.

"You boys looked a little tired. I felt a little hungry so came looking for something to eat…and here I am."

"Well, boys, let's grab a quick bite to eat and then let's get on the road. You're paying eh Adi?"

Adolf nodded and smiled. It quickly became obvious who was going to be funding this "road trip."

Back in Germany, a concerned President Luxemburg was wondering what had happened to her husband. He seemed to be missing in action, not having heard from him since he had called her from the Mayflower Hotel upon his arrival in the United States. Later that day, she was told by one of her assistants that Adolf was wiring for more money from a bank in Pittsburgh, Pennsylvania. She did not think that Pittsburgh was on his itinerary but approved the wire transfer anyway. She knew that Adolf needed a break from being the president's husband and if he wanted to visit Pittsburg then so be it.

One stop that Jackson really wanted to make in Pittsburgh was the Carnegie Museum of Art. All four of the men ran into the museum to see what was new and not so new. They spent several hours in awe of the great works there. Adolf was especially fond of the Picasso exhibit, recalling old times with the painter and more so recalling his times with Maria.

After completing their tour of the museum, they grabbed a quick bite to eat and then headed on the road again. They didn't stop until they got to Chicago, trading off drivers including Adolf who had never driven an American car like an Oldsmobile, but he did his duty none-the-less. While they traded out drivers the other three would sleep. When they arrived in Chicago they stopped for a deep-dish Chicago pizza at a local establishment. Adolf was quite intrigued by the "colossal piece of bread with tomato sauce on it." They then took in a Cubs game at Wrigley Field. Adolf had never seen a baseball game before and found it enlightening. Next to golf, he had never seen so many men running after a white ball before. He wasn't quite sure what the point of the game was but he enjoyed it when the baseballs were hit toward him in the bleachers – he had to duck a couple of times to get out of the unpredictable orb's way. The men admonished him to enjoy a Chicago dog and a beer while they watched men run around in a square shape after hitting the ball. It was all enjoyable for Adolf as it was a beautiful day in the Windy City.

After the game they visited the aquarium for a couple of hours and then headed over to the Museum of Contemporary Art. Adolf was delighted to find that his *Valencia Beach*, seascape that he had done when vacationing with Maria back in the thirties was on display. He could see the bright orange and yellows he used for the piece attracting a lot of viewers. Even Jackson, Jack and Willem were impressed.

After downing a few beers at another eatery where barbequed spare ribs were served, the four men climbed back into the Oldsmobile and were off again. They continued to change out drivers until they hit Minneapolis. Somewhere between St. Paul and Minneapolis they lost Willem. They had visited a bar that was on the Mississippi. Willem had met a girl and they soon departed the bar. When the three other men decided to depart, they found a note on the car scrawled with writing indicating for the three to continue on and that he would find his way back to New York. The three men laughed and were on their way.

A few days later the men arrived in Seattle. They had made a brief detour to Yellowstone to see the geysers and hopefully a moose or two but were back on the road within an hour and a half. In Seattle, Jackson was desperate to have fresh salmon. They found a restaurant overlooking the Puget Sound and the men dined on oysters, mussels and fresh salmon. They spent the night in a hotel in downtown Seattle, visiting a bar where they downed a volatile sum of a locally brewed beer. When Jackson vomited all over the bar, Adolf had to pay reparations and the three retired back to the hotel.

The next morning, they began their southern approach down the illustrious Highway 101 toward Hollywood. They again traded drivers, not stopping for a hotel until they arrived in San Francisco. In San Francisco they stayed a couple of days, visiting Chinatown, the Embarcadero, and Fisherman's Wharf. Again Pollack indulged his taste for fresh seafood, ordering lobster, oysters, Clams casino, swordfish and four bottles of champagne. The three of them woke up in a back room of the restaurant the following day. A barmaid had recognized them and asked the owner if they could use the apartment that was in back of the restaurant. It was at that point that Adolf was really starting to regret the whole idea of the trip. Granted it was 2,000 miles into the trip, but he was now seeing Jackson Pollack in a new light. It seemed he was in search of something but not finding it, Jack as well. It seemed that the only solace they could find for "it" was alcohol. Adolf decided it was better to just go along with them – perhaps they would need his help at some point. He did truly like the men, but could see that their lives were rather empty. In any event, he did want to visit Hollywood and hopefully meet up with some of his friends from Germany.

After another two days on the road, the three men finally arrived in Los Angeles. They booked into the famous Beverly Hills Hotel and immediately took a spin down the Sunset Strip. They eventually pulled into the Brown Derby restaurant to have a bite to eat and for Jackson and Jack to also partake of multiple glasses of wine and other cocktails. After getting extremely drunk, Jackson and Jack began to pretend they were waiters and started to serve plates of plants they had pulled out of the nearby pots that were situated throughout the restaurant. Jack presented a cactus to Jimmy Stewart who did not seem amused. Jackson took his napkin and put it over his arm like a high profile maître d', walking over to Jerry Lewis' table with a potted fern. Jerry liked the creativity and especially so when he recognized that it was Jackson Pollack, one of his favorite artists.

While this was all happening, Adolf decided to have a glass of wine and pretend he didn't know who the two lunatics were. Eventually the real maître d' kicked them out of the restaurant and they were back in the Oldsmobile. This time Jackson, feeling somewhat invincible decided to drive up into the Hollywood Hills. They wound their way up Laurel Canyon Blvd where near the top they could view out over Hollywood and out toward the Pacific Ocean. Jackson kept picking up speed as he wound his way through the Hollywood Hills, the other two occupants had enough to drink that they were not noticing. As Jackson turned onto Mulholland Drive, he began to increase his speed. When they came to a sharp turn near Groves Overlook, he began to swerve and then lost control of the car. The car bounced over the curb and crashed into some nearby trees and bushes.

An ambulance was called to the scene and the three men were rushed to the UCLA Medical Center. All three men were unconscious but in stable condition. Given the stature of the men, news reports of the accident hit the airwaves pretty quickly. Back in Germany, President Luxemburg was in a staff meeting when she was given word of Adolf's accident. She immediately rang up the hospital and asked to speak to the chief of staff. She introduced herself to the chief-of-staff and demanded to know what was the state of Adolf.

"President Luxemburg, your husband is fine. He took a little hit to the head when the car made impact but he should be fine – he had a mild concussion. Other than that he has some scrapes and cuts but again should be fine."

Not totally convinced by the doctor, she immediately ordered the Consul General from the German Consulate to go and visit Adolf immediately. Conrad Adenauer the Consul General made haste to the medical center to visit Adolf and report back to President Luxemburg. Upon arrival, Adolf was awake and doing well. He was able to eat and seemed to be lucid. After reporting Adolf's state to President Luxemburg she told Adenauer that as soon as Adolf was well and could leave the hospital that he was to be escorted to the Los Angeles Airport and put on a Lufthansa flight back to Germany.

The next day, in the hospital room of Jackson Pollack, Adolf was wheeled in. Jackson was sitting up in bed and smiled as Adolf was steered near his bedside.

"How are you Jackson?"

"Fine Adi – a little woozy and a bit of a headache but otherwise fine. And you?"

"I'm fine -a bit of a bump to the head but I will be okay. I came to tell you that they will be discharging me today. Unfortunately, I have to go back to Germany."

"You do…why?"

"My wife is threatening to not give me anymore funds if I am 'going to misbehave' like this, she says."

"Wow, what a ball-buster eh? Look I'm sorry I got you into this crash and everything, but I understand if you need to leave. Good old Jack and I will make it back to New York somehow."

Adolf smiled and reach out his hand to shake. The nurse turned Adolf and wheeled him out of the room. That would be the last time that Adolf would ever see Jackson. Pollack would be killed less than four year later in a car-crash near his home in Springs, New York – it would be alcohol-related.

As the nurse took Adolf down the elevator and to the front entrance of the hospital, Conrad Adenauer and his staff were waiting for him. There was a large limousine outside waiting to take Adolf to the Los Angeles International Airport. It seemed as if the key to the city was being handed to him as he walked into the terminal. The mayor of Los Angeles, Ronald Reagan was there with some of his staff to greet Adolf. Rosa Luxemburg would be paying a visit to Los Angeles late in the year and he wanted Adolf to start priming the pump. At the boarding gate there were two flight attendants to escort him onboard to his first class seat. The quick success of the H-1000 had now expanded to non-stop flights from the west-coast to Europe breaking new distance records. Again Adolf didn't care about that, he just sat back and opted for spring water on this trip, remembering the hang-over he first had when he arrived in Washington DC. As the plane took off over the Santa Monica Bay, Adolf craned his neck to look down at the coastline as the plane had done a 180 degree turn and was now flying eastward over the Hollywood Hills. Adolf began to smile, remembering his time with Jackson and Jack – it was a time he would not forget.

CHAPTER 19

Back in Germany, Adolf was greeted by one of Rosa's assistants who escorted him to a nearby limousine. The limo quickly made its way to the Reich Chancellery where Rosa was waiting for him.

"My dear husband, it's so good to see you well," she said in a somewhat mocking tone.

"Yes darling it's good to see you." He walked up to her and planted a kiss on her cheek.

"It seems as if you have been keeping yourself busy wandering the American countryside…did you learn anything?"

"Yes. Don't go on a road-trip with Jackson Pollock and Jack Kerouac," he said with a grin that was met with steely eyes.

"Look, Rosa, I am sorry for my behavior. It won't happen again."

"Are you unhappy with your life Adi? I know as of late you seem to be always bored, always looking for something to do?"

"Yes…I don't know. I feel a little lost right now."

Adolf shook his head and looked at Rosa. She was looking particularly feminine that day. She wore a lace dress with high-heeled shoes. She had pearls around her neck and seemed to have caught a little sun which made her look radiant. Normally her look was a little neutral gender-wise. She had started a craze of women wearing pantsuits. She had been on the cover of Vogue magazine and was now not only the most famous woman on the planet politically, but also now in a fashion sense.

"I guess some times, I feel a little emasculated."

"Really, I never thought you felt that way Adi. You've always seemed to be secure in your manhood. I've never seen you act in a superior way to any woman or to look down at a successful woman."

"No, I adore women. That love affair started with my mother, my sisters, my niece – I've always looked to the fairer sex with great respect...I guess though, sometimes I feel I was made to do more."

Adolf walked to a nearby window and looked out over the city of Berlin.

"I think back to the early days in Berlin when we first met. I really liked politics. At first I was just looking for something to do. Later I was just wanting to look like a politically aware artist, but later I was thinking that maybe I would like to run someday for a position...a senator...I don't know, leader of some kind."

"Why don't you?"

Adolf laughed as he poured himself a glass of water from a nearby picture.

"Why do you laugh – I think you could do a good job in politics."

"Well thank you but no. Anyway, anything I would accomplish, everyone would just say that you had given me the position or had seen to it that I had won the election..."

"You mean I would use my influence unethically?"

"No, not in reality, it's just what a lot of people would believe."

"Well...have it your way. But if you want to consider leadership opportunities I am here to help. Now why don't we go to the restaurant and then get an early night tonight?"

Adolf smiled and then wrapped his arm around her shoulder.

"You're a good woman Rosa. I mean that – not only as a great leader but as someone who really cares."

"Thank you Adi. That's nice to hear."

The two then strolled hand in hand to the front of the Chancellery where they were met by their state limousine which whisked them off to their favorite restaurant.

As the couple ordered their dinner, Rosa noticed that Adolf was not ordering any meat dishes.

"Has your trip to America made you a vegetarian darling?"

Adolf pursed his lips and thought.

"I don't know. On our road-trip we accidently ran over a fox on our way through Montana. It seemed like after that I was put off by meat. Now all I can think about is potatoes and cabbage and vegetable broth. It's probably just a phase."

Adolf smiled at Rosa and took a sip of champagne. Rosa knew that Adolf had a deepness to him but sometimes he was a little too mysterious for her liking.

******

The next morning, Adolf woke up with a feeling of incompleteness. He looked over at Rosa, gave her a kiss and walked into the kitchen. He made himself some instant coffee, made some toast and ate a banana. He could hear Rosa rustling in the bedroom and eventually heard the shower turning on. Having the night to sleep on it, Adolf was now contemplating politics. He waited for Rosa to join him in the kitchen before he would screw up enough courage to broach the subject again.

"Good morning darling, you look wonderful…very business-like."

"Yes, I'm flying to Moscow today…I'm meeting with Leibknecht. It's the unveiling of the power grid node that we are supplying them."

"Oh, sounds marvelous. Can I get you some coffee?"

"Yes darling that would be nice."

Adolf poured her a cup of coffee while she played with some papers she had in a brief case. He didn't look too closely but figured it was a speech she had for the occasion.

"I was thinking about what we discussed yesterday and am having second thoughts?"

"About a career in politics?" She said while perusing her speech.

"Yes, I am concerned about others having concerns about nepotism."

Rosa looked up from her papers.

"Well, one thing I didn't mention to you yesterday is that we will be holding general elections in 1956. Perhaps I will not be re-elected. Maybe you could run then?"

"Hmmm…I would be 67 by then. If I do this I should probably do it now."

Rosa could see he was serious and decided to sit down. She looked into his eyes and smiled noting a different tone to him.

"Alright. What do you want to run for?"

Adolf thought for a moment.

"Well I guess prime minister is a too lofty…what do you suggest?"

Rosa giggled at his joke of running for prime minister. She grabbed his hand and continued to giggle.

"Why don't you start with something small…councilman?"

"Councilman…what do they do?"

"Well, they work for the mayor. You could work for the mayor of Berlin – Ketty Guttmann."

Adolf began to think about that not looking too convinced.

"What type of work would I be doing?"

"Well, it depends on the mayor. Typically, council members would head up various committees. For example, if the mayor wanted to build a park she might create a parks committee and she might choose you to preside over it."

"Hmmm…then what would happen?"

"Then you would be in charge of that project. You might need to do a feasibility study. You might need to work with the city engineer. You would probably need to work with the finance department. You would then go back to the mayor and say what your recommendation are?

"Hmmm…sounds boring, but I guess I have to start somewhere."

"Well, why don't you go down to the mayor's office today and have a talk with Ketty. Anyway, I must run my darling, good luck." Rosa gave Adolf a kiss on the cheek while he imagined himself as a city councilman. After showering and dressing, Adolf proceeded to the city hall to talk with Ms. Guttmann. He walked up to the reception desk and asked to see the mayor.

"I'll see if she's available," said a very feminine man behind the desk. Adolf, having been involved in the height of Berlin bohemianism had met many homosexuals and transgendered individuals but the man, or what he presumed was a man behind the desk, definitely had him guessing. The only thing he could think that perhaps indicated maleness was the suit he was wearing. But wearing a suit did not necessary mean male – Marlene Dietrich would often wear suits.

As if running from a horde of bees, Ms. Guttmann came careening out of the elevator toward Adolf. She immediately offered her hand to shake.

"Please Franz, we shouldn't keep Herr Hitler waiting like this."

Franz was a little confused, thinking to himself that he had just asked if she was available. Adolf looked at Franz and smiled nodding his head.

"Ah Franz!" he continued to nod his head which made Franz even more confused.

"Please Herr Hitler, let us go to my office."

"Thank you Mayor Guttmann, and please call me Adolf."

"Thank you Adolf and you may call me Ketty."

The two seemed to be euphoric with their encounter as the elevator doors closed. Franz continued to look at them puzzled.

"I am a huge fan of your wife. Of course, I wouldn't have had this job unless she had appointed me."

With that bit of news Adolf became a little disappointed. He felt he would never escape his wife's long shadow. The two arrived on the top floor and walked into the mayor's office. It was a beautiful office full of the art deco objects that Adolf had loved from the thirties.

"So what would you like to talk about Adolf?"

"Well, I was interested in making a run for some political office and my wife suggested speaking to you about a possible post in the mayor's office."

"Oh yes, absolutely, I can set you up with something right away."

"But, wouldn't I have to run first?"

A confused look ran over the mayor's face.

"I'm not sure I follow?"

"My wife seemed to think that for me to be a council member I would have to be elected?"

The mayor sat back in her large chair and pondered the significance of Adolf's statement. Was this a trick question? If Rosa Luxemburg wanted something it was the mayor's job to fulfill whatever it was she wanted.

"Well…typically, that is how it works."

There was a long pause and the mayor looked intently at Adolf like he was about to give her a secret code or the magic word and then everything would make sense. Adolf just smiled back.

"Ok, how do I get started?"

"When would you like to start?"

"Oh right away."

"Ok great. Why don't you come in Monday morning? By then I can have an office ready for you."

Adolf's forehead began to crinkle.

"Office? I thought I had to run first?"

The mayor had a look of confusion.

"Oh, yes, right. Ah…let me see…" the mayor seemed to search the ceiling above for an answer.

"Give me one moment and I will be right back." Before Adolf could blink the mayor was out of the room. She returned less than a minute later with a pamphlet. She handed it to Adolf with a nervous look in her face. Adolf became concerned like maybe there was something on his face. He pulled a handkerchief out of coat pocket and began to dab around in hopes of removing whatever errant object had adhered itself to his face.

"Ah, this pamphlet will give you an idea of how to start your campaign," her hand began to shake like she was experiencing an earthquake.

"Are you alright Ketty?"

"Oh yes, yes of course!" She practically screamed causing Adolf to move back in his seat.

"I'm sorry Adolf, I think I had too much coffee this morning…I get a little high strung sometimes."

Adolf smiled and nodded.

"Well, thank you very much Ketty, I will review this pamphlet and get my campaign started."

"Terrific Adolf. And please, please let me know if there is anything I can do to help."

For a moment Adolf thought that Mayor Guttmann had winked at him. He did a double-take to make sure he wasn't imagining anything. He did walk out of her office with a little extra bounce to his step. Perhaps this would be a whole new adventure for him – a whole new horizon. After having some lunch at his favorite bistro and reading the latest edition of the Berlin Times and the Bild. He took a walk through the city to look at what might one day be his subjects. He knew he was letting his imagination run away with him but why not – he had nothing better to do.

He then suddenly remembered his days back in Paris and the dream he once had. Edmond James de Rothschild had interpreted his dream of a flock of sheep falling off a cliff as Adolf not being a leader or not being able to lead or something along those lines. He couldn't remember exactly what Edmond had said. Unfortunately, soon after his return to Germany, Edmond had passed away. Adolf began to try and rake his mind but it was no use – he couldn't remember exactly what Edmond had said. Maybe it wasn't meant for him to be in politics?

In any event, Adolf walked back to the Reich Chancellery apartment he shared with Rosa. When he got there he was surprised to see Rosa.

"Rosa? You're back so soon?"

"Yes darling, I was just there for the unveiling. That new Heinkel jet got me there in 2 hours. I think we were in Moscow all of forty minutes and were back on the plane back to Berlin."

Adolf shook his head with awe, unable to understand how his wife could have been to the Russian capital and return all that same day – it was a new age!

"Oh, a funny thing just happened. I just spoke with Ketty, she mentioned you met with her today. I guess I should have spoken to her first before I sent you over there. She seemed confused by your questions. She thought she should be giving you the council member's job." Rosa began to laugh, but Adolf wasn't amused.

"Well so much for avoiding the appearance of nepotism," Adolf sighed.

"Look darling as much as I would like to help you, you are married to the president of the country. Everyone is going to think that I had something to do with whatever advantage you obtain…unless of course it's in art…you've obviously earned your way in the world of art."

Adolf became quiet and walked over to the main balcony window.

"What's the matter darling?"

"I don't know. Ever since I got back from the United States, I've just felt lost…not knowing what to do."

"Well, go into politics. Whether or not people think you got your position because of me, you can prove to them that you were the right person for the job."

She put her arm on his shoulder and pulled him toward her.

"What have you got to lose?"

"My dignity, my self-respect."

"C'mon…this is not the Adi I married. The Adi I married saved me from the Freikorps. He became a master painter. You know you can do anything you set your mind to!"

Adolf smiled and gave her a hug.

"Okay, I'll give it a try."

Rosa smiled and nodded her approval.

******

For the next several weeks Adolf worked on his campaign. There was one council member position that would be available in the next few weeks and so he began to work on his strategy. Ketty made one of her secretaries available to help Adolf with his work. Elsa Baumgartner was a tall blonde who appeared to be in her early twenties. Elsa would come over to Adolf's apartment and work with him throughout the day on anything from making posters and postcards to giving him ideas such as going door-to-door to meet his constituents and writing speeches.

When Rosa would come in to find the tall buxom blonde helping her husband it was a little difficult to not feel jealousy. She tried to remember the age difference but she also knew that many women, including herself, were attracted to older men.

On the day that he registered himself as a candidate for the position, he found out who his opponent would be. Marian Von Stautten was a retired librarian and had been active in her support of Ketty Guttmann. She was married to a man who spent much of his time examining the interior of the local hofbrauhaus. She looked like a typical librarian; conservatively dressed, large rimmed glasses, hair in a bun, but she ruled her house like a dictator and hence the absence of her husband. As previously mentioned she had been an active supporter of Mayor Guttmann, continually writing letters to her advising her of what she felt about the city government. She now wrote Fraulein Guttmann with the news that she would be running for council member and would appreciate her support. For Fraulein Guttman's part, she really didn't care who won as long as it did not affect her relationship with President Luxemburg.

With the news of his opponent, Adolf set to work on his campaign. As Fraulein Baumgartner suggested, he went door-to-door with stickers that said "Vote for Hitler!" He then would take the time to explain to the occupant of the house the reason he was door-to-dooring and the reason why they should vote for him. Most occupants just took the sticker and slowly closed the door. Adolf soon realized that the majority of the constituents in his district were older – aged pensioners he had reckoned. Occasionally, he would find a supportive ear to listen to his thoughts.

Adolf's next step was to purchase advertising in the local Berlin newspapers. He then had his likeness slapped onto the sides of buildings, park and bus benches just about anywhere that was legal to slap things on. Surprisingly Fraulein Von Stautten had similar ideas – bumper stickers on cars, her likeness spread about on various objects around Berlin and then she did one better – she slapped her likeness onto a van and had her husband drive her around town as she bellowed out of a bullhorn to people walking about urging them to vote for her. Adolf was incensed. How would he one up the old librarian? Rosa suggested he start making speeches around town, and that's just what he decided.

He started to pin up notices that he would be making a speech that Thursday in the park at the large bandstand. He noted that anyone attending would be offered coffee and donuts.

And so it was that the following Thursday arrived and Adolf made ready at the park bandstand. Fraulein Baumgartner helped prepare a nearby table with many a treat all covered up so as not to tempt the local gentry. With the news of donuts on their minds, many a local showed-up in front of the bandstand. Fraulein Baumgartner gave Adolf a big thumbs up. She had rehearsed the speech with Adolf multiple times and felt he was ready.

"Ladies and gentlemen, thank you for hearing me today. I would just like to speak to you with regard to my candidacy for councilman with the Berlin mayor's office. I feel especially honored to be thought of as a candidate for councilman and know I would do an excellent job assisting in creating an even better Berlin. As you know, I am a world renowned artist, so when I put my mind to something, I see it through."

As more people began to gather, the accumulating crowd caught the attention of some local policemen, a couple of them were on horseback. The policemen strolled through the park on their horses trying to present an imposing figure. Adolf noted their arrival with some interest and concern.

"I am sure, that if elected, I will do a terrific job. There is so much that can be accomplished. Why look at this park – while quite attractive, it offers little in the way of family recreation. I propose that we erect various play areas where mothers can bring their children. With the hustle and bustle of the street, I know mothers want a safe place for their children."

The statement brought some applause from various mothers in the crowd.

"Where would we be today without a strong family unit? That is why we must provide opportunities for Berlin's youth – our teens. I propose that we construct more gymnasiums for them to train and to exercise. We do not have enough physical activities for our youth. We need to develop youth sports. Yes, there are football academies around Germany, but we need more of them here in Berlin…"

As Adolf was proposing the support of the youth, he noticed two young boys beginning to snoop under the blanket of the table. Ms. Baumgartner shooed them away, but like bees they seemed to keep hovering, even from a distance.

"I am proposing that in the northeast quadrant of this park, the city of Berlin construct a large youth complex to allow for the young people of the city a place to meet, to play sports…hey, get away from that table you young monsters!!!"

As Adolf shouted at the two young boys, the two police officers came nearer to check on what the commotion was about. One of the boys came away with a donut and immediately ran into one of the horses which frightened the horse causing it to rise up on its hind legs. The other horse followed suit sending its rider into the table of donuts, causing multiple cream tarts and pastries to go flying. Not wanting to be without their allotment, the crowd immediately converged on the table and began to abscond with whatever they could take.

Adolf was in a daze, trying to figure what on earth was happening. He tried to yell at the assembled with the microphone but nothing was going to stop the stampede. He quickly collected Fraulein Baumgartner and they ran out of the park away from the madness. Adolf returned to the apartment and reported the news to Rosa who couldn't stop laughing. Adolf had other feelings.

Despite the debacle of his speech, Adolf was feeling optimistic when election day arrived. He and Rosa went and voted first thing in the morning. Rosa's presence at the local precinct gathered quite a crowd and it was hoped it might aid Adolf's chances. That night however, the news was grim as it was clear that Fraulein Von Stautten had won. Rosa tried to comfort Adolf but he was not in a good mood. The truth of the matter was that Fraulein Von Stautten had been a fixture in Berlin for years. She was a respected librarian and was also a major contributor to her church and the city. When one really thought about it there was no surprise that she had won.

"I think I will turn to drink." Adolf said somberly.

"Don't be silly, you can't allow this one defeat to get you down."

"No, I think that's it. I just don't have the energy for politics. I can see that I am not a politician. I should have listened to Edmond back in France – he said I did not have the ability to lead. I think I will go back to art…maybe take up photography."

"There you go Adi, that's the spirit.

Although down for several weeks after the loss, Adolf did turn his spirts around. He did take up photography and decided to travel the world. He took a trip to Machu Pichu, in Peru, took a safari in Kenya, visited the Great Wall in China, camped in the Outback of Australia and learned to scuba dive in Tahiti. He had finally felt productive again and really enjoyed photography.

When he finally arrived back in Berlin three months later, Rosa could see he was a changed man. While he had failed at politics, he now found a hobby that would keep him occupied. He was soon doing photography for a local theatre which did live shows. He would take photos of the actors and various scenes of the plays that would later be used for advertising. For the next several years he did nothing but focus on photography.

In 1956, Rosa had won reelection as a second term as president of Germany. The things she had accomplished had been incredible. Germany's atomic power grid had now spread all over Europe with the exception of the Iberian Peninsula, both Spain and Portugal saying they wanted to stay independent of Germany. President

Luxemburg had stated publicly that there was no allegiance that had to be offered – only monthly payments. Still Spain and Portugal would not budge. Perhaps it was because of what some of the other countries had done. In the case of Romania, they had become the Germanic State of Romania. Romania, while not losing their cultural identity wanted to align themselves with Germany to be able to have a stronger ability to negotiate trade with other countries. As Romania rose in economic status, many other countries wanted to join this Pact. Soon there the Germanic State of Finland, Denmark, Poland, Hungary, Austria, Bulgaria, Albania and Estonia (The Soviet Union having been completed dismantled into its original states). Clamoring for similar agreements were the Ukraine, China, Greece, Norway, Sweden, North Korea, India and much of Africa.

The German Power Grid was now in almost every part of the world with the exception of the Western Hemisphere. Rosa's plans were to expand there next and she had meetings planned in 1957 to meet with all the leaders of both South and North America. Rosa was anxious to meet the new president of the United States Earl Warren. Warren had served as Thomas Dewey's Vice President. When Dewey was indicated and later sentenced to prison, Warren became president. He then won another term as president in 1956. He was anxious to meet with Rosa to help the United States with multiple projects – amongst those the ability to produce an atom bomb. Rosa was not anxious to give any other country the ability to develop nuclear weapons. She wanted to keep things the way they were. But she was not against the idea of building a power grid in the United States. While Warren did want the atomic power via the German grid, he wanted more and would try to convince Rosa that the United States would be eternally grateful to Germany if they would help them develop a nuclear arsenal. Rosa just advised the U.S president to be patient.

Rosa was the most powerful person on earth, and it felt good. She knew the work she was doing was helping everyone – men, women, children, in all parts of the world. She had brought electricity to the remotest parts of the world; villages in Africa, farms in China, huts in India, all with the use of atomic power plants throughout Germany. Nodes from these power plants would deliver supercharged electrical particles through long pipelines that would then charge nodes in the receiving country. The power then would be channeled to the rest of the country through various means; power lines, underground cables, etc. And Germany would enjoy trillions of Deutschemarks in revenues each year. And true to Rosa's words, "All Germans would benefit from the technology of Germany." And they did. Anyone who wanted to own a house and a car could. All education and medical treatment was paid for – it was truly a utopian society.

And yet for Adolf Hitler, he paid little attention to the state that his wife had built. He just travelled within the empire she had created in first-class style. He would seldom attend any state dinners or government functions. He just worked in his dark-room that he had created in the basement of the Reich Chancellery. Fraulein Baumgartner continued to work as his assistant, helping him with travel arrangements, or getting Adolf photographic and art supplies.

Later toward the end of the fifties, Adolf started to establish himself as quite a gifted photographer. He also began to combine painting with photography creating montages and collages. Adolf was also himself quite a celebrity. He was earning himself a reputation as quite an enigmatic recluse. People could only find him near Mount Kilimanjaro or Mount Fuji. Rumors too began to fly that he and Fraulein Baumgartner were having an affair. Rosa would hear the gossip but at her age she no longer cared what he did. She would often find herself in the company of young male politicians who would keep her entertained.

One such person was a young man by the name of Lee Harvey Oswald. He seemed like a nice enough young man to Rosa. He had sought asylum in Germany, swearing allegiance to Germany's communist ideals. He was a fan of Marx and Lenin and could quote many statements from the communist pioneers. He had asked to meet with the president and in a highly charged meeting she had offered him asylum. The United States offered no real resistance which started to make Rosa think that he was planted there as a spy. Her meetings in 1957 and 1958 with President Warren had only yielded small benefits for the United States. While a transatlantic pipeline was in the works to transfer atomic power, what the Americans really wanted was denied them by Rosa.

After contacting the United States Department of Justice as well as the FBI, it was decided that Oswald could live in Germany. While his German was at a beginner's level, he would be offered on-going language lessons. It was decided that Oswald would be given a position within the government to become an English-German translator. With many projects pending between Germany and multiple English-speaking countries it would be imperative to get as many translators as possible. One side benefit to Rosa was that Oswald and Fraulein Baumgartner had become romantically involved. While she doubted Adolf's interest in her, there was always the chance that a healthy male would find the young woman attractive at some point.

CHAPTER 20

Entering the 1960's it appeared that Germany would continue to lead the world as the one true "Superpower". Rosa won re-election again in 1960, and she began to make multiple trips to the United States which Adolf would sometimes join her for.

President John Kennedy and his wife Jackie would entertain Rosa and Adolf, giving them tours of the many areas of the White House. They would then top off the day with a state dinner attended by many members of the United States Congress and Senate. Rosa Luxemburg was the center of attention at these state dinners and was held in great esteem as someone who could build a strong partnership with the United States.

Building on the old telegraph cables that had been laid in the late 19th century by the German company Siemens, it was with similar cabling that would provide high-powered energy to nodes in the United States. The alliance between the United States would be mutually beneficial, more technology and engineers would be coming to America and Germany would have access to more of the Western Hemisphere for more power projects.

The relationship between President Kennedy and President Luxemburg became a very important one. Eventually it was determined that Germany could have private military bases in the United States if Germany shared their military and atomic secrets. Through several treaties it was decided that the only nuclear secrets that would be shared would be to build reactors and other power plants. There would be full-time German contractors and engineers in the United States to help build and maintain them.

On November 22, 1963, The first nuclear reactor outside of Germany was commissioned in Savanah, Georgia. President Luxemburg flew to the United States to meet with President Kennedy for the great occasion. A new level of technological partnering had been reached between Germany and another country – it was a true milestone. With this new landmark achievement, Rosa picked that day to announce her retirement as President of Germany. Her vice-president, Hannah Hoch would take over as leader of Germany. It was a sad day for many around the world.

On a smaller note, that same day, Lee Harvey Oswald married Fraulein Baumgartner – Adolf gave the bride away.

******

For the rest of the sixties, Adolf began to slow down. Adolf retreated more and more to his house on the outskirts of Berlin. He would also make time at his house in Bavaria. While his new art form of photography mixed with his sketches and paintings continued to sell well, he seldom ventured beyond the studios of his Berlin home.

In 1967, he was asked by the British rock group the Beatles if he would put together the cover for their new album they were about to release St. Pepper's Lonely Hearts Club Band. He spent a month in London working on the project, getting to know John, Paul, George and Ringo. He especially liked Ringo – down to earth and comical he thought. John and George appeared to be distant and under the influence of something while Paul was a little too upbeat for his liking. In any event, the final photo shoot was a success and the Beatles liked the outcome. Adolf later heard that the album was a smash success and considered offering his services to other "rock-n'roll" bands. He did get some correspondence from a group called the Moody Blues, but he lost interest and never responded back to their manager.

For the rest of the decade Adolf did little more than read newspapers at his favorite bistro in Berlin. Rosa would occasionally join him, but after leaving office she had seemed to age quickly. There was one more event that she would turn out for and that was at the German Space Center where on July 21st, 1969, Wernher von Braun's first rocket-ship landed on the moon. It was a joint venture with England, France and the United States. The first person on the moon though was German. Commander Elena Fasbinder would become the first person to walk on the moon. She would be immortalized along with Christopher Columbus and Amelia Earhart. It was truly a remarkable accomplishment and almost all of the world witnessed it – of course it was on television screens made by the German electronics company SABA.

For Hannah Hoch, President of Germany it was a momentous day. She commissioned Wernher von Bran to make ten more flights to the moon and on flight ten to begin preparations to colonize the moon. The idea would be to put an atomic power-plant on the moon that would provide everything necessary to start a human colony. Wernher von Braun was ecstatic about the idea. And so Germany committed that by 1979, there would be humans living on the moon.

******

In a rare and sad coincidence, on March 5th, 1971, on her one-hundredth birthday, Rosa Luxemburg passed away. Her body lay in state at the Reich Chancellery for three days. Former President John F. Kennedy and his brother, the current president of the United States, Robert Kennedy were in attendance. Almost every major head of state was there or a representative was sent in their place. The world mourned for a week with many television shows presenting programs showing all that she had accomplished. In many countries there would now be a "Rosa Luxemburg Day". Adolf, looking withdrawn and sad attended the funeral and was given the state flag after the ceremony.

After the funeral, Adolf was seldom seen. He later became a recluse and seemed to go into hiding. Art collectors and promoters trying to get in touch with him had to go via circuitous routes which involved Fraulein Baumgartner-Oswald and one of Adolf's sisters. The usual answer that was given to them to give to the inquirer was "no".

Adolf later went on a drinking and eating binge that saw him gain weight and become less and less mobile. He would often just sit in the back porch of his Bavarian home and look into the Alps seeming to search for the meaning of life.

On April 30th, 1975, at the age of 86, Adolf Hitler passed away. His aid Fraulein Baumgartner-Oswald happened to visit that day and contacted the local doctor, coroner and priest to go up to the Bergdorf. When the news hit the world that Adolf had passed there was a great renewed awareness and remembrance of all that Adolf had contributed to the world of art. There were many around the world who mourned his passing.

For the next several days there were many tributes and remembrances made in Adolf's honor. At the Vienna Institute of the Arts their flags were lowered to half-mast. Many students there were regaled by professors of the impact of Adolf's art. Similar tributes were made at the Berlin Institute of the Arts. The Carnegie and Guggenheim museums in the United States all put on extensive art shows of Adolf's work. Messages poured in from around the world to his studio in Berlin. Fraulein Baumgartner-Oswald had to find box after box to put them in. It was clear that the world had loved Adolf. He had been put on a path to create some of the world's great art. He would be remembered always as a man of great passion and love and forever immortalized and spoken of in the same manner as Picasso, Von Gogh and Pollack.

CHAPTER 21

On April 30th, at 1:23 in the afternoon, Adolf Hitler's heart stopped beating. At 1:29pm, his spirit left him. He awoke in a strange dark place. It seemed to be a dream of some sort. The darkness evolved into a grayish fog, like he often found when he was in London. He looked at the ground – it seemed to be dirt or something that was dark brown, although that was hard to see at times from a thick mist that enveloped everything. He began to walk to see if he could find something…anything. He seemed to hear whispers or faint talking but could not make out what was being said. He looked around and tried to orient himself but there was nothing to be seen. He felt a slight chill but after that nothing – he could not distinguish if he were in a cold or warm place, there was nothing much he could decipher. As he continued to walk he wondered if he was in hell or purgatory. From everything he had read on the subject it seemed to be devoid of fire and brimstone so that was a relief. But perhaps hell was something else? Perhaps it was the complete absence of people…of God?

As he walked and walked he could not find anything. There were no plants or trees or bushes. No sound of birds or anything. He began to worry, wondering where he had landed.

"Hello Adolf."

Adolf turned with a fright. He peered into the gray fog but could not see anyone. Slowly he began to make out a shape in the fog and he was soon presented with a man. He seemed to be a familiar individual but couldn't quite place his face.

"Do you remember me Adolf?"

Adolf looked deep into the man's face, trying to remember. His voice certainly sounded familiar.

"Think back Adolf. Do you remember your time in Amsterdam?"

Adolf nodded, unable to vocalize anything, feeling as if his tongue had been removed.

"Remember when you were in prison?"

"Paul!" Adolf shouted. He walked to Paul to try and hug him but as he did so his arms just went right through him. He looked at his hand and arms and wondered how they could have gone through Paul's body.

"You are in another world now Adolf, you are no longer on the earth."

"Where am I?"

"Well, you are in a place that is between heaven and hell…some refer to it as purgatory, the boss refers to it as the waiting area."

"The boss?"

"Yeah, I like to refer to him as the boss, makes him more down to earth so to speak."

"You mean God?"

"Yep, you catch on quick Adi!"

"So are you some sort of angel?"

"The simple answer to that is yes. I was sent to help you at various points in your life."

"You're my guardian angel?"

"Precisely."

"I remember you in the Amsterdam prison, but what other times did you help me?"

"Do you remember that time when you were a little depressed and you were sitting in the beerhall in Vienna? You had sold some painting but were running out of money. On that day a small breeze wafted through one of the windows in the beerhall. At your feet was deposited a flyer announcing that applications were being taken for the Vienna Institute of the Arts."

Adolf began to search his memory. It was a dark day for him, not meteorologically speaking, it had been a bright sunny day, but his spirit was dark at the time and he was feeling depressed. As he began to flog his memory the flyer became visible in his mind and he began to nod his head. Paul smiled at Adolf as the memory became more vivid.

"On that day you determined that you would apply for the school, and look what happened to you and your career."

Adolf smiled and nodded.

"Do you also remember the day you were accepted to the institute?"

Adolf again began to search his memory.

"Well there was a lot of debate going on with regard to that decision. Two of the professors wanted you but the other was not so convinced of your talent. This is where the power of prayer comes in. Your mother had prayed for you for years…for your life, for your career. Those prayers of course had risen to God, but one of them also came to you. Because of your mother's urging you then also sent up a prayer. Your faith at times has waned but at that moment you asked God in faith to help you and He did. You were accepted into the arts institute."

A bright smile began to grow on Adolf's face as he remembered that day that he asked God on his knees in humbleness to help him.

"You see Adolf, there are many times that we do not make the right choice. You sometimes did not make the right choice but many times you did. There were times you were tempted to put your ego ahead of everything else – to abandon the faith that your mother had chiseled into your psyche. You know things could have been very different for you."

Paul began to walk several feet away from Adolf. He then pointed to an area off in the distance. The fog began to scattered and something like a large movie screen appeared. Like a movie starting in a movie theatre a great light from behind him shone through the mist. He turned around to see where the light was emanating from. The light was brighter than anything he had ever seen – it was like staring into the sun but it didn't bother his eyes, in fact it seemed to stimulate him like nothing ever before. It also gave him a warm, happy feeling to look into the light, he was tempted to start walking toward it but then Paul asked him to turn back.

As the images began to appear on the screen, they became quite focused almost larger than the screen. There were explosions and men running around crying and screaming. Adolf shuddered as he looked at the pain of the men. He started to see that they were wearing uniforms and it was clear they were soldiers fighting a war. Then the scenes became even more painful to watch as tanks and armored vehicles were moving over injured men, crushing them. There was blood everywhere. He wanted to turn away but couldn't. Then more scenes appeared, it looked like the ruined streets of a city, but then there were scenes of other ruined cities with smoke and fire. Then there was a great screeching sound from the sky and planes could be seen dropping bombs on the cities…the bombs were hitting men, women and children…little children, babies. It looked as if the whole world was ablaze.

Then another scene appeared. It looked intensely familiar. It was a scene of a young boy with a Star of David pinned to the lapel of his jacket. He looked dirty and in dire need of medical attention. The poor boy was running down a street and then into a building. He tried to hide himself and as he did so in a room he could hear the voices of men following him – he had a look of terror in his eyes. He immediately remembered that he had dreamed of that boy a long time ago when he had lived in Paris.

"Paul, what is this?!!! What does all of this mean?!!!" Adolf cried out in grief. Paul looked at Adolf. He waved his hand and the light and the screen disappeared.

"This could have been you Adolf. This could have been the destruction you wielded."

"What do you mean, I don't understand you. I could not have caused such terror, such pain and grief?"

"You have to remember Adolf that human beings are subject to good and evil. The devil can tempt us to do things we cannot even imagine and it is only with God's love can we do the right thing. On that day when you prayed you set yourself on a path toward the light, toward good. Your decisions could have easily led you in another direction."

"How do you mean?"

"Do you remember that in Paris you also had a dream about sheep being led to a cliff where they all jumped off?"

"Yes, yes, it was one of the most realistic dreams I ever had."

"That dream was a manifestation of the leadership role that was lying in you since you were little. When you were little and you led kids on your block in that little gang.

When you were in Vienna and you would lead some of your buddies around, telling them what to do with their lives. You had leadership qualities, but you also had the potential to misuse them. Luckily, you chose art over leadership and by doing so you saved yourself and the world – millions of people."

Adolf looked confused. He had no clue how he could have possibly done so much damage by making the wrong choices.

"Life Adolf is a series of obstacles and choices. Depending on how you maneuver around or through those obstacles and depending on what decisions you make can lead to life or destruction. Jesus himself said it is the narrow path that leads to life and the wide path that leads to destruction. You were lucky, you had your mother, you had me, you had God and you decided for God and not for yourself. Many people will take a little good thing like applause or compliments and use them to puff themselves up, to make an idol of themselves. Some make idols out of money, out of over indulgence in food, out of drugs and alcohol, yet many make idols of themselves. Many of the Roman Emperors made themselves idols. People who desire fame, like the movie stars and musicians you met along the way. But you stayed humble. You didn't always make the right decisions and so you are here in purgatory, but you decided that Adolf was not to be a god. Adolf was not to be an idol. But, as you can see from the images I just showed you, you could have easily gone down that path, the path of self-absorption, the path of power and greed. Most people, without some times realizing it choose to put themselves ahead of the needs of others. But we are here to serve and not to be served. Now look over there." Paul motioned to look into the distance. A great light began to beam down upon what looked like a plain. It looked like a grassy plain that one might find in a great field in Russia or in the Midwest of the United States. In the distance the sky began to turn a beautiful blue, a color of blue he had never seen before. Way in the distance, what looked to be hundreds of miles beyond the plains was a large mountain. Without telling him what to do, Adolf began to walk toward it. He had no idea what he was doing but knew that he needed to head toward that mountain, no matter how far away it was.